ANCIENT INDIAN TRADITION AND MYTHOLOGY

Translated by
BOARD OF SCHOLARS

Edited by
DR. G.P. BHATT

VOLUME 71

ANCIENT INDIAN TRADITION AND MYTHOLOGY SERIES

[PURĀṆAS IN TRANSLATION]

Volumes Released

ŚIVA 1-4
LIṄGA 5-6
BHĀGAVATA 7-11
GARUḌA 12-14
NĀRADA 15-19
KŪRMA 20-21
BRAHMĀṆḌA 22-26
AGNI 27-30
VARĀHA 31-32
BRAHMA 33-36
VĀYU 37-38
PADMA 39-48
SKAṄDA, PARTS I-XXIII, 49-71
VĀMANA 72-73

Volumes Under Preparation

BHAVIṢYA
BRAHMAVAIVARTA
DEVĪBHĀGAVATA
KĀLIKĀ
MĀRKAṆḌEYA
MATSYA
VIṢṆU
VIṢṆUDHARMOTTARA

THE SKANDA-PURĀṆA

PART XXIII

Translated and Annotated by
SHRIDHAR BALOONI
PRATOSH PANDA

Book VII : Prabhāsakhaṇḍa
Section IV: Dvārakā Māhātmya

MOTILAL BANARSIDASS PUBLISHERS
PRIVATE LIMITED • DELHI

First Edition: Delhi, 2011

ISBN: 978-81-208-3428-6

MOTILAL BANARSIDASS
41 U.A. Bungalow Road, Jawahar Nagar, Delhi 110 007
8 Mahalaxmi Chamber, 22 Bhulabhai Desai Road, Mumbai 400 026
120 Royapettah High Road, Mylapore, Chennai 600 004
236, 9th Main III Block, Jayanagar, Bangalore 560 011
Sanas Plaza, 1302 Baji Rao Road, Pune 411 002
8 Camac Street, Kolkata 700 017
Ashok Rajpath, Patna 800 004
Chowk, Varanasi 221 001

UNESCO COLLECTION OF REPRESENTATIVE WORKS—*Indian Series*
This book has been accepted in the Indian Translation Series of the UNESCO Collection of Representative Works, jointly sponsored by the United Nations Educational, Scientific and Cultural Organization (UNESCO) and the Government of India

Published by Narendra Prakash Jain for
Motilal Banarsidass Publishers Private Limited,
Bungalow Road, Delhi 110 007

PUBLISHER'S NOTE

The purest gems lie hidden at the bottom of the ocean or in the depth of rocks. One has to dive deep into the ocean or delve into the rocks to find them out. Similarly, truth lies concealed in the language which keeps on changing with the passage of time. Man has to learn that language before he discovers that truth.

But he has neither the means nor the leisure to embark on that course. We have, therefore, planned to help him acquire knowledge by an easier course. Our goal is to universalize knowledge through the most popular international medium expression. Thereforc, wc havc started the series of *Ancient Indian Tradition and Mythology* under which we plan to publish Purāṇas in English translation.

Acknowledgement

It is our pleasant duty to put on record our sincere thanks to Dr. R.N. Dandekar and the UNESCO authorities for their kind encouragement and valuable help in the publication of the volumes in this series.

CONTENTS

SKANDA-PURĀṆA

BOOK VII : PRABHĀSAKHAṆḌA
SECTION IV: DVĀRAKĀ MĀHĀTMYA

ABBREVIATIONS

Common and self-evident abbreviations such as Ch (s)—Chapter(s), p—page, pp—pages, v—verse, vv—verses, Ftn—Footnote, Hist. Ind. Philo.—History of Indian Philosophy are not included in this list.

AGP	S.M. Ali's *The Geography of Purāṇas*, PPH, New Delhi, 1973
AIHT	*Ancient Indian Historical Tradition*, F.E. Pargiter, Motilal Banarsidass, Delhi
AITM	*Ancient Indian Tradition and Mythology Series*, Motilal Banarsidass, Delhi
AP	*Agni Purāṇa*, Guru Mandal Edition, Calcutta, 1957
AV	*Atharva Veda*, Svādhyāya Maṇḍal, Aundh
BdP	*Brahmāṇḍa Purāṇa*, Motilal Banarsidass, Delhi, 1973
BG	*Bhagavadgītā*
BhP	*Bhāgavata Purāṇa*, Bhagavat Vidyapeeth, Ahmedabad
Br	*Brāhmaṇa* (preceded by name such as Śatapatha)
BsP	*Bhaviṣya Puraṇa*, Vishnu Shastri Bapat, Wai
BVP	*Brahma Vaivarta Purāṇa*, Guru Mandal Edition, 1955-57
CC	*Caturvarga Cintāmaṇi* by Hemādri
CVS	*Caraṇa Vyūha Sūtra* by Śaunaka, Commentary by Mahīdāsa
DB	*Devī Bhāgavata*, Guru Mandal Edition, 1960-61
GDAMI	*The Geographical Dictionary of Ancient and Medieval India*, N.L. De/Dey, Oriental reprint, Delhi, 1971

DhS	*Dharma Sūtra* (preceded by the author's name such as Gautama)
GP	*Garuḍa Purāṇa*, ed. R.S. Bhattacharya, Chowkhamba, Varanasi, 1964
GS	*Gṛhya Sūtra* (preceded by the name of the author such as Āpastamba)
HD	*History of Dharma Śāstra*, P.V. Kane, Gaekwad Oriental Series
JP	*Purāṇa* (Journal of the Kashiraj Trust), Varanasi
KA	*Kauṭilya Arthaśāstra*
KP	Kūrma Purāṇa, Venkatesvara Press Edition, Bombay; also Kashiraj Trust Edition, Varanasi, 1971
LP	*Liṅga Purāṇa*, Guru Mandal Edition, Calcutta, 1960; also Motilal Banarsidass, Delhi, 1981
Manu	*Manusmṛti*
Mbh	*Mahābhārata*, Gita Press, Gorakhpur, VS 2014
MkP	*Mārkaṇḍeya Purāṇa*
MN	*Mahābhārata Nāmānukramaṇī*, Gita Press, Gorakhpur, Vikram Samvat, 2016
Mtp	*Matsya Purāṇa*, Guru Mandal Edition, 1954
MW	M. Monier-Williams' Sanskrit-English Dictionary, Motilal Banarsidass, Delhi, 1976
NP	*Nāradīya or Nārada Purāṇa*, Venkatesvara Press, Bombay
PdP	*Padma Purāṇa*, Guru Mandal Edition, 1957-59
PE	*Purāṇic Encyclopaedia*, V. Mani, English Version, Motilal Banarsidass, Delhi, 1975
PR or PRHRC	*Puranic Records on Hindu Rites and Customs* R.C. Hazra, Calcutta, 1948
ṚV	*Ṛg Veda*, Svādhyāya Maṇḍal, Aundh
Śat Br	*Śatapatha Brāhmaṇa*
SC	*Smṛti Candrikā* by Devanna Bhaṭṭa
SkP	*Skanda Purāṇa*
SP	*Śiva Purāṇa*
VāP	*Vāyu Purāṇa*

VR	*Vālmīki Rāmāyaṇa*
VdP	*Viṣṇudharmottara Purāṇa*
VmP	*Vāmana Purāṇa*
VP	*Viṣṇu Purāṇa*
VrP	*Varāha Purāṇa*

SKANDA PURĀṆA

BOOK VII : PRABHĀSA KHAṆḌA
SECTION IV: DVĀRAKĀ MĀHĀTMYA

CHAPTER ONE

Does God endure in the Kaliyuga?

Obeisance to Lord Gaṇeśa. Section Four of the seventh book of Skanda Mahāpurāṇa describing greatness of Dvārakā commences.

Śaunaka said:

1-2. Sūta, please tell as to how in this harsh epoch known as Kaliyuga with pre-ponderance of atheists and proliferation of narrow-mindedness among people, Madhusūdana (i.e. an epithet of Viṣṇu) can be obtainable? After the phasing out of the three Yugas in which people's behaviour was always marked by the pursuit of righteousness, arrived the difficult Kaliyuga. Hence (the question arises) where is Lord Viṣṇu?

Sūta said:

3. After Daśaratha's offspring, the great king Rāma's attainment of divinehood (i.e. death), the earth's surface got afflicted with the burden of wicked kings.

4. Then, with the purpose that actions of gods meet the desirable accomplishment as well as the earth gets relieved of the burden, Janārdana (an epithet of Viṣṇu) manifested himself in bodily incarnation in the house of Vasudeva.
5. Sucking the vigour out of Pūtanā's body, the God then went to the region of Braja in the kingdom of Nanda. There, after killing Tṛṇāvarta, he got the epithet of Śakaṭa for himself.
6. He also tamed the Nāga, i.e. a cobra called Kāliya and killed the demon Pralamba. Bearing the mountain Govardhana, he rescued Gokula.
7. Getting the milk of cow named Surabhi sprinkled on himself, he shattered the joy of Indra. Then engaging himself in dancing with other goddesses he killed the demon Keśi by tearing him apart.
8. Then as per the instructions of Akrura (i.e. an uncle of Kṛṣṇa) Hari went to Mathurā and there he killed the tormenting group of wrestlers and their robust king.
9. Then after killing Kaṅsa—the king of Bhoja under the watchful eyes of the gods and the demons, he got Ugrasena crowned as the king of the city of Yadupura considered as the stronghold of the Yādavas.
10. He killed the formidable Jarāsandha and his troop of barbarians. While doing his part of coordination in the conduct of the Rājasūya Yajña (i.e. the sacrificial rite performed by a monarch as a mark of his sovereignty) he killed Caiddya (i.e. an epithet of Śiśupāla).
11. After the conclusion of the Mahābhārata war which had badly affected the earth with its aftermath, Kṛṣṇa took all the members of the Yādava dynasty to Prabhāsa region under the pretext of a journey.
12. Addicted to drinking and engaged in mutual infighting to kill one another, the Yādava dynasty there was on the path of ruin.
13. Then Janārdana (i.e. Kṛṣṇa) giving up his body went inside the infinite underground surface of the earth and making the holy fig tree his resort, remained seated there.

14. But while he was at that state, an arrow from a hunter hit him. He left the wounded part of his body behind and moved to his own abode. At that time Pārtha, i.e. Arjuna again came to him.

15. Yadupura, the stronghold of Yādavas got completely flooded and submerged under the sea. Then Arjuna made an abode, i.e. a temple for Kṛṣṇa in Indraprastha.

16. With this came to an end the epoch of Dvāpara—a mixture of both righteous and unrighteousness. Then came the terrible yuga which is defined as the Kaliyuga.

17. With the gradual decay in upright religion, unrighteousness began to acquire gigantic form (in this Kaliyuga). With the expulsion of debates over Vedantic dictates, the attendant religious activities/rituals began to wear out. The single-footed religious conduct based on Varṇāśrama system was also abandoned.

18. Under such unsteady state of affairs in this epoch, all sages like Garga, Yavan and Bhārgava *et.al.* assembling together in forests began to deliberate and consult one another.

19. There were also sages like Asīta, Devala, Dhoumya, Krantu, Uddālaka as well as others who began to speak to one another in a greater manner in this regard.

20-22. (The sages said amongst themselves) "O sages! All of you see that the Kaliyuga is expanding in such form breaking all limits. The thieves are also running here and there, harassing subjects everywhere. Men have become very unrighteous. Truth and straightforwardness have been driven away. So how could we, as virtuous sages attain God Viṣṇu? Who can prevent such downfall and help the society to successfully cross over? Can it at all be possible for Madhusūdana to appear in the Kaliyuga as in the previous three yugas? Can it at all be possible for us to move about in this Kaliyuga without him, the lotus-eyed, i.e. Kṛṣṇa."

23. When the ascetics were getting worried as such being sad within themselves, the sage Uddālaka began to speak out.

24-26. Uddālaka said, "The virtuous sages, as long as we do not get ourselves involved in the mischiefs of Kaliyuga, all of us together can go to that world of Brahmā without any blame on our part. As far as the question regarding presence of Viṣṇu in the Kaliyuga of the Creator (i.e. Brahmā) is concerned, if Viṣṇu will not be there alongwith Rudra and Brahmā in the same yuga, we shall give up our bodies without the Lotus-eyed Kṛṣṇa, for who can put up in this Kaliyuga without God?"

27. After hearing these words of the sage, all the ascetics– the diligent followers of any vow taken up in the mind, said "well-said, well-said" and then went to Brahmā.

28. Feeling satisfied within and then remembering and narrating amongst themselves the stories of Viṣṇu and his various forms all the ascetics then came near Brahmā.

29. They happened to see Brahmā seated in his primary position but surrounded by actual bodily-beings as well as by those without bodies.

30. Seeing the four-faced God (i.e. Brahmā) they (the sages) paid their honour falling flat on the ground and by reciting the hymns to please him.

31. The sages said, "Obeisance to you having birth from the lotus, the four-faced, the unperishable and indestructible. Obeisance to you the grandfather and the creator."

32. When the devout sages recited hymns in this manner the God born from lotus (i.e. Brahmā) became very pleased. Then he intended to ask the assembled sages who offered him water at his feet, flowers, etc. and prayers in honour.

33. Brahmā asked, "The sons, what is the reason that prompted you to come here? Tell me the fact behind the same. Is everything all right with you, the fortunate souls, regarding your sons, your disciples and your companions in the spiritual domain?"

34-36. The sages said, "By your grace, we have attained fruits of our penance. It is by virtue of penance that we happened to have a look at the teacher of all gods—the

Lord himself. Śambhu (an epithet of Brahmā), listen to the reason behind our coming to you. After passing out of the three yugas like Kṛta, Dvāpara, etc., the formidable Kaliyuga has arrived. But then where is Lord Viṣṇu on earth after taking a look of whom can we ultimately attain liberation becoming free from bondage?"

37. Brahmā said, "The best of Brāhmaṇas, I do not know the principal image of Viṣṇu. He, the God is known to me only in his form as fish and as a tortoise."

38. The Sages said, "O father! if you do not know the whereabouts of Viṣṇu, then we may go to Prayāga where we can forsake our bodies."

39-40. Brahmā said, "Let there be no sorrows for you people. Hence, for your welfare, I can advise that all of you proceed to hell where a virtuous demon, dwells. Going there, ask Prahlāda— the virtuous demon for the Brāhmaṇas, he must be aware of the factual whereabout of Hari."

41. Hearing these words of him (i.e. Brahmā), the Brāhmaṇas for whom real wealth lay in observance of penance left in that direction (i.e. the hell) after bowing down to the God of gods.

42. With pleasure in mind, they hurried up in that direction constantly (praising the demon within themselves) saying, "It is only the great fortune of the demon king to know the whereabouts of Janārdana."

43. Thinking like this, the Brāhmaṇas then reached deep into the surface under the earth.

44. After arriving at his city there, they began to enter into his beautiful hall. Seeing them from a distance to be heading towards them, Bali, son of Virochana along with Prahlāda got up and moved ahead towards them with all eagerness to welcome them.

45-46. He offered them the mixture of five substances (like honey, curd, ghee, milk, sugar, etc.) in their honour. He too also made gifts of cows to them and offered water at their feet. Remarkably happy within himself, he then told them bringing together both of his palms in salutation,

"Welcome to you all great souls. My night today will pass off well as I have got a sight of yours. Please say what can I do for you."

47. With such befitting welcome by the demon king, the good-hearted Brāhmaṇas became very happy and then told his son.

48-54. The sages said, "We have come here for our task as you, the strong soul being the lover of Hari can only save us from getting washed away in the ocean of this worldly life. How could we be without fear in this formidable and harsh age known as "Kaliyuga" without Viṣṇu? In this yuga unrighteous-ness has won over righteousness which is eternal. Falsehood has won over truth and the low castes are claiming themselves as Brāhmaṇas. The cunning are claiming to have acquired knowledge of the pathways laid down in the Veda while women are gaining an upper hand over men. The outcastes are posing a threat to Brāhmaṇas claiming themselves to be kings. With the putting aside of the Varṇāśrama system, the same appears to be on the verge of expulsion. The paths laid down as per the Veda seem to be on extinction. So where is Lord Viṣṇu given such circumstances? Give us the secret as to how to attain God (i.e.Viṣṇu) without knowledge, without contemplation and without controlling the sense organs. O king of demons! you are our dear friend and path-finder. You, the highly fortunate one, tell us where is Keśava?"

55. In this way, the Brāhmaṇas put their question to the virtuous demon who in turn with all happiness in mind offered them his salutation with due regard.

56. He also paid his obeisance to other gods as well as Brahmā—the Supreme Soul. Then to fulfill their (i.e. the Brāhmaṇas') request, he, with due devotion towards God, began to tell them.

CHAPTER TWO

Durvāsā cursing Rukmiṇī

Prahlāda said:

1. In all beings—be they demons or giants or be they the gods or the average ones, He—the adorable is present.
2. As per your approval, I shall inform you about the abode of God Kṛṣṇa by His grace.
3. In earlier times there was a city named Kuśasthalī founded by Kuśa near the sea on the western coast of India.
4. The river Gomatī had met the sea here in its natural course of flowing. By the name Dvārāvat (i.e. Dvārakā) it used to invoke adoration of people and its fame had spread out.
5. Adorned with sixteen qualities and in twelve imagery form of idols, Hari—the universal soul and the giver of all wishes resides there.
6. That is the best of places and that is his ultimate place. That is the fortunate (and auspicious) Dvārakā where Madhusūdana is present.
7. Lord Kṛṣṇa is heard to be present here like a door-frame with conch, disc and mace in his hands. Men can attain liberation by going there in Kaliyuga.
8. After hearing these words of the great soul Prahlāda, the devout sages became very surprised and they in turn asked him.
9-11. The sages said, "When the Yadu dynasty met with its downfall, then the best of the Yadu, i.e. Kṛṣṇa had rescued the earth from its resultant burden and had then left for his own place, i.e. Prabhāsa. When flooded by sea, Dvārāvat got washed away. So how could God's name be used to be taken with all glory there in the Kaliyuga? How could Viṣṇu stay back in this region on earth's surface evoking adoration of people? Tell us in details."

Prahlāda said:

12. When king Ugrasena was ruling on the earth, then Kṛṣṇa was adding to the glory of the city of Yadus, i.e. Yadupurī from all sides.
13. Once, along with his beautiful wife, Kṛṣṇa was seated in a meeting which itself was offering a pleasant sight.
14. Different discussions bearing varied accounts of people were going on there. Uddhava happened to apprise Kṛṣṇa about the happenings all around.

Uddhava said:

15. Undergoing pilgrimage to get rid of his evil deeds Durvāsā happened to be there in the auspicious place called Cakratīrtha on the banks of the river Gomatī.
16. Hearing that, the all powerful, i.e. Kṛṣṇa with pleasure of mind got up immediately from his seat and headed for the house of Rukmiṇī.
17. Then coming near Vaidarbhī (i.e. an epithet of Rukmiṇī) he told her that by virtue of his great penance, Durvāsā—the son of Atri had virtually washed out most of his sinful deeds.
18. By fulfilling all duties towards treatment of him as a guest as well as by serving him as a Brāhmaṇa we can earn our upliftment for visiting the home of a person having no wife is futile for a deserving party/person.
19. The gods do not accept his worship. So do his forefathers do not accept his libations. Hence, let us go and invite him for a dinner.
20. After saying like this the God then got onto the chariot and then getting himself seated on it along with Rukmiṇī headed towards the place where Durvāsā was for the time being.
21. Then they saw him engaged in burning penance near the sea-shore covering himself fully with a garland of skulls.
22. Then before putting his questions, the God offered him, his regards. The daughter of soil of Vidarbha, i.e. Rukmiṇī also paid him her obeisance.

23. Durvāsā also seeing them to have come to meet him, enquired everything about their wellbeing as a matter of greeting.
24. Durvāsā said, "Where do you Kṛṣṇa put up at the moment? Tell me the details regarding everything of yours—your financial state as well as the overall condition of your subjects."
25-26. Śrī Kṛṣṇa said, "The sea has gifted me land measuring about eight miles. While residing there, the city has become a golden city to me, the Brāhmaṇa. The palace there is adorned with nine lakh gold. Out of your grace, I am staying there hale and hearty and without any fear."
27. After hearing these words of him (i.e. Śrī Kṛṣṇa) Durvāsā was completely taken aback. With a little smile on him, Durvāsā began to ask Madhusūdana slightly sarcastically.
28. (Durvāsā asked) "Then there must be your able-bodied sons and other kith and kins who must be staying there with you! Please tell me about their number."
29-31a. Śrī Kṛṣṇa said, "O Brāhmaṇa! I have got more than sixteen thousand and eight queens out of whom the daughter of king of Vidarbha (i.e. Rukmiṇī) is very dear to me. Each one of them, the sage, has got ten sons and ten daughters. There are fifty-six crore kith and kins of mine. The factual position with regard to the number of the remainder is not known."
31b-32. Hearing this, the sage began to wonder as to how could it be. (He told himself) "Oh, this is based on the magic of limitless seed. All these deeds are manifesting the disposition of eternity."
33. Durvāsā said, "I welcome you, the strong and powerful. Please tell what is intended to be executed by me. As my mind is full of pleasure by getting a sight of yours."
34. Śrī Kṛṣṇa said, "Lord, if you are pleased, come along with me to my house. There I shall sanctify myself by making my forehead touch the water offered at your feet."
35. Durvāsā said, "What shall you, Mādhava do taking me along, the person having such a high degree of intolerance.

You can take me along only if you intend to follow my words together with your wife."

Prahlāda said:

36. Having said that it would be like that, the God then left on his own chariot. Seeing Viṣṇu leaving, he (i.e. Durvāsā) began to laugh and said humorously.
37. Durvāsā said, "You do not know Durvāsā. Leave aside your efficient horse and along with your wife, be yoked onto my chariot."
38. Śrī Kṛṣṇa said, "I shall do as you said, the Lord. By your grace, the Brāhmaṇa, I can cross over (the worldly life) along with my relations."

Prahlāda said:

39. Then both of them including the Goddess got themselves yoked onto the cross-bar of the chariot with the sage directing the lotus-eyed (i.e. Lord Kṛṣṇa) to move ahead while himself controlling the reins in his hands.
40-41. Seeing Hari pulling the chariot, all the gods began to tell one another amongst themselves: "Well done and well done." They said, "The love of God for the Brāhmaṇa is remarkable indeed that along with his wife, he has taken the weight of the cross-bar of the chariot on his shoulders and both of them are pulling the same."
42. Then while the gods continued showering flowers on Janārdana, he along with wife took the chariot towards Dvārakā.
43. Subsequently, in the process of pulling the chariot, Rukmiṇī felt thirsty out of exhaustion. Then Vaidarbhī (i.e. Rukmiṇī) with all eagerness writ-large in her eyes told Kṛṣṇa.
44. (Rukmiṇī said) "I have become exhausted pulling this chariot heavy with the weight of this irritable Brāhmaṇa. Darling, give me some water and then take me back to our abode."

45. Hearing these words of hers, the God then striking his feet on the ground brought out the auspicious Gaṅgā having fluency in three directions.
46. Then seeing clean, cool, aromatic and pure water before her, the thirsty Goddess Rukmiṇī quenched her thirst by having the water of Jāhnavī (i.e. an epithet of Gaṅgā).
47. Seeing her drinking water the astute sage began to burn with anger, his eyes got red in anger and he thus, cursed the supreme Goddess.
48-49. Durvāsā said, "Rukmiṇī, as you have taken water without seeking my permission, you will always remain occupied with the habit of drinking and there will be no doubt about this. You have drunk the water without taking the yoke of the chariot off your shoulders and without asking me. Hence you will bear separation from Kṛṣṇa."

Prahlāda said:

50. After saying so, the Brāhmaṇa with his eyes red-shot in anger got off the chariot and sat down on the ground.
51. Cursed in this way, the Goddess then got perturbed and began to cry. Bringing her pitiable state to the knowledge of Kṛṣṇa, she told him as to how could she stay without him.
52-53. Śrī Kṛṣṇa said, "Everyday, I shall come twice to your residence, the Goddess. Those who will have a sight of mine then, will get a look of yours here at the same time. If men having a sight of mine do not take a look of yours here with faith, the fruits of their visit here will get halved."
54. By giving assurance to his dear wife in this manner, the God thus evinced his kindness towards the vehement Brāhmaṇa, Durvāsā.
55. Then outside his (i.e. Durvāsā's) house, the God (i.e. Hari) worshipped him, washed his feet with water and then taking in hands the water offered at the Brāhmaṇa's feet got his head touched with the same.
56. Then he offered him water through both his palms joined together in form of a cup. He gifted him with cows as

well as offered him the mixture made of five ingredients (viz. milk, ghee, curd, honey, sugar, etc.) with faith. He also offered him palatable food consisting of six tastes and flavours as per accepted procedure.

CHAPTER THREE

Relief of Rukmiṇī

1-4. The sages said with a note of exclamation: Oh! despite his limitless power, Kṛṣṇa gave due importance to the words of a Brāhmaṇa sage and acted in such a manner that the sage's words did not become futile. In any case, it is well-known that despite bearing the circular disc (as a weapon) in his hand, Janārdana—the guardian of the unanimously accepted righteous path (i.e. *dharma*) did not get angry when *Bhṛgu* humiliated him by striking feet on his chest. On the other hand, he continued to bear that footprint on his breast. So how could the Goddess stay separately from her dear husband as directed by the Brāhmaṇa? Please narrate us the story of her staying all alone. We are very eager to know about this story of Dvārāvat. Our earnest desire to get enlightened about this is solely out of the wish to get rid of the lamentation in our mind.

Prahlāda said:

5. Listen to all the factual details that I am going to narrate regarding the sorrows arising out of the curse upon Rukmiṇī and how subsequently she—the dearest of Hari, got free from the same.
6. Due to the curse of Durvāsā, the wife of the king of the Yādavas (i.e. Śrī Kṛṣṇa) began to weep immediately.
7-14. Rukmiṇī said, "Reliance on such unbelievably good happening can only be possible on earth for the presence

of water either in a well or in the seas cannot be evidence enough for more water. It is highly fortunate for me to have the Lord of the world as husband. Otherwise, I would have had to bear the consequences for disregarding the sage belonging to the Pulastya clan (i.e. Durvāsā) all alone. On one side there is Hari full of all gracious qualities and the repository of all goodness. But on the other side there is me—the beautiful woman excessively restless and obstructive, with lesser qualities of goodness. Despite this, the wise God has tried his best to bear with the pain of separation from a poisonous and sinister woman as a part of sticking to his words. Otherwise anyone else in his place as a master of all castes and completely imbued with the wisdom of scriptures as well as knowledge of weapons would have definitely been tired of a woman like me. He has made my heart hundred times stronger and as a result impregnable like lightning. Otherwise, it would have simply broken down with distress of separation from the pleasurable company of him. By observance of persistent penance I attained the first Puruṣa as my own. That is how without having sons I did not meet death in five days. Hence, I could successfully bear with such harsh pain. Otherwise, this destabilizing evil which I committed for myself would have definitely grown by lakh of times."

15. Lamenting excessively in this way and with sorrows, her deplorable condition was almost like that of female cranes making sounds in distress. Obsessed with the fear of separation integral to the curse of the Brāhmaṇa, her condition became pitiable and she, as a result, fell unconscious.

16. Thus Rukmiṇī—the beloved of Kṛṣṇa was cursed by Durvāsā and with her consequently becoming unconscious her father—the sea, arrived there.

17. With water full of particles of nectar and the air perfumed with pollens of lotus, the sea surrounded Rukmiṇī—the beloved of Kṛṣṇa.

18. In the meantime, Nārada with his vīṇā in hand and singing the glory of God reached there in the pathways of the sky.
19. Then learning that the sea came down to assure the mother of universe (i.e. Rukmiṇī) Nārada was heard saying as follows.
20-30. Nārada said, "O mistress of God! the curse of the Brāhmaṇa on your husband has already faded away. Hence, the giver of all goodness, be patient. You are the manifest Goddess and Lord Kṛṣṇa—the best Puruṣa. He has descended on earth in his incarnation as per your will to relieve the earth of its burden. The God Kṛṣṇa, as the Supreme Brahma, is above all sorrows of mind. You, on the other hand by your propensity to engender attachment, are the cause of the dissolution of creation ultimately. Inhering the whole—the totality within, the Lord by nature remains separately in the heaven. Despite this, the Lord of the universe could hardly separate himself from you. Inseparable forever from you, He, the God of gods is the Lord of the world. All his dramatic incarnations are only based on your support. There cannot be either the meeting or separation of God from you—the flawless. The God's assuming different forms is only with an eye towards the welfare of everything existing. The desire for prosperity should always be preceded with earnest efforts towards worshipping of the best Brāhmaṇas. One need not excessively excite the ascetics—the learned in the knowledge of truth. As per your perception, this is the way people become fragile consequent to their separation from near and dear ones. But it is Hari who, in the guise of sages curses the treacherous. Kalyāṇī, you may remember, how taking birth for himself in the Raghu dynasty Hari had evinced enthusiasm to stoop low for the sake of relieving the earth of its burden. Don't you know Rukmiṇī that God—the Lord of the world is relatively more important than the very life itself. The universe is filled both inside and outside by Him. Hence, the question that occupies my mind, O the ardent follower of all religious vows! is how

the Lord, who by nature, is free from keeping any specific company, can incessantly have your company?

31. It appears to me that you have employed all his powers in this task. Hence, get rid of your pre-occupied mental distress with regard to having his company in an exclusive garden. O mother! get reminded of your form and holding patience onto the mind, remain free from obsession with regard to your reunion with him."

32. After Nārada's (i.e. the sage of the gods) speaking like this, the Lord of rivers (i.e. the sea) began to speak out gently and with well-thought of and delineated terms.

33-42. The sea said, "All that the sage of gods has told you, are true, the Goddess. The Vedas have always described you as the companion of Viṣṇu. The ultimate masculinity which is devoid of any particular form or appearance, assumed a body onto itself in the form of your Lord and with your support created and established the universe on its sweet will. And its assuming body is only possible beside you and it cannot be any other way than this. Hence regret or repentance does not behove you. The permanence of your company is there forever and is like the curl of hair on the chest of Śrīvatsa (an epithet of Viṣṇu). This Bhāgirathī (i.e. Gaṅgā) has come down here as per my orders. It will continue to entertain you—the Goddess in your embodied form. (Further) this region, full of its fresh water will be a giver of immeasurable happiness to you. Full of varieties of trees, creepers along with shrubs forming arbour and accompanied with elephants and the gentle humming of bees, the place will offer a beautiful and attractive sight to behold. The place will brim with new sprouts apparantly in all eagerness to break forth, with bunches of beautiful flowers, with fruits having nectar-like juice and with rows of buds. Thus embellished, this garden would be fit to appeal and stand out in the mind. Indeed, the garden here will forever be beautiful. As it is we always address you and treat you like the mother. You are the image of inaccessible knowledge. So how can we fully comprehend you? Thus the supreme Goddess, be graceful and allow both of us (i.e. the sea and Nārada) to leave. All our homage to you, the mother of universe. Kindly accept our repeated homage to you which is always there for you."

Prahlāda said:

43. Having said so to the bearer of the world (i.e. the Goddess) both of them then left in the same direction they had come from. Bhāgīrathī—the Goddess then got herself placed there on her own.
44. (As per words of the sea and Nārada) A forest got materialized there always attended with abundant beauty. Endowed with the wealth of flowers and fruits, it became fit for service of the entire world.
45. As a matter of grace for living beings, Gaṅgā—the destroyer of all evils began to ornament the region as a river known as Viṣṇupadī (i.e. an epithet of Gaṅgā).
46. Thus with the persistence of Goddess (i.e. Gaṅgā) there as per the words of the sage and as a result of the assuring presence of Gaṅgā, that particular region not only became beautiful but also hale and hearty.
47. Then after hearing the Goddess Viṣṇupadī's (i.e. Gaṅgā's) meeting the sea, all rivers from here and there reposing faith in her began to assemble there.
48. The inhabitants of Dvārakā also got enchanted with the beauty of the forest and began to frequent the same, i.e., the Rukmiṇī's forest.
49. After hearing all these about the cunningness of Śambhu (an epithet of Śiva) Durvāsā got highly enraged, but with a smile on himself said as follows.
50-54. Durvāsā said, "Who could change or give a different shape to my words in the three worlds? Even among gods, the primordial Brahmā would not dare so. Is the world not aware as to how Śakra (an epithet of Indra) got deprived of the prosperity of the three worlds as a result of my heightened anger? Aware of the fact of my reputation as a giver of curse,

how could Rukmiṇī roam about there in the forest which is like the Nandana forest in heaven and in the service of the people. Hence, let the fruits of all trees in existence in this garden be unfit as eatables for people. Let the fortune of flowers and the bunches of buds wean away and let these fall off. Let this river standing at the helm of all rivers get burnt by my curse and let the boon of taking its water as a blessing no more hold validity."

Prahlāda said:

55. Then everything existant there got burnt out and ruined as per the words of the sage for it is Viṣṇu himself who had rendered the basic strength behind actuation of the words of Brāhmaṇas.
56. Then the Goddess, witnessing the unsurmountable misfortune for herself became intensely depressed and began to solicit death for herself time and again.
57. Then realising that death is the sure remedy for sorrows she (i.e. the Goddess) then fastened a portion of her stole around her neck.
58. Then becoming aware of everything happening there, the all-abiding and benevolent Lord (i.e. Visṇu) hurried up and arrived there seated on his career bird, the Garuḍa.
59. Then he saw the Goddess in such a condition in which she happened to be hanging herself below the branch of a tree with her neck trapped in a noose and with her eyes shut.
60. Ornaments on her body had fallen down. Her body had emaciated like a creeper. Nearer to death, her lotus-like face had virtually become pale. The God offered his compassionate salutation to her—the image of grace and kindness, the giver of all happiness and the bearer of qualities.
61. With her wretched condition accompanied with screaming and her lotus-like eyes shut up, she appeared like being completely overpowered. With the lower portion

of spine turned around and with her wet eyes, she appeared as if she had offered herself in reverence to the Lord of her life.

62. Herself thrilled up, imbued with the feeling of love, she was equally presenting a sight of one being ashamed of the filth of her love and thus equally angry. With herself full of two-times of sorrow she was like a present of varied emotions to the sight.

63. Then as a matter of medical treatment the God separated the noose from her neck by his own hands and then to infuse life into her began to recite the life-giving sacred incantation taking her hands in his.

64-68. Śrī Kṛṣṇa said, "O Goddess! how could you dare to commit this cowardly act of killing yourself without getting into the necessary act of reasoning prior to it. Now tell the cause behind your sorrows. If you are wisdom, I am the supreme consciousness. I am the God, if you are illusion. As you are the wisdom, I am the living being. So how can there be separation between both of us. Enchanted by you, both Brahmā and Śiva wander. So why do you get restless. Are not you aware of your own position? Bound by you, the sages perform their activities. So how can the same sage curse you who is the receptacle of all excellences. O Goddess! all my endeavour in this way has been to educate the worlds. Men act helplessly completely taken over by my illusion. Look, how the chief of the sages taken over by intense anger has calmed down."

Prahlāda said:

69. Sobered down with devotion and accompanied with due deliberation, the virtuous sage Durvāsā then began to repent.

70. Saying (onto himself) how could I do all this, he (i.e. Durvāsā) then came nearer to them and with eyes full of tears, fell flat before them on the ground offering his homage.

71. Making himself pitiable, he began to make entreaties before the father and the mother of the world seeking their pardon. To please them, he began to utter hymns in a mysterious manner of devotion.
72. He said, "O Lord of the world! if you are kind enough towards me, please fulfill my wish through your union with the Goddess as pre-ordained."
73. Then Govinda (an epithet of Viṣṇu) with a pominent laughter said, "Your words—the virtuous sage would be given due importance so that those would not go in vain."
74-78. He said, "O Brāhmaṇa! how could I dismantle the bridge (i.e. the rule of law here) which I have arranged governing relationship among and between beings. The bridge based on good conduct has been effected to protect the world. Twice, everyday I shall come here, the virtuous sage and in the process I shall entertain the virgin daughter of the sages according to their wish. I get pleased by worship and by no other means including words and deeds. As I get worshipped, so will accrue my love and affection. The great sage, on my ascending onto Vaikuṇṭha (i.e. the heavenly abode of Viṣṇu) all my brightness will enter into and reside in my dwarf incarnation. Rukmiṇī will again join me in the form of an idol. The Bhāgīrathī (an epithet of Gaṅgā) will also be blessed with qualities similar to a sea and putting aside all sorrows she will proceed on the pathways of happiness."
79. In this way, after obliging the sage, Keśava (an epithet of Kṛṣṇa) left for his own abode giving up his apparel and along with the sage. And this is how, the sage's putting up close to the God was decided.
80. The Goddess, on her part, becoming fully conscious of the efforts of God towards favouring the sage, became free from her mental distress.
81. Like this event of the Goddess, i.e. the beloved of Hari becoming free from distress, Bhāgīrathī has been spoken since then, as the liberator of all sorrows.

82. A man conforming to the ritual of taking a bath here in this auspicious meeting place of Gaṅgā with the sea either on the new moon or full moon day gets completely relieved of his sorrows.
83. All the desires of those, who have a sight of Rukmiṇī either on the eighth or ninth or the fourteenth day of a month, get accomplished.
84. This is how I have described to you the narrative with regard to how the Goddess as well as the sage got liberated from their sorrows by virtue of God's grace. What more do you wish to listen to?

CHAPTER FOUR

Commendations of Dvārakā visit

Śrī Prahlāda said:

1. Honoured by Hari, the best of the Brāhmaṇas (i.e. Durvāsā) became fully satisfied and asked Keśava to put forth the desired boon in his mind.
2. Śrī Kṛṣṇa said, "If the revered personality is pleased, I may be granted with the boon by which he will remain always present here and under no circumstances should he forsake this place."
3. Durvāsā said, "If I have to stay here Kṛṣṇa then you Keśava too have to give me the word that you will remain ever present here along with your sixteen attributes."
4. Śrī Kṛṣṇa said, "The virtuous Brāhmaṇa, whenever the devotees will have a look of yours here, they will simultaneously have a sight of mine also. So the revered being, tell me what fruits will you grant such devotees?"
5-6. Durvāsā said, "O Kṛṣṇa! Whoever takes a bath here in this particular meeting place of Gomatī (i.e. an epithet of Gaṅgā) with the sea, my boon will cause them to be free

from all sins. Kṛṣṇa! also listen to another thing that is going to materialize here—those who will make offering of wealth to me as per my requirement, after taking a bath here, their wealth will grow sixteen times of the proportion offered."
7. Śrī Kṛṣṇa said, "I shall grant that man that particular state of liberation which is even a rarity for gods, if after worshipping you, he follows it up with worship of mine."

Prahlāda said:

8. In this way both Kṛṣṇa and Durvāsā remained delighted in granting boons to each other. Since then, the master Brāhmaṇas! both of them stayed put there. As per their boons, undergoing the religious ritual of pilgrimage there has been stated to result in realisation of all desires.
9. By virtue of the boon awaiting the religious ritual of taking a bath here, a man obtains thousands of cows as fruits, for the place is already blessed with the boons from Viṣṇu and Durvāsā beforehand.
10. Since then, the foremost Brāhmaṇas, Hari has been present in Dvārakā. Bound by his words to Durvāsā, he never leaves this place.
11. Beside the idol representing the dwarf incarnation of Viṣṇu here, flows the Gomatī. By coming in association with and taking round of this centre of pilgrimage men succeed in their endeavour towards liberation.
12. When Hari gave up his body at Prabhāsa (i.e. a centre of pilgrimage near Dvārakā) all his attributes (i.e. the so-called sixteen qualities) integral to his brightness got embedded in this idol of him.
13. Hence, the Brāhmaṇas, nowhere else can Hari be found except here in the Kaliyuga. If Kṛṣṇa is your mission, go there without fail.

The sages said:

14-16. Let there be your well being O best devotee of Viṣṇu and the path-finder. Such awareness could only be possible for you and we could never know this. What fruits can be had by going there and by having a sight of Lord Kṛṣṇa? Besides, what are the other centres of pilgrimage there and which are the other gods to be found out there. O King of the demons! in which months, in which period and during which festivals men must visit there and if they do so what offerings they have to make during such visits?

Sūta said:

17. When the Brāhmaṇas asked like this, the ardent devotee of Viṣṇu (i.e. Prahlāda) accompanied with his earnest devotion, began to speak as follows.

Prahlāda said:

18-37. Listen to this which is ultimate and eternal, yet lying concealed. I am going to speak about this in greater details which in any case, has hardly been described. When-ever one makes up his or her mind to visit Dvārakā, his or her forefathers in the heavenly world seem to sing that he or she has been liberated from the hell. Whenever a man makes his steps on the pathways towards Kṛṣṇa, fruits equivalent to those accruing from the ritual of sacrificial fire accompanied with offerings of horses, await on each of his progressive step. One who motivates people to come here to have a sight of the God undoubtedly attains the position of a Vaiṣṇava. He who provides a resort to rest for those visiting Dvārakā and speaks to them politely, gets blessed with a life of playfulness like in the heavenly garden of Nandana. A man providing conveyance to the tired visitors on the way gets the opportunity of passage to the heaven on the aerial pathway by the carrier drawn by swans. Listen to all that which can happen to one who offers cooked rice (i.e. food in other words) to the hungry passengers on their way to this destination with due devotion in the middle of the day (i.e. noon hours of the day). The meritorious act of offering rice here promotes the satisfaction of one's forefathers and equals the holy fruits that accrue to humans through the conduct of *śrāddha* (i.e. the religious ritual conducted in memory of one's forefathers) at Gayā. By gifting footwear while on his way to Dvārakā, a man gets the opportunity to move around seated on the back of an elephant, by the grace of Kṛṣṇa. An individual creating hurdles on the pathway to Dvārakā is foolish enough to get himself or herself plunged into the dreadful world of hell as a matter of law. One who gifts water-pots to the passengers on way, gets the fortune to be blessed with thousand times the fruits that await upon putting up sites offering free drinking water to passers by in the daily chores of life. One who offers a bit of caring to the tired feet and limbs of the passengers on the way or washes their feet, gets all his desires accomplished. There is nothing more fortunate for one than listening either to the religious verses or singing them in the name of Viṣṇu or making offering of gifts to Brāhmaṇas while on the way to Dvārakā. The sight of palace of Kṛṣṇa appears like the summit of Kailāśa mountain as well as that of a clear sky to the best of men. After seeing the temple with golden aura, joined together with the flag and pitcher, one leaving aside his/her vehicle begins to roll down on the ground. By proceeding on the pathway to Dvārakā one gets rid of the sins accruing due to accidental killing of insects, worms and moths by use of appliances at home as well as those arising from lowliest deeds on one's part. (All the) sins arising from usurping other's food or drink or by touching the untouchable get destroyed by having a sight of the flag on the temple of Lord Viṣṇu. One who reads the book in eulogy of Viṣṇu containing his one thousand names and recounts the verses in the praise of Viṣṇu, he slowly proceeds ahead on his way reading out the deliverance in the name of the excellent elephant. In this way, the very act of singing about Viṣṇu as well as his many appearances on earth not only makes one to dance accompanied by happiness time and again, but also the very act of dancing conjoined with happiness fills the devotees with a sense of delight, while approaching the God's temple. In this playful manner one approaches Viṣṇu—the giver of deliverance and by having a vision of this, the urge for emancipation arises in men in the Kaliyuga.

Prahlāda said:

38. Earlier, after paying his earnest homage to Bṛhaspati with all devotion, Indra—the king of gods asked the great mind.
39. Indra asked, "Be kind enough to describe me the greatness of Dvārakā by which individuals can obtain the share of religious righteousness as per their due and which has been on a continuous path of enhancement throughout the four yugas."
40. The virtuous sages! after hearing these words of the great Indra, Bṛhaspati began describing to him who was also equally surrounded by other gods.
41-46. Bṛhaspati said, "O meritorious God! as described by revered sages, the four yugas are virtually the Kṛta yuga, the Tretā yuga, the Dvāpara yuga and the Kaliyuga. Dharma in Kṛta yuga had four bases and accordingly the fruits were described in the Veda. These (bases) were pilgrimage, making of donations, penance, knowledge, meditation and longevity of life through freedom from diseases. One-fourth of these got lost in the Tretā yuga, the Lord, with the Dvāpara yuga happening to retain only two of these. In the beginning of Kaliyuga all these in each of its compartment began to lose vibrancy by wearing out in many proportions. And there is no doubt that there will be destruction of all these as the yuga moves ahead. Mantra i.e. sacred prayer, centres of pilgrimage, yajñas, meditation on divine forces as well as the Vedas and Śāstras will proceed on the path towards extripation. The lowly and the meanest will be rulers on earth and the society will deprecate the ascetics who are followers of some mental vows within themselves."

Prahlāda said:

47. The Brāhmaṇas, after hearing such words of Bṛhaspati regarding the state of affairs coming to wait upon centre(s) of pilgrimage, the gods began to tremble solely out of fear of their co-existence with the mean and the lowly.
48-50. Then they, with all sobriety, began to ask Bṛhaspati—their preceptor, "Is it that the sins which are bound to arise through comixture with meanness will not be flown away by Gaṅgā? Be kind enough and specify the place which would be free from the affectations of the Kaliyuga and by residing where, we would be able to retain our utmost repose. With our difficulties gone, we shall be free from sorrows in that place. We shall regain our upfront of goodness. Please tell us the centre of pilgrimage keeping in view our welfare in this regard."

Prahlāda said:

51. After hearing these words of gods including Indra, the chief of the Angirā clan and the gods' priest after receding into a state of utmost concentration for a while spoke as follows.
52-56. Bṛhaspati said, "Free from the defects of Kaliyuga and in the reputed place of pilgrimage known by the name of Dvārakā, there is a leading and excellent pilgrim centre known as Pañcakośa. Founded by Viṣṇu, this shows the right ways to human society. In the period of Kaliyuga it acts towards the deliverance of people who are bereft of knowledge. This place is well above (i.e. affectations of) human deeds. Imbued with merit, it kills all sins. Evils do not shoot up here. Sins committed earlier get destroyed. There are half of thirty crore centres of pilgrimage on the earth's surface. As an emancipator, there is Dvārakā in this world, which as it is, is full of centres of pilgrimage. Blessed with the good human life, every one must make efforts to serve it.

Prahlāda said:

57-58. After hearing what Bṛhaspati said, Indra then said, "Sir, you have narrated me all about Dvārakā. Tell me as to what fruits, have been said, to result, after going and having a sight of the Lord Kṛṣṇa there. The preceptor, please tell me about the other centres of pilgrimage there having importance as has been said and with regard to the fruits of the sprinkling of water at the confluence of Gomatī with the sea there."

59-110. Then after endearingly addressed Indra as father, Bṛhaspati said, "Listen to the greatness that evolves out of Dvārakā which I am going to narrate. The Lord in his human form of incarnation as Keśava engages in his sports here. He is the Lord Nārāyaṇa encompassing the entire world. Fix your mind on Him as He, the chief God is present here in the Dvārakā city. Putting forth or taking successive steps towards Dvārakā result in yielding thousands of merits for embodied beings in the Kaliyuga. The best of men who visit the beautiful city of Kṛṣṇa (i.e. Dvārakā) in the Kaliyuga, along with one crore members of their ancestral clan, they get enabled to set foot on Hari's abode. Those after making up their mind with all firmness and proceeding towards Dvārakā, can be understood to have made an offering of all of their sins committed in previous birth. Thousands of sins of one simply disappear if the same embodied soul gets fully awakened towards having a sight of Kṛṣṇa and upon his/her taking a look of the face of Lord Kṛṣṇa. Those after visiting Dvārakā and meeting with death in the vicinity of Lord Kṛṣṇa never return to the repeated cycle of worldly existence till its final deluge. For human society in the Kaliyuga, it is easy to get Mathurā, Kāśī, Avantī, Ayodhyā and for that matter even gods. But Dvārakā is difficult to obtain. It is a known truth, the best of gods! that those who after going to the city of Kṛṣṇa spend six months in his (i.e. Kṛṣṇa's) vicinity and take a look of him, get fully liberated from life. The leader of evil spirits, i.e. Yama washes away all sins from within those who endearingly desire for this sportive place of Lord Kṛṣṇa. Sins with all ferocity persist in the body till a man makes a visit to Dvārāvat (i.e. Dvārakā) in the Kaliyuga. Brāhmaṇas in olden times could quantify the deeds holding merit like the various centres of pilgrimage, the nature of donations as well as the studies to be made. But somehow the Dvārāvat (i.e. Dvārakā) of Kaliyuga could not touch upon their perception. However, if by any way a human soul visits the Cakratīrtha (i.e. an epithet of Dvārakā) he, besides himself, facilitates twenty-one of his previous generations to attain the supreme place. Even one visiting Cakratīrtha motivated by greed or crime or audacity or treachery never has to make a retreat to the worldly existence. The fruits resulting from the immersion of bones of the deceased have been renowned. But hundreds and thousands of the same happen to result from immersion of bones of the dead at Cakratīrtha. Among the various centres of pilgrimage in the world this centre has been highly glorified. Known as Cakratīrtha, it has reputation as the destroyer of sins accompanying Brahmicide. All the succeeding future generations in a clan go to the abode of Viṣṇu by virtue of men in their clan previously happening to immerse bones of deceased at Cakratīrtha. What use of having so many sons only for the sake of counting. Having one son happening to visit Cakratīrtha turns out to be a boon. What use undergoing the arduous process of penance or for that matter of making charities and studies? One gets relieved of all circumstances by visiting the city of Kṛṣṇa. Even if a man has faulty activities of a severe nature in the Kaliyuga, a mere sight of the face of Lord Kṛṣṇa will make him not to be sullied by the same again and forever. Making donations and studies or for that matter undergoing purificatory rites become of lesser importance for one born in a low caste or for that matter a soul afflicted with sins by simply visiting the city of Kṛṣṇa. One-half of the proportion of fruits effectuating from visit to Vārāṇasi, Kurukṣetra and Narmadā get materialized by regular visit to Dvārāvat. He is the blessed one and if a god, so among the gods who never allows his thoughts dither from being fixed on Kṛṣṇa even for a while. It has been heard that one after undergoing abstract meditation on the twelfth day of a month and thereafter following it up with taking a look of the face of Kṛṣṇa after taking a bath in the confluence of Gomatī with the sea, scarcely gets defiled by evils. As it is, if a man simply goes and takes a look of the sportive city of Kṛṣṇa as the 12th day of a month approaches, he becomes free from the abysmal worldly existence. O the king of gods! those whose life-force gets departed here in the abode of Kṛṣṇa, never return from heaven for crores of years. My dear child, a man's condition on earth is understood to be of one like in the womb if he has not happened to have a sight of the God—the killer of Kaṅsa present at Dvārāvat. Inhabitation in Dvārakā is difficult to obtain. So is also a sight of Kṛṣṇa. Getting an opportunity for a bath at Gomatī is difficult to obtain, as is also the husband of Rukmiṇī. Penance was of ultimate value in Kṛta yuga while deliverance was the backbone of knowledge in the Tretā yuga. *Yajña* (i.e. sacrificial fire) had the highest value in Dvāpara yuga while in the Kaliyuga it is celebration of the glory of Keśava. A crore time of the fruits accruing to making donation of one thousand *palas* weight of gold, result by having a sight of the face of all-giver Hari. Charities made at Dvārakā as well as the extirpation of shells here and so also the ritual offering balls of cooked rice in the memory of one's forefathers here become imperishable. Donations of cows and buffaloes here is similar to making donations of gold and dwelling units. Making gifts of bulls and the booties of land here become the same as that of gifting beautiful and virgin daughters. God Indra! besides all this, there are three more places where charities are to be made. Engendering liberation, such action is stated to bring emancipation for one's forefathers as well as for one's ownself. This place has been commended as having higher importance in the human world. All charities made here have been proclaimed to cause liberation by the great sages. Donations in whatever quantity made here or even the undertaking of bathing here out of playfulness, have been stated to cause immeasurable results out of grace of Lord Madhūsudana. Neither ghostly spirits are going to hurt him nor the fear of pain of the hell of Yama is going to affect him, who has complied with taking a look of Kṛṣṇa after visiting Dvārāvat. Complying with the ritual of *śrāddha* for one's forefathers by a mere offering of water of the Gomatī in the Kaliyuga brings them appeasement forever and until the final deluge of world. The best of gods! those while leading family life never fail from visiting this city of Kṛṣṇa everyday, earn the salutation of the entire world as well as of gods. Knowledge of the supreme being, the *śrāddha* at Gayā, death through getting meshed up in a cluster of cattle and inhabitation at Dvārakā are the four ways of liberation for human beings. There can be deliverance of one by virtue of knowledge of the supreme being or by having the last breath at Prayāga. This apart, a mere bath at Gomatī in the vicinity of Kṛṣṇa enables one to attain liberation. Even the great ocean expresses its gratefulness for acquiring merit. It proclaims that its body of water has been sanctified by virtue of Gomatī flowing into it. Even the acute and severest of sins continue to persist as long as the body home to them does not take a bath in the evil-snatcher water of the Gomatī. By taking a bath in the Rukmiṇī pool in the river Gomatī at Cakratīrtha and thereafter by taking a look of the face of Kṛṣṇa a man succeeds in enabling one hundred members of his clan to tide over the ocean of worldly life. Accompanied by devotion towards Hari, if men continuously remember Kṛṣṇa as well as Dvārāvat, then getting themselves cleansed with all certainty of all their sins, they attain a passage to the supreme world of Murārī (i.e. an epithet of Kṛṣṇa). After washing one's feet, one has to bow down first before Gaṇeśa. By this one certainly and beyond doubt lets all hurdles destroyed. Bow down before Kṛṣṇa—the son of Devakī dancing on the petals of dark-coloured lotus. Then fall flat on the ground to dearly pay homage to his elder brother (i.e. Balarāma). Sins committed during childhood as well as during boyhood and youth get destroyed without any doubt by a sight of God Kṛṣṇa. Sins accumulated over thousands of births either through words or by deeds or intentionally by the mind get destroyed here beyond any doubt. A crore time of the fruits obtainable by making donations of gold measuring one thousand *palas* in weight, result by taking a look of Kṛṣṇa. Bow down to the lotus-eyed God at Dvārakā which is protected by Durvāsā along with Maheśa. Any one coming to Dvārakā taken over with supreme devotion happens to be right in front of the auspicious door to heaven. After resting for a while and thereafter in the company of friends and relatives, chanting the vedic incantations after assembling all equipments meant for conducting the activity of worship and by calling together the Brāhmaṇas give effect to the undertaking of pilgrimage there (i.e. to Dvārakā)."

CHAPTER FIVE

Penance of Sanat kumar: Appearance of Viṣṇu and the emergence of Gomatī

Prahlāda said:

1. All of you—the best of Brāhmaṇas, therefore go to the abode of Kṛṣṇa at Gomatī without any hesitation. A sight of him (i.e. of Kṛṣṇa) relieves one of all sins. The state of liberation from all sins can only be obtained through intimate identification with the idol of Kṛṣṇa.
2. Bowing down to the water of Gomatī fulfills all human desires striking far away the destructive forces on the path of human well-being.
3. As a great destroyer of all sins, it gives added momentum to the striving against sins to those who visit her (i.e. Gomatī). Bowing down to the water of Gomatī whets up the merits earned in earlier life which have somehow got subdued.

4-5. The sages said, "O the demon king! we have a doubt in our mind as to how could Gomatī be here or for that matter who brought her down here? The great mind! please remove the doubt from our minds. What for this waterbody came up here? O the chief devotee of Viṣṇu! please tell about all this in greater details to us."

Prahlāda said:

6. Once, in ancient times the mobile and the immobile got submerged in the sea and in the process got ruined. Then as commanded by Viṣṇu, Brahmā picked up his weapons in hand.
7. As commanded by the Lord, Brahmā thus created varieties of people. This is how, the creator acted in all earnestness as per the directions of Hari and for the purpose of creation.
8. With a firm desire in mind, Brahmā thus created his youthful son Sanaka instantly whom he asked to procreate further descendants.
9-10. After hearing these words of Brahmā, all of them (i.e. the descendants) with folded hands in supplication told him, "O Lord, O God, we desire to have a sight of your appearance in the form of Viṣṇu. We cannot tie ourselves up remaining bound up with attending to the unassailable obligations of creation in visible forms." Having said so, all boys of Sanaka began wishing if they could be horses fit to be sacrificed.
11. Then placing themselves on the western shore of the sea, they remained engaged in the most difficult penance to actuate their mental resolve. The entire scene began to present one with a bright picture illuminated with radiance of these great meditating souls.
12. Then after a lapse of thousand years, becoming pleased, the bearer of earth, i.e. Viṣṇu pierced out of water manifesting, his unassailable bright form.
13. The tamer of innumerable demons, the personality known for tearing apart so many weapons and the beautiful

God, the bearer of the discus and reflecting the brightness amounting to crores of sun became manifest on the scene.

14. The sons of Brahmā got struck with wonder seeing him. Seeing Viṣṇu they began to feel among themselves as if they got the best of arsenals.

15. Seeing him as well as after hearing the incorporeal voice, the sons of Brahmā began to think that the God himself would soon appear before them.

16. For the purpose of worshipping Viṣṇu, the Brāhmaṇas then hurriedly prepared a weapon resembling the discus of the Lord of the world (i.e. Viṣṇu) as an offering to satisfy the venerable God.

17. In the mean time a voice from above declared that Sudarśana (an epithet of Viṣṇu) appeared to be pleased with them.

18-19. The sages said, "We bow down to you the resplendent and supreme Hari. Our homage to you—the eternal and the master of thousands of gambling. Our homage to you having the appearance of Sun and having the form of supreme being, i.e. Brahmā. We bow down to you—the Amogha, the infallible and the chariot of song."

20. Thus they worshipped him gracefully with whole and unbroken grains.

20. They uttered varieties of eulogy and sang hymns in honour of the supreme Hari. After that they nurtured all eagerness for a vision of the paramount Lord hoping that he would be kind enough to do so.

21. Then learning that the Brāhmaṇas were worried for forefathers of their own caste and tribe, Brahmā then told Gaṅgā as follows.

22-24. (Brahmā said) "O best of the rivers! hurry up and descend down to the surface of earth for the sake of Hari. You, the venerated soul raise yourself to the occasion in keeping with the high esteem that I have for you. Higher up in the regions above, you shall be well-reputed by the name of Gomatī. Then following Vasiṣṭha you be there fast on the surface of earth. Like a daughter following her father, you be the daughter of Vasiṣṭha."

25. Proceeding ahead she, the Goddess (i.e. Gomatī) left towards the reservoir of water. Vasiṣṭha kept moving in the front while Gaṅgā followed him from behind.

26. Seeing her, the fortunate one along with Vasiṣṭha, moving on the western side of the sea, all humans bowed down and paid their homage to her.

27. As they were placed ahead in the front in their movement, then visualising the fulfillment of his desire, the four-armed God, i.e. Brahmā, appeared then and there and in his apparant form of Hari was fittingly delighted.

28. He saw Gaṅgā following Vasiṣṭha and everything happening to be fortunately brightened up with an aura and gracious mind.

29. With mind full of happiness, he worshipped her with beautiful garlands as well as with perfumed incense and with offering of whole and unbroken grains. He kept on repeatedly uttering "let there be your well-being."

30. Seeing Vasiṣṭha leading ahead from the front, the Brāhmaṇas became happy within. Elated as they were, after conforming to all sacred rituals and making offerings to him, they said as follows.

31-34. (They said) "As you have brought the best of rivers to this world, it will therefore have its reputation in the world as your offspring. As this place has been esteemed to be its right place after being brought down from the heaven, it will therefore, have reputation in the world by the name 'Gomatī'. A mere sight of hers (i.e. of Gomatī) will land men in a state of liberation. By undergoing the ritual of taking a bath here again followed up with the activity of making charities, people will earn the passage to the abode of Hari. Those accomplished among the ascetics who after making their offerings as part of worship, sing hymns in eulogy of Hari, they will entitle themselves to the supreme masculine status as per the Ṛg Vedic Puruṣasukta and the status of Śeṣasāyinām (i.e. an epithet of Viṣṇu)."

35. As a result of their (singing in) eulogy, Hari appeared draped in yellow cloth, decked up with the garland made of wild flowers (Lord Kṛṣṇa generally wears such garland) and with parts of his body embellished with beautiful garlands and ornaments.
36. Then as the God assumed his ultimate position, he became visible in his beautiful stature with more than one weapon raised in his hands with his resplendently bright crown and his gleaming earrings in the shape of Makara, i.e. crocodile.
37. Taking resort of the powerful arms of Śrīvatsa (an epithet of Viṣṇu) gives peace of mind to the devotees, takes away all their fears and makes them always happy.
38. Seeing him in the beautiful and eye-catching position when Lakṣmī was happening to gently rub his feet out of deep attachment and faith, the sages got transported to the height of happiness. Then they tried to appease Viṣṇu by singing the hymns as prescribed in the Veda.
39. Following their hymns in his eulogy, Viṣṇu—the God known for his compassion for the poor and distressed, began to speak to the virtuous Brāhmaṇas with himself full of heightened pleasure.
40-45. The gracious God said, "O boys! I am pleased with you and shall grant you that as sought for in your mind. It will so happen that all of you will be united with that knowledge which has so far been inaccessible and by my trick only. The Brāhmaṇas making offering of water to me here solely guided by the desire for liberation, will have all their desires fulfilled as a reward of this supreme centre of pilgrimage. Any Brāhmaṇa, who to oblige this Sudarśana discus of mine here out of devotion, becomes the first to come before me after taking a dip in the water here, will earn the same fame as is the reputation of this centre of pilgrimage known as Cakratīrtha. Like me, he will continue to reside here in this great body of water forever. If by the time, men take a bath here, like the best of Brāhmaṇas at Cakratīrtha, liberation will be there for them in their hands.

The very activity of staying put here in the evening by the Brāhmaṇas after their completing the sacrificial fire here will turn out to accomplish all desires extending over land, air and the space."

Prahlāda said:

46. Hearing all this, Gaṅgā with all happiness and for the purpose of making offering as a matter of worship, took water in her hands for the purpose of washing Hari's feet and touched her head to the same.
47. For this purpose, she then entered the water body and as soon as she did so, Gomatī, the exterminator of all sins, flowed towards the sea.
48. Granting the boon then and there, Viṣṇu disappeared. Sanaka as well as all of Brahmā's sons remained assembled there.
49. This is how Gomatī which finally flowed into the sea, came up there. Stated to be an abductor of all sins, she was heard of as Gaṅgā earlier.

CHAPTER SIX

Importance of bath at the confluence of Gomatī with the sea

The sages said:

1-4. "Let there be your well-being, the highly fortunate and the virtuous king of the demons, Prahlāda. Without you, we perhaps could not have had a vision of the God Hari in this Kaliyuga. The words from your mouth are like the water of river Sindhu and are like nectar. While our ears have completely taken in the same they have failed to deliver in evoking our (i.e. the sages') satisfaction. Hence, the powerful, please tell us in details about the pilgrimage here. We also need to go there where flows the river Gomatī for the God himself, looking after the centre of pilgrimage called Cakratīrtha, puts up there. O father ! we are fallen in this ocean of worldly existence. Kindly rescue us from this ocean. O the great mind ! please tell us the ways and procedures of undergoing pilgrimage.

Prahlāda said:

5. After going near the banks of Gomatī, all of you bow down falling flat on the ground. Then after washing your hands and feet, take the ***kuśa*** (i.e. religiously considered as holy grass) in hands.

6. Then carrying an auspicious fruit along with some unbroken and whole grains in hand, make offering to worship and according to the laid procedure, facing the East.

7-8. While making the offerings say, "O auspicious daughter of Vasiṣṭha! you have descended down from the world of Brahmā. For the purpose of cleansing all my sins, I am making such offerings to you—the Gomatī. O daughter of Vasiṣṭha and the glorious Goddess! the gods salute you. The three worlds sing your glory. O Gomatī! take away my sins."

9. After uttering like this, O the best of Brāhmaṇas! then carrying a bit of earth in hand, remember Viṣṇu in mind and utter this mantra.

10-11. (The mantra is as follows) O earth! the horses run over you. So also the chariots and the God Viṣṇu. The Lord Kṛṣṇa in his incarnation as boar with one hundred hands rescued you. O earth! take away my sins accumulated earlier. By your taking away the sins, I shall be purified and another hundred years will be added to my life.

12. In this way after anointing the body with the mud of earth there, take a bath as per laid down procedure. Then listen to the fruits that result after taking a bath in such manner.

13. Similar merits result by virtue of a mere bath in Gomatī in the vicinity of Kṛṣṇa like by having a bath at Kurukṣetra during eclipse of the sun by Rāhu.
14. After complying with the ritual of taking a bath here with devotion, get engaged in activities as stated. Accompanied by feelings make libation of water in honour of gods, forefathers as well as other human beings.
15. Those who have obtained a place for themselves in one of the hells or have got the dreadful condition of insects get freedom beyond any doubt by making offerings of the water of Gomatī.
16. Even without making offering of whole and unbroken grains or without the sacred *kuśa* grass or even without being attended by due feelings, the offering of water of Gomatī in memory of one's forefathers simply enables one to derive the same results like that of *śrāddha* conducted at *Gayā.*
17. Then after inviting the Brāhmaṇas knowledgeable in the Veda and who happen to make the river bank (i.e. Gomatī's) their habitat, worship the universal God and observe the *śrāddha* ceremony of forefathers.
18. Then after completing *śrāddha* there as per procedure, make sacrificial gifts (to the Brāhmaṇas) in the form of gold and silver with yourselves full of highest faith.
19. Then donate a little female calf with its horns adorned with gold, its hoofs embellished with silver, with its tail decked up with jewels and with itself covered fully with clothes and its back decked up with copper.
20. Then by earnestly saluting the Brāhmaṇas and by offering them cloth, wealth, ornaments as well as seven-fold corns, one can earn endearment of Viṣṇu.
21. After that becoming free from sensory attachments, make the Brāhmaṇas reach the final boundary of their territory. After this make donations to the poor, the blind and the miserly as per your ability and affordability.
22. Gomatī, anointing the body with cowdung, making donations of cows, having the sandal on the idol of Kṛṣṇa applied on one's self and taking a look of the Gopīnātha

(the Lord of protectors of cows—an epithet of Kṛṣṇa) are the five tasks most difficult to obtain.

23. Hence making present of cows on the banks of Gomatī is the best duty. O the best of Brāhmaṇas! by doing this, a man gets gratified.

24-25. Those who might have gone to the most dreadful hell or those who might have attained the passage to the ghostly world or those who might have gone to the inanimate state due to evils committed in previous lives or even those born in a lineage on that particular day requiring sacrificial rites either for the father or the mother—all of them obtain the road to liberation by a sight of Gomatī in the Kaliyuga.

26. O the best of Brāhmaṇas! men who conduct the religious ritual of *śrāddha* after taking a bath in Gomatī, obtain the fruits equivalent to that of the rites of the sacrificial fire involving horses beyond doubt.

27. The merit which has been proclaimed to be earned by virtue of taking a bath at the confluence of Gaṅgā at Prayāga, can be equally yielded if human beings conduct *śrāddha* at Gomatī.

28. Their forefathers as well as their incoming future generations go to the world of Viṣṇu. The sins of thousands of rebirths disappear without any doubt.

29. All sins committed through words or intentionally by deeds go into liquifaction by a sight of Gomatī.

30. O Brāhmaṇas! the God Viṣṇu along with Lakṣmī—the Goddess of wealth, undoubtedly get pleased with the man who conforms to the ritual of having a bath in Gomatī during the month of Kārtika, i.e. during October-November.

31. One needs to make oblations to fire everyday with all earnest application. One must make offering of the six auspicious things produced from the cow's milk everyday as food to the Brāhmaṇas.

32. With all eagerness in devotion one has to worship God Kṛṣṇa everyday. By whatever religious observance it may be, but the chiefs of Brāhmaṇas, one has to remain here by observing certain religious rule.

33. By following completely a religious vow as per the approval of Brāhmaṇas, a man can obtain the sight of Lord Viṣṇu on that particular eleventh day in the month of Kārtika (i.e. October-November) when the Lord is believed to come out of his sleep.

34. One needs to prepare the bathing water for God by mixing the five sweet things (viz. milk, sugar, curd, ghee and honey) with the water of the centre of pilgrimage here. After this one, with all devotion has to anoint the Dāmodara (an epithet of Kṛṣṇa) with a mixture of sandalwood, saffron and the musk.

35. Then worship Garuḍadhwaja (an epithet of Viṣṇu) with aquatic flowers (i.e. lotuses), with *tulasī*, (i.e. basil) with the *kaner* as well as with all other flowers found in the region

36. Then please Viṣṇu by offering the eatables that he is fond of. Then read out the books in his name and sing, dance and play instruments in his honour.

37. Remaining awake throughout the night utter the varieties of hymns in the God's name. Invite the Brāhmaṇas and feed them as per your ability and affordability.

38. Then O chief Brāhmaṇas! even after the completion of the month of Kārtika, worship the God seated on the chariot with eagle on its flag staff, in this spot of confluence of Gomatī with the sea.

39. After taking a bath, worship Janārdana (an epithet of Viṣṇu) while making libations of water in memory of forefathers. Offer salutations to Rāma (i.e. Lord Viṣṇu) by adorning him with gold. Then consider that your religious vow has reached the point of completion with the consent of Brāhmaṇas.

40. In this way, O the chief Brāhmaṇas ! whoever takes a bath here in the vicinity of Kṛṣṇa in the month of Kārtika, entitles for himself a passage to the world of Viṣṇu becoming free from all sins.

41. By virtue of undergoing the ritual of bath with due faith along with one's wife here in the Gomatī during the

rising hours of sun in the month of Māgha (i.e. February), a man remains ever contented.

42. Sesame with turmeric is fit to be given to the virtuous Brāhmaṇas. Every time one must be intent upon presenting sweetmeats mixed with jaggery to them.

43. Sesame seeds are always for use in the sacrificial fire. Hence it is always the duty of men to sprinkle them onto fire to break open. Similarly fire is always for the sake of sacrifice. It must never be used to dispell the cold.

44. One needs to take bath with all devotion in the month of Māgha (i.e. February) which is, as it is, dear to Kṛṣṇa. After that one may donate red-coloured clothes as well as warm robes.

45. Donate shoes and with devotion, offer saffron specially. Viṣṇu can be endeared by offering of blanket as well as food prepared in oil.

46-47. A bath in Gomatī in the month of Māgha (i.e. February) has been stated to result in the same passage beyond any doubt as has been recounted for those who meet death while engaged in action for their masters or in the melee of weapons in the battlefield or for losing their lives for the sake of protecting cows and the Brāhmaṇas. A bath in Gomatī has been stated to sum up the fruits of all charities as well as of all pilgrimages.

48. A man goes to the eternal world of Viṣṇu by having a bath (in Gomatī) in the month of Māgha. Earnest worship of Janārdana also results in realization of all desires.

49. A man who directs himself so and spends the entire month of Māgha (i.e. February) in the place of confluence of Gomatī with the sea and follows the same as per the instructions of Brāhmaṇas, attains fulfillment with all completion.

50. O the best of Brāhmaṇas! even the evil-doers by virtue of a bath in the waters of Gomatī attain the state of those who perform sacrifices as per Vedic precepts by grace of the bearer of discus in hand, i.e. Lord Viṣṇu.

51. Even that particular position of the discus-bearer in hand (i.e. Lord Viṣṇu) which is higher than Brahmā and Śiva has been stated to be obtainable by virtue of a mere bath only in the Gomatī in the vicinity of Lord Kṛṣṇa.
52. The sins that attend upon treachery towards friends or by murder of a teacher apply in equal intensity upon one who tries to create hurdles on the path of journey of one here (i.e. this centre of pilgrimage).
53. The sins that result from robbery of the wealth of Brāhmaṇas or that of the sacred places like temples get purified beyond doubt by dint of a mere bath here in the Gomatī.
54. Similar merit like the one earned by providing security to the frightened, is equally earned by a man by only a bath in Gomatī.
55. By providing security to the frightened, one gets blessed with a son undoubtedly and that too without specifically nurturing a desire in that regard. Backed up with a desire for wealth, one gets blessed with the capability to earn enormously in that regard.
56. If one comes in close contact with the water of Gomatī in its place of confluence with the sea as per a wish nourished in this direction since birth, one becomes grateful O chief Brāhmaṇas! for his will gets fulfilled and he becomes free from debts towards his forefathers.
57. All sins made either in mind or through words and deeds go away by coming in contact with the water of Gomatī in its place of confluence with the sea.
58. Dressed in yellow clothes and seated on the carrier drawn by Garuḍa—the chief of birds, adorned with garland made up of wild flowers and with his body covered with the beautiful and scented sandalwood, he goes, O Brāhmaṇas! to the abode of Viṣṇu becoming independent of all signs of rebirth.
59. By dint of a bath only in Gomatī, a man, without any doubt becomes free from all sins and proceeds towards the eternal abode of Lord Viṣṇu.

CHAPTER SEVEN

Eminence of Cakratīrtha

Śrī Prahlāda said:

1. Then O best of Brāhmaṇas! go to that particular ocean bearing the discus of Viṣṇu in a part of its body. A sight of the mark of Viṣṇu's discus on the stones here brings in liberation for one.
2. Those who happen to worship the lord of the universe, i.e. Jagannātha accompanied by earnest feelings can expect to have a sight of Janārdana forever without blinkling of their eyelids.
3. The God Viṣṇu as Kṛṣṇa directly looks upon everyone from here. Having a mark of discus of the God on its body, this centre of pilgrimage is the best among pilgrimages as far as having a look of the supreme Hari (an epithet of Viṣṇu) is concerned.
4. It has the highest reputation in the three worlds extending over both the animate and the inanimate. It is considered greater than Prayāga as a holy place and as a liberator.
5. The gods as well as the embodied beings certainly worship this discus marked here in the body for six months.
6. Just by having a look of this, a human being gets free from sins in whatever circumstances the same may have been committed. It is due to this that it is counted as the best among the centres of pilgrimage.
7. After coming there, O best of Brāhmaṇas! wash your feet as well as hands. Thereafter, pay your salutation falling flat on the ground.
8. After paying your homage, collect five gems in your hands as well as other things like flowers, unbroken grains, incense, fruits, gold and the sandalwood meant for offerings in the ritual of worship.

9. After through with the things to be offered in worship, go to the western side of the ocean and then facing it, utter mantra (i.e. the sacred prayer as per Vedic hymns) as follows:
10. *Om namaḥ Viṣṇu rupayaḥ, Viṣṇu Cakraya te namaḥ. grahanārghya mayā dattam sarva kāma prado bhava."*
This means "homage to you the discus of Viṣṇu and representing the form of Viṣṇu. Please accept the offerings of mine given as a matter of worship. Let this cause fulfillment of all my desires."
11. Then O Brāhmaṇas! saying, "O fire! O resplendent! O Mṛuda! (an epithet of Śiva), O Rudra! (again an epithet of Śiva) O bearer of the seed of progeny! (i.e. Retodha) and O the paramount and eternal Lord Viṣṇu," enter into the master of rivers, i.e. the ocean for a bath.
12. Take a portion of earth trickling down from the hands of gods raise the same to your heads and then take your bath as per laid down procedure.
13. Then offer libations to forefathers, gods and men in the same stated order. Then after washing things, do the sacrifices to fire with ghee and due devotion.
14. O best of Brāhmaṇas! the fruits that are obtainable after conducting of thousands of sacrificial fire involving sacrifice of horses, have been stated to accrue by just having a bath at Cakratīrtha.
15. O best of Brāhmaṇas! the fruit as has been stated to result by the worship of Mādhava (i.e. an epithet of Kṛṣṇa) at Prayāga in the month of Māgha, i.e. February, results through a bath only at Cakratīrtha.
16. Do the *śrāddha* ceremony in honour of forefathers there with due regard. Make donations of gold as well as of silver to the universal gods and forefathers respectively.
17. Offer food to the afflicted and the tormented. Endow them with clothes and ornaments as well. Give presents to the poor, the blind and the miserly as per your own ability.
18. O virtuous Brāhmaṇas! in Cakratīrtha—the leading centre of pilgrimage, the Lord of the world can be gratified by donations of weaved material studded with gems.

19. Donating a cart yoked with oxen to be driven and complete in all respects is gratifying for Viṣṇu.
20. One may offer a well-disciplined, well-trained horse with good conduct after duly adorning it and along with one's donations to a Brāhmaṇa.
21. O best Brāhmaṇas! by doing so a man becomes accomplished in doing that which is worth doing. His forefathers extending over three generations of his clan attain liberation by this.
22-23. Those who might have reached the womb of ghostly spirits or those who might have got the life of worms/insects onto themselves or even those who might be getting themselves roasted in the hell so defined as dreadful—they all get contentment by the influence of Cakratīrtha. The fruits of *śrāddha* at Gayā can equally be had here, the best of Brāhmaṇas, through a conduct of *śrāddha*.
24. The fate that awaits devoted allegiance to one's mother or the regular conducting of sacrificial fires can be gained through a bath at Cakratīrtha.
25. O the master Brāhmaṇas! the best results of *śrāddha* can be had here on the new moon day. Similarly, the *śrāddha* conducted on a day of solar eclipse is specially remembered for bestowing one with the results obtainable following similar rites at Kurukṣetra. The activities like *śrāddha*, the religious ritual of taking a bath here, making charities and offering of libations of water in memory of forefathers have been recommended on such occasions.
26. The Cakratīrtha is the best one, the excellent one. Never think of actions anywhere else other than here.
27. O Brāhmaṇas! the Cakratīrtha always remains holy and there can be no doubt about this. Man comes here to conduct *śrāddha* in memory of his forefathers.
28. O the best Brāhmaṇas! come to Cakratīrtha for the purpose of worshipping Madhusūdana (an epithet of Kṛṣṇa). The master Brāhmaṇas, by saluting him here, one can get closer to Viṣṇu.
29. Sins are earned through words or through deeds committed intentionally. But all such sins get destroyed by

only a bath here and nowhere else. There can be no doubt about this.

CHAPTER EIGHT

Eminence of a bath at Gomatī's confluence with the sea and of Cakratīrtha.

Prahlāda said:

1. O the best Brāhmaṇas! there is no need of going to the godess-like river, i.e. Gaṅgā or the Kālindī (an epithet of river Yamunā). If you have to go, visit the spot where the river Gomatī meets the sea.
2. It is beyond doubt that all desires can be accomplished here without any difficulty for it is the sea that plays sport here in the waves of the river Gomatī.
3. As it is, men attain their welfare on the banks of the river Gomatī which echo the forces of destroyer of sins. By its meeting with the sea here, this place has been imbued with the power as a great destroyer of sins.
4. O the best Brāhmaṇas! Gomatī's flowing into the sea (here in this spot) has been spoken as a gateway to liberation (in the Kāliyuga) and there is no doubt about this.
5. The bundle of merits obtainable at the place of confluence of Gaṅgā with the sea are equally obtained at the confluence of Gomatī with the sea.
6. Hence you all pay your salutations to the Lord Gomatī as well as the master of river, i.e. the sea. With the sacred grass *kuśa,* make your offerings enjoined with the worship and as per laid down procedure.
7. O the master Brāhmaṇas! make your offerings by mantra as part of the worship as per laid down procedure and while doing so, perform it after going there with

Brāhmaṇas and along with other inhabitants of the same centre of pilgrimage.

8-9. (The mantra is like this) "My homage to you having the form of God. I am offering all this as a matter of worship to you - the God and the supreme soul with due faith just to liberate me from the awful sins. My salutations to you, the ruler of pilgrimage and the gem-like great reservoir of water. I offer my reverence so that the Lord Govinda accepts my offerings made through worship along with Gomatī.

10. After completing the offerings as part of worship, you then tie the hairs on the crown of your head into a lock and then remembering the God, i.e. Lord Viṣṇu, stated to be lying on the water-bed you take a bath there either facing East or West.

11. After bathing there with devout faith, you make libations of water to your forefathers. Then by worshipping all gods of the universe conduct the *śrāddha* ceremony in memory of your forefathers.

12. Make such presents which have been stated to evoke Lord Viṣṇu's pleasure. O the virtuous Brāhmaṇas! donate gold in particular.

13. Along with Lakṣmī, the pleasure of the Lord of the world, i.e. Viṣṇu can be earned by making presents of clothes meant for a couple, i.e. a husband and wife including their warm apparel.

14. Big donations made at the place of confluence of Gomatī with the sea have been glorified for not only to yield one with the lordship of seven islands but also land one in the abode of Viṣṇu.

15. Presenting cotton at the spot of confluence of Gomatī with the sea has also been equally acclaimed to land one with lordship of seven islands as well as in the abode of Viṣṇu.

16-17. That man who donates gold or silver equal to his weight or makes donations of clothes, saffron, fruits and liquids at this spot of confluence of Gomatī with the sea, he not only gets blessed with immense enjoyments but also with all delights of life. He earns a place of salvation from the three directions and finally gets a passage to the abode of Viṣṇu.

18. The donations of gold, silver as well as of horses and cows at the place of confluence of Gomatī with the sea also makes all desires attainable.

19. No one is considered more fortunate than him who after making donation of land here in the confluence of Gomatī with the sea follows it up with the purificatory rite of having a bath here and then remembers Hari (an epithet of Viṣṇu).

20. If a man makes gift of unmarried daughters or hands over learning to others and thereafter takes a bath at the confluence of Gomatī with the sea, he attains the position of Brahmahood.

21. One may make presents of gold, cows and of ghee made of cow's milk with all earnestness. Besides these, if one donates the entire universe, one can earn limitless merit.

22. By donating a lovely or a well-nourished cow at the confluence of Gomatī with the sea one can obtain that ultimate position.

23. If one takes a bath here in the confluence of Gomatī with the sea and makes libations of water covering all festivals and auspicious occasions extending over all *yugas* in memory of his forefathers, one attains that indestructible region of the world.

24. A man desirous of that imperishable position, can have that by having a bath in the confluence of Gomatī with the sea in any of the months of Āṣādha (i.e. July), Kārtika (i.e. November) and Māgha (i.e. February) and by offering libation of water in memory of his forefathers and by conduct of *śrāddha* attended with worshipping through *havan,* i.e. the sacrificial fire and making of charities.

25. O the highly fortunate souls! *śrāddha* at the confluence of Gomatī, yields the inexhaustible satisfaction of one's forefathers in the same manner as at Gayā.

26. O the foremost Brāhmaṇas! have your bath as well as offer libations of water in memory of forefathers here in this

confluence of Gomatī either on the fifth or the seventh, eighth or ninth day following the full moon in any of the months stated earlier.

27-28. Particularly take bath here in the confluence of Gomatī and do charities as per procedure on that particular full moon day falling on Monday or that auspicious sixth day named after the sage Kapila or on the twelfth day of a month. By doing so one goes to that sacred place which is free from sorrows.

29. Offering of balls of cooked rice at the confluence of Gomatī with the sea on dark half of Bhādrapada (i.e. September) particularly appointed for observing obsequecial rites for paternal relations, yields the same higher merit of śrāddha at Gayā.

30. Hence, with all efforts, the best of Brāhmaṇas, observance of *śrāddha* on the dark half of Bhādrapada (i.e. the month of September) otherwise known as Pitṛpakṣa, is desirable at the confluence of Gomatī with the sea.

31. One may conduct *śrāddha* for ancestors on the paternal side for days together under the guidance of Brāhmaṇas well-versed in the Veda. But the merit accruing to this can be yielded by observance of *śrāddha* only for a day on Bhādrapada (i.e. September) at the confluence of Gomatī with the sea.

32-33. One may be devoid of faith. One may fail in mantras or in having association of worthy persons to conduct the *śrāddha*. Or for that matter one may not have the requisite material or may simply not have time or may be in an unhealthy state mentally. Despite all this, libations to gods by putting ghee into the consecrated fire here at the confluence of Gomatī with the sea, ensures and fulfills satisfaction of all of one's ancestral forefathers.

34. The three rivers, viz. Gomatī, Kamalā and Candrabhāgā join the sea at this point of Gomatī's confluence with the sea.

35. Fruits equal to offering balls of cooked rice at Gayā or immersion of bones of the deceased at Prayāga, can be had

by man by *śrāddha* at the confluence of Gomatī with the sea on the particular new moon day appointed for obsequial rites in honour of forefathers on the paternal side.

36. One might have sprinkled the water of most of the centres of pilgrimage onto oneself as a matter of pastime. But with all devotion, one must take bath at the confluence of Gomatī with the sea.

37. Those who observe *śrāddha* invariably on the particular day appointed for obsequial rites in memory of paternal forefathers, the same reaches its point of completion and fulfillment at the confluence of Gomatī with the sea.

38-39. O Brāhmaṇas! by performing *śrāddha* in the Pitṛpakṣa on the new moon day, those who happen to be without sons or those who happen to be merely contemptible barren women, get blessed. Even the defects with those happening to get sons as still births, get done away with by their undergoing the ritual of bath here at the confluence of Gomatī with the sea. A bath, yields them a son with long life consequently resulting in their obtaining happiness.

40. Whatever charities have been stated to be possible in the world, must be offered at the confluence of Gomatī with the sea.

41. O the master Brāhmaṇas! always and especially during all festivals, one needs to take bath at the confluence of Gomatī with the sea without fail.

42. The venerable Brāhmaṇas! sins get destroyed by having a look of it. Salvation brings content in the mind and a bath effects liberation.

43. *Śrāddha* causes unending satisfaction of the forefathers while charities result in realization of desires of the mind without any doubt.

44-45. O foremost sages! one can deem oneself to be fortunate enough to have offered libation of water in memory of one's forefathers and to perform *śrāddha* in their honour at the confluence of the river (Gomatī) with the sea. And the same *śrāddha* includes those performed on days specifically appointed or chosen for obsequecial rites involving the paternal relationships or the maternal relationships or even the relationships extending over the level of in-laws, friends and relatives.

46-47. One might have become inert, i.e. immobile. One might have accessed the state of beauty or loveliness. Some might have attained the state of ghostly spirits. Some might have gone to the womb to have birth as animals or some still might have just become worms/insects. But by virtue of only a bath at the confluence of Gomatī with the sea, all of them attain liberation and there can be no doubt about this.

48. Human beings through performing *śrāddha* as well as by making charities at the place of confluence of Gomatī, attain liberation beyond any doubt.

49. After taking a bath at the confluence of Gomatī with the sea on that particular twelfth lunar day having the union of *Śravaṇ* star, one becomes free from all sorrows and attains liberation.

50. Keeping aside all centres of pilgrimage, if a man takes bath, performs *śrāddha* at the confluence of Gomatī with the sea and then worships the dwarf incarnation of Lord Viṣṇu, he attains the next world by His grace.

51-52. A man who after taking bath here in this confluence as per laid down procedure, worships Garuḍadhwaja (an epithet of Viṣṇu) he gets clothed with yellow robes and adorned with beautiful ornaments. Then summoned by Garuḍa—the carrier of Lord Viṣṇu, he proceeds to the abode of Viṣṇu while the divine women watch him doing so and the Sages in the appearance of Caturbhuja (again an epithet of Viṣṇu) decorated with garlands made of wild flowers continue singing hymns in his glory.

53-54. Human being can consider himself fortunate after taking a bath at the confluence of Gomatī. The powerful Viṣṇu had given effect to killing of a demon here and before doing so Kṛṣṇa himself had washed his discus with the water here. O Brāhmaṇas! it is due to this that this place is famous in the three worlds by the name of Cakratīrtha.

55. There happens to be a stone here bearing the mark of the discus of Lord Viṣṇu which as it is, is a giver of liberation. Worship of it gives one the proximity of Kṛṣṇa—the universal Lord.

56. Here also, one can get glimpse of stone bearing marks of twelve discuses together.

57-58a. As a giver of liberation to all embodied beings, it is understood as the twelve-souled. With mark of one discus on the stone, it shines at Dvārāvat. Named as Sudarśana, it only grants the single fruit of liberation.

58b. The stone bearing marks of two discuses named Lakṣmī Nārāyana gives fruits of happiness and liberation.

59. The stone bearing marks of three discuses is named Trivikrama and gives three kinds of fruits while the stone having marks of four discuses takes away enemies and induces wealth/ prosperity.

60. Known as Vāsudeva, the stone bearing marks of five discuses takes away the fear regarding life and death. The stone bearing marks of six discuses gives fruits like prosperity and fame.

61. The stone bearing marks of seven discuses bearing name Balabhadra has been glorified, while stone bearing marks of eight discuses is known as Puruṣottama and it induces faith and devotion.

62. Difficult for even gods to obtain, the stone bearing marks of nine discuses grants everything while the stone bearing marks of ten discuses reflects the ten incarnations of Lord Viṣṇu and yields kingdom for one.

63. The stone having marks of eleven discuses bestows one with power and might, while the stone bearing marks of twelve discuses blesses one with salvation.

64. Higher than all these stones is placed the stone bearing the mark of the Kṛṣṇa's own discus, i.e. the Sudarśana discus which gives the great fortune of happiness and liberation.

65. A touch of all these stones, takes one above the den of sins. Hence, after taking a bath at Cakratīrtha, human being must imprint a mark of the discus of Kṛṣṇa on his body.

66. Hence, one needs not only to worship Hari—the bearer of discus but also needs to continuously meditate on Him - the eternal. A human being doing so can neither remain childless nor can he become pōor or afflicted with diseases.
67. All sins accruing to Brahmicide or acquired mentally and through words and deeds get buried by a sight of the good-causing stone bearing mark of the discus.
68. If the auspicious mark of the discus is found in a land inhabited by the outcastes, there can be no doubt that the same land like the exclusive region of Hari is also a giver of liberation.
69. If a human soul meditates upon Hari or makes a mark of His discus on any limb of his body as death approaches, he attains the ultimate position.
70. By bearing the mark of discus on one's breast, one instantly gets sanctified. With the protective shield of Kṛṣṇa's discus on the body, the messenger of Yama then becomes fearful to approach or come near him. One goes to the abode of Viṣṇu. Nothing other than this can be thought of.
71. A bath at the confluence of Gomatī and a visit to Cakratīrtha emancipates a human being from severe sins. There can be no doubt about this. This equally applies to those who usually remain engaged in sinful conduct. So what is the need to spell it out again specially in the context of the religious and the meritorious souls?
72. People endowed with the quality of *rajas,* i.e. passion also embrace virtue and goodness under the influence of eternal *Vaiṣṇavism.* This is how the eminence of the same region has been extolled.
73. Both the people endowed with *tamas,* i.e. vicious qualities and the *rajas,* i.e. passion get humbled by the slightest degree of worship of Viṣṇu on their part and get union with virtue / goodness like a river finally meeting with the sea in its natural flow downward.
74. O Brāhmaṇas! it is indeed difficult (to be blessed with a fortune) to go to Dvārakā. So also it is difficult to have a

touch of the (auspicious) water of Gomatī. More difficult, it is to sit up throughout the night to be a part of a religious ceremony invoking Kṛṣṇa. Finally, it is equally but very difficult to have a sight of Kṛṣṇa.

CHAPTER NINE

Eminence of Lake Rukmiṇī

Prahlāda said:

1. Then O the foremost Brāhmaṇas! go to that place having seven basins together, i.e. *saptakuṇḍa* which has been well-heard of. This not only redeems all sins but also enhances one's intelligence.
2. (Hari) the Lord of the world along with Lakṣmī had appeared there when the sages worshipped him by reciting hymns in his honour.
3. Then they got up, formed a circle amongst themselves, for coronation of Padmā (an epithet of Lakṣmī) seated on the left of the God and worshipped her with the water of the divine river Gaṅgā.
4. Then, O Brāhmaṇas! the sons of Brahmā like Sanaka *et. al.* and the seven sages stated to be created from mind began to worship separately with requisite offerings and sprinkling of water onto the Goddess. When they thus made sprinkling of water an ocean came up there.
5-6. Then so named after the Goddess, this pool of water was spoken as Lakṣmī lake. As the *dvāpara yuga* came to an end, the same lake with the support of Rukmiṇī retained its reputation as Rukmiṇī lake in the *Kaliyuga.* Also happened to be served by Bhṛgu, it is remembered as Bhṛgutīrtha.
7. Hence, the great fortunate souls, after going there, better wash the dust off your feet and then bearing the sacred *kuśa* grass in hand, sip water as a matter of the religious ritualistic practice facing the east which has been upheld to be sanctifying.

8-9. Then after making full arrangement with regard to fruits, flowers, the unbroken whole grains required for making offerings as a part of worship, raise a silver onto your head and then recite the mantra saying, "I am making offering of all these for worship in the lake named after Rukmiṇī so that I shall earn the pleasure of Rukmiṇī and all my sins shall wither away."

10. Then continuing to hold the silver on the crown of head, the Brāhmaṇas, take your bath. Then offer libation of water to the gods, human beings and your forefathers in particular.

11. Then perform *śrāddha* there after inviting Brāhmaṇas with all faith. Also make offering of your religious fee to them in silver and gold.

12. Then O the best of Brāhmaṇas! give them juicy fruits in particular. Besides feed sweet food to married couples.

13. Worship wives of the Brāhmaṇas as well as other women also. Give them bodices and red clothes to earn the pleasure of Rukmiṇī.

14. O the foremost Brāhmaṇas! human beings can consider themselves to be fortunate enough by doing so. By doing so, all desires of one get fulfilled and he succeeds in going to the abode of Viṣṇu.

15. Lakṣmī is stated to reside in his house without any doubt. He becomes free from diseases and with a contented mind, anxieties hardly affect him.

16. His forefathers get inexhaustible satisfaction and his children get to enjoy a settled life. Feeling of meanness never gets onto him and man gets blessed with long life.

17. One who takes a bath in the Lakṣmī lake becomes rich/ wealthy from all sides. Neither Lakṣmī deserts him nor the fear of losing wealth ever haunts him.

18. One who takes a bath in the Lakṣmī lake will neither have any enemy nor does he have to get embroiled in any battle. He gets free from the repeated cycle of coming in and going out, (i.e. making exits) from worldly life.

19. One who takes a bath in the Rukmiṇī lake does not have to worry about sorrows and bereavement. Getting free from all sins, he gets purged of all fears.
20. Getting all his desires fulfilled/ accomplished, he goes to the abode of Viṣṇu.

CHAPTER TEN

Eminence of Kṛkalāsa alias Nṛga Tīrtha

Prahlāda said:

1. Then O the best of Brāhmaṇas! go to the Kṛkalāsa reputed as the Nṛga tīrtha which takes away sins.
2. After assuming the body of a lizard onto himself here, the king Nṛga had attained the ultimate passage by the company of Kṛṣṇa.

The sages asked:

3. Who was this king named Nṛga and how could he get associated with Kṛṣṇa ? By virtue of what deeds did he become a lizard? Please speak in details in this regard.

Prahlāda said:

4. O Brāhmaṇas! the king Nṛga was very powerful, intelligent, firm, astute and endowed with all qualities.
5. There were hundreds and thousands of kings in his lineage and he was well-equipped with forces having elephantry, cavalry, charioteers and a considerably large number of infantry.
6. With the mine of soldiers, he was thus invincible. He used to remain incessantly engaged in devotion for his teachers and in the worship of Gods.
7. O the master Brāhmaṇas! the king used to make varieties of charities every day. The virtuous king also used to gift thousands of cows regularly.

8-9. After washing their feet with faith, he used to make the Brāhmaṇas seated on beautiful seats and then with himself putting on the auspicious silken cloth, he used to annoint them with perfumed ointment. After this, he used to worship them with flowers, garlands and perfumed incense. Then he used to offer cows with devotion to the Brāhmaṇas with betel leaves as a matter of religious fee saying, "Let me have the pleasure of Lord Viṣṇu".

10. O the best of Brāhmaṇas! in this way by making charities, performing Yajñas and having enjoyments of life for himself, his time used to pass.

11-12. Once, the king with utmost regards and with folded hands told Jaimini, the Brāhmaṇa thorougly accomplished in observance of religious vows and equally averse towards accepting any donation in return, "O greatly fotunate soul and the reservoir of penance! please be kind towards me by accepting the cow which I am offering as a gift".

13. After hearing such words, the Brāhmaṇa despite unwillingness on his part but in honour of the king said, "It would be like that" feeling ashamed of himself.

14-15. After this, the king then washed his feet and raised water to his head. Then he got a cow, adorned its horns with gold, its hooves with silver, its udder with copper and its body with a white cloth. Then after worshipping it, he offered the same cow as a religious fee to the Brāhmaṇa.

16-17. Then the king became happy to see the Brāhmaṇa leaving after taking the cow. Bearing the colour like that of a white swan, the young cow was being heard by the name of Harsī. The virtuous Brāhmaṇa took the cow back to his home, got it tied up with a rope and gave it moist grass as fodder.

18. The cow's appetite was satisfied with the grass. But at noon it began to feel thirsty and then the Brāhmaṇa took the cow as tied up towards a pond.

19. But after seeing elephants, horses and camels on the way, the cow got terrified and sensing danger, she broke away from the hands of the Brāhmaṇa and ran away.

20. The great Brāhmaṇa looked for the cow hither and thither, but could not locate it. Frightened, the cow fled back into the herds of king's cows.
21. The virtuous king invited Brāhmaṇas again the next day. As per customary practice he worshipped them devotedly and gifted them with clothes and ornaments.
22. In keeping with customary practice, the king donated a cow to the saintly Brāhmaṇa Somaśarmā who taking the same along left for home from the royal palace.
23. (While on his way) He went on proclaiming the king to be efficient and having knowledge of dharma. Incidentally, the other Brāhmaṇa Jaimini happened to be moving around here and there in search of his cow very sadly.
24-26. Seeing Somaśarmā passing by the way with a cow behind him, he (i.e. Jaimini) then went near him and said, "You, the robber! where are you taking my cow after kidnapping it?" Somaśarmā became very surprised hearing such words alleging him as a robber. He instead thought, "I got this cow as a gift from the king and am taking it back to my own house. So how could the virtuous Brāhmaṇa cast aspersion on me as a robber of cow?"
27-28a. The Brāhmaṇa (i.e. Somaśarmā) retorted, "As a gift of the king, this cow is mine beyond doubt. So how could you—the Brāhmaṇa take it away till I remain alive? I have got it today as a gift only."
28b. The other Brāhmaṇa (i.e. Jaimini) said, "Why are you telling me a lie as I got it yesterday? Why do you intend to take it by force?"
29-30. With anger Somaśarmā kept on saying "this is mine". While burning with anger and with eyes red-shot, the other Brāhmaṇa repeated the same in turn. Fighting with each other in this way, both Brāhmaṇas then came near the door of the palace. So severe was their mutual duel, it appeared as if they were out to give up their life.
31. Visibly angry and cursing each other both the Brāhmaṇas wished to convey the same to the king.

32. The king however did not pay any heed to the two Brāhmaṇas fighting with each other on the height of anger. His mind got agitated with fear and he did not bother to come out.
33. Thus continuing to argue with each other they remained there for three nights. Sensing the king's disregard of their matter, they got angry with the king.
34-35. With anger they stated that the king was not coming out of his palace out of sheer disrespect. Despite being the ruler of the people he was not coming out with a decree towards justice. Hence the king would become a lizard without any doubt.
36. Cursing like this, the two Brāhmaṇas then gave away the cow to someone else. Hungry and thirsty as they were, they were equally exhausted. So they got up to move towards their homes.
37-38. As they were about to leave, Nṛga came to the doorstep. After falling flat at their feet to offer salutation, he told them with folded hands, "Your words will never go in vain. Indeed, it will happen and in no way can there be anything different from this. But, be kind towards me and apprise me of the duration of the curse."
39-40. After hearing these words from him they told the king, "After the *dvāpara yuga*, the God Hari will appear in his incarnation as the son of Devakī in the house of Vasudeva. By his touch, you will be liberated from the curse."
41. Having said so, both the Brāhmaṇas then left for their own abodes. The king experienced varieties of luxuries. He also made abundant charities.
42. He made prayer to God through varieties of *yajñas*. Finally death occurred to him and the Brāhmaṇas! he went to the abode of king of dharma, i.e. Yama.
43. After welcoming him honourably as a guest, Yama told the king, "O king! whether you intend to enjoy the fruits of your meritorious deeds first or those of your bad deeds? You may spell out the same for those are to be executed by me only."

44. Nṛga said, "First of all, grant me the fruits as per my misdeeds, if any." Then he assumed the entity of a lizard as per the approval of Yama and had his existence in that entity for a thousands of years.
45. O Brāhmaṇas, one day, all the princes of Yadu dynasty along with Kṛṣṇa were moving about in the forest with an eye for hunting deer.
46. Being thirsty, they began to look for water and reached a pool at noon hour of the day. They all sighted the lizard there in the pool.
47. The Yadu princes made all efforts to rescue it. But it was relatively heavier in weight and given the operation of gravitational pull it could not be moved about.
48. When none of them could bring the lizard out then all of them brought it to the attention of Kṛṣṇa and Balarāma. By just having a glance, Kṛṣṇa could sense it to be Nṛga and began to laugh.
49. By just putting his left hand playfully into the water, the Lord of the world threw the lizard out of water and by touch of the God, it soon got free of the burden of curse.
50-51. Giving up the body of lizard, the king then got himself annointed with sandalwood paste and adorned with beautiful garland. Then with earnest devotion and with folded hands the king said, "Obeisance to you—the protector of the world, its creator, its rearer and the ultimate destroyer. My homage to you— the thousand-headed, the all-powerful and the eternal Brahmā."
52-53a. The God-incarnate as son of Devakī then said to the king that he had been pleased with him (i.e. the king) and was prepared to grant him the boon playing rounds in his mind. (He said) The king would be blessed with a divine vision by the touch of God.
53b-55. As the God said so, the king got excited with happiness and said, "If you are pleased to grant me a boon then Keśava let this hollow spot here acquire fame by my name. Let those offering libation of water to their forefathers

after taking a bath here with due devotion obtain the world of Viṣṇu by your, i.e. Govinda's grace."
56. After saying, "Let it be so" the God then returned to Dvārāvat again.
57. Getting adorned with beautiful garland and his body smeared with sandalwood paste, the king also proceeded in a space car to the palace of Viṣṇu served by gods.

Prahlāda said:

58. O master Brāhmaṇas! since then has this well been named after Nṛga. This is a holy place for all embodied (living) beings with the boon of Kṛṣṇa.
59. O best of Brāhmaṇas! go there, make offerings as part of your worship as per laid down procedure. Your offerings as part of worship must contain fruits, flowers, unbroken grains including rice as well as sandalwood.
60. While making offering say, "Obeissance to you the omnipresent and the supreme soul Viṣṇu. Please accept our offerings as part of worship made at the well named Nṛga."
61. Then take some earth in your hands and anoint your bodies with it. Take a bath after this. Then follow it up with libation of water to forefathers, Gods and human beings in the stated order.
62. Then observe *śrāddha* with due respect in memory of your forefathers. Feed Brāhmaṇas as well as give religious fees to them as per your capability.
63. Donate a decorated cow along with calf in particular. Give away beds as well as any other article of household use which yields Viṣṇu's pleasure.
64. Always make charities to the poor, the blind, the miserly as well as the inhabitants near it. Make charities as per your own capabilities and without any streak of dishonesty.
65. O the master Brāhmaṇas! fruits are obtainable by only a bath here and through giving cow in charity. With observance of *śrāddha* here one does not get debased or ignominous birth.

66. By doing *śrāddha* at *Kṛkalāsa tīrtha* as well as by offering libation of water in memory of one's forefathers, a man goes to the abode of Viṣṇu along with his forefathers.
67. A visit undertaken to this *tīrtha* for the purpose of realization of one's desires nurtured in the mind yields success. Fruits of all centres of pilgrimage are obtainable at this *tīrtha* and there is no doubt about this.

CHAPTER ELEVEN

Eminence of Viṣṇupada Tīrtha

Prahlāda said:

1. Then O the foremost Brāhmaṇas! visit Viṣṇupadodbhava *tīrtha*, i.e. the centre of pilgrimage where the foot of Viṣṇu has come up. Taking only a sight of this yields the fruits of having a bath in Gaṅgā.
2. O the virtuous Brāhmaṇas! I have already narrated about its origin earlier. By simply remembering its glory, sins get destroyed.
3. Hari had brought down Gaṅgā here to please Rukmiṇī. By just having a mouthful of its water one can obtain the fruits of *yajña* involving sacrifice of horses.
4-5. Gaṅgā here emerges below the foot of Viṣṇu. Hence it has been referred to as Vaiṣṇavī. Therefore you—the highly fortunate souls, go there and make offering as a part and parcel of your worship and as per accepted procedure. Offer your salutations to Goddess Bhagavatī, i.e. Gaṅgā emerging below the foot of Viṣṇu saying, "O Gaṅgā! please accept our offerings as part of the worship along with Viṣṇu."
6. O the foremost Brāhmaṇas! after making this utterance, pick up some mud in hand and then facing East take bath remaining as far as possible in one spot.

7-11. After this it is desirable to do libations to gods, one's forefathers and other human beings with seasame and unbroken whole grains. Then after inviting Brāhmaṇas there one may make offering of gifts. The adept must perform *śrāddha* attended with earnest faith and offer gold and silver as religious fee as has been stated. The virtuous Brāhmaṇas, make charities for the poor, the blind and the miserly as per your own affordability and donate gold in particular. Make presents of footwear as well as water pitchers to the Brāhmaṇas. Give them curd added with water and salt. Also give them cooked spinach added with cumin seeds. Give red clothes with blouses which Rukmiṇī wears. Make offering of gifts to Brāhmaṇas as well as their wives to earn pleasure of Viṣṇu.

12-14. O the foremost Brāhmaṇas! a man can consider himself fortunate by doing so. His forefathers attain inexhaustible pleasure by all these like that of the *śrāddha* at Gayā. His forefathers extending over three lineages go to the abode of Viṣṇu. And while alive, blessed with prosperity that man gets bestowed with sons and grandsons. Besides Rukmiṇī, Kṛṣṇa gets pleased for ever by *śrāddha* here and grants him all objects desired for in this as well as the next world.

15. This is all about the eminence of the Tīrtha where the foot of Viṣṇu has come up. One gets free from all sins by listening to this with all devotion in Hari.

16. The merit earned by listening to as well as reading it leads to liberation from all sins.

CHAPTER TWELVE

The Maya lake—its formation and greatness

Prahlāda said:

1. Then O the best of Brāhmaṇas! visit the foremost Tīrtha called "Gopracāra". By taking a bath here with faith, a man obtains the fruits of making charities of cow.
2. The Lord of the world had bathed here when gods from above had showered him with their appreciation. The virtuous Brāhmaṇas, a bath here on the twelfth day of a month is spoken as Katadānam.

The Sages said:

3. O king of the demons! how could the Gopracāraka Tīrtha come up there and for that matter, for which purpose did Janārdana take a bath there?

Prahlāda said:

4. After killing Kaṁsa—the king of Bhoja with his limitless power, the great God Kṛṣṇa then got Ugrasena coronated as the king of Mathurā.
5. Then given his fondness for Gokula, Kṛṣṇa sent Uddhava there keeping in view his hearty and loving wishes for friends and for both the male and female inhabitants there.
6. After offering his salutation to Govinda, Uddhava proceeded towards Gokula of Nanda. He was dressed up in a similar way like Kṛṣṇa and adorned with jewellery and ornaments.
7-10. Seeing Uddhava, the dear servant of Kṛṣṇa well-dressed and adorned with ornaments towards the fag end of the day, i.e. in the evening, Yaśodā offered him her respect. Then she served him food and while putting him to take rest, enquired about the well-being of her son Kṛṣṇa

with tearful eyes and her voice choked out of affection for son, saying, "Is everything running happily for both my sons and the best of the Yadus—Balarāma and Kṛṣṇa? Is Govinda at all remembering his other companion cowboys? Will Govinda—the Lord of Mathurā ever come back to the region of Gokula and help its sons of the soil to cross over the ocean of sins?"

11. Saying this with tearful eyes and with choked voice both Yaśodā and Nanda wept pitiably and persistently subjugated by affection for son.

12-14. Sensing both of their lives to be at stake Uddhava then amiably conveyed them the message of Kṛṣṇa to boost up their spirits saying, "Along with his elder brother, he has asked me to convey his regards to you. With everything fine with him, he desires to be apprised of your well-being and health. He, the light of the Daśaī clan will come back soon with venerable Balarāma and after coming here, he—the Lord of the World, will lay down the system as per your welfare."

15. In this way Uddhava assured the Nandas and being welcomed by them slept off with all happiness in their house.

16-17. Seeing the chariot in front of the door of Nanda's house, the Gopīs became surprised. As it is they were eagerly waiting for the advent of Kṛṣṇa. Hence they began to say, "Who was it, who was it? Who was this being having the brightness like sun, having long arms and having the same apparel on his body like Kṛṣṇa to have arrived in the house of the King of cowboys?"

18-20. Coming together and discussing among themselves all the women of Braja, as it is afflicted with sorrows due to separation from Kṛṣṇa began to ask the same messenger of him in seclusion. The beautiful Gopīs said, "Wherefrom have you come here and for what purpose? Do you intend to abduct us in the guise of a dacoit? As it is Kṛṣṇa has aleady hurt our heart. He has fled making us, the womenfolk drink the abominable poison."

21. Saying like this and after seeing the attendant of Kṛṣṇa before them the Gopīs impatient with sorrows fell unconscious on the ground.
22-23. Uddhava on his part could realize all of them to be bewitched coming under the resort of Kṛṣṇa's love and affection. Hence to give them assurances, he began to make the following words soothing to their ears. Uddhava said, "O Gopīs! the God alias husband of ten women is equally afflicted with the arrow of Kandarpa, i.e. the Lord of lust and desire. Obsessed with the same, day and night, he is neither drinking nor eating anything."
24-26. Hearing these words of him one of them named Lalitā became relieved of her anger and with her eyes reddened due to crying, she told Uddhava, "Kṛṣṇa is cruel and dear to the cruel people. Hence, do not lie me by stating that which does not fit those failing to evoke respect. Shame on the cruel and evil-doer Hari who despite the good wishes of the women folk has left for Dvārāvat by evincing his bad temperament."
27. Śyāmalā said, "Why to speak about a being having low fortune, less merit and a bad temperament? Speak something other than this that fits him."
28. Dhanyā said, "Who has brought this messenger of that bad person here? Let him also equally follow that evil path following which Kṛṣṇa did not turn back."
29. Viśākhā said, "His birth is only to hurt women for he does not know how to honour nor does he have a good family lineage nor does he fear sinful activities. Seeking company of such a person is meaningless for he lacks in the basic quality of manhood."
30. Rādhā said, "It cannot be tenable to accept that one who does not have the slightest sense of fear of sin for killing living beings, can at all have the hesitation to hurt women."
31. Śaivyā said, "O greatly fortunate one! please tell us the truth as to what the best of Yadus doing? For that matter why should he at all remember us when he is having the company of city-bred women?"

32. Padmā said, "O greatly fortunate Uddhava! will it ever be possible for the God dearer to wicked women to be attracted towards lotus with its broad leaf?"
33. Bhadrā said, "O Kṛṣṇa! O best of the Gopas (i.e. the protectors of cows) O darling of the Gopīs (i.e. women protector of cows) O immensely powerful and the strong one! rescue the Gopīs from the ocean of worldly existence."

Prahlāda said:

34. The women of Braja constantly weeping in this way and remembering their yearning for Kṛṣṇa were making varied voices of concern albeit in a well thought of and organized manner.
35. Uddhava became utterly surprised hearing them crying and then with himself taken over with affection said faithfully, "all right, all right".
36-37. Uddhava said, "These women of Braja are indeed fortunate enough to follow Hari whose inherent nature could not be comprehended by Brahmā, Hara, other Gods and even the great sages. Their birth as well as their youth has become fruitful through such unshaken faith in Lord Kṛṣṇa."
38. The Gopīs said, "O noble soul! show us Govinda, show us Ballabha and take us there where Kṛṣṇa has placed himself firmly."

Prahlāda said:

39. After hearing all this as they said and bearing in mind their persistent weeping over the same, Uddhava got overpowered with affection and said, "Let it be so."
40. Attached as they were to Kṛṣṇa then all those women of Braja began to follow Uddhava in the same direction with a desire for Kṛṣṇa.
41. Singing the couplets bearing fondness for Kṛṣṇa as well as containing accounts of his childhood days, the women of Braja proceeded slowly along with Uddhava.

42. They reached Yadupurī and thereafter coming across the gardens and series of groves there they thought that they would have an opportunity to have glance of the Nandana garden of Kṛṣṇa.
43-45. By going to Dvārāvat and by meditating upon the master of Lakṣmī (i.e. Viṣṇu) all of their sins would get destroyed and they could be free from such bondage. As they reached the pool built up by Maya, Uddhava bowed down to those Gopīs who were inclined to consider him as the God Kṛṣṇa and after endearingly addressed them as mothers said, "You all stay back here. The strong-armed the lotus-eyed (i.e. Kṛṣna) will come here and will arrange your welfare."
46. The Gopīs said, "Who has made this lake here richly decorated with lotuses of varied colours and with white as well as blue water lilies?"
47. Uddhava said, "There was a great and famous demon by name Maya in the world. As a prolific trickster he seemed to have built this white lake here and it is by his name that this lake has become renowned in the world."
48. The beautiful Gopīs said, "O virtuous soul! please bring along the unmovable Govinda fast here. We will be delighted to see him. So also the three kinds of our lamentation will get wiped out."
49. Soon after hearing such words of the Gopīs, Uddhava then called for Kṛṣṇa through a messenger.
50. Then he saw the son of Devakī coming fast seated on a vehicle, with his body radiating brightness and adorned with a garland made of wild flowers.
51. His crown was burning with brightness and his dangling earrings in the shape of alligator were shining. With the mark of bunch of hairs in the shape of a coil on his chest the strong-armed and powerful was dressed in yellow clothes.
52. With an umbrella over his head and accompanied by his ancestor Vṛṣṇi and with songs and hymns recited in his honour by Nandī from behind, it was offering a delightful sight.

53. People from all over the city as well as those from the city belonging to Viṣṇu who happened to pass by there could see the lake richly full of Indian cranes as well as groups of cranes in copulation.

54. Witnessing the arrival of permanently fixed Kṛṣṇa having the most attractive body in the world and whose loveliness is indeed captivating for the mind, the women of Braja got fully enchanted.

55-58. Then composing themselves after sometime they began to weep saying, "O Lord, O embodied beauty captivating to the mind, O Kṛṣṇa and the master of Braja! We are related to you since your childhood. We have reared you up as a child and have played with you while you were a boy. So how could you be pitiless and cruel to give us up? Neither you are following dharma by doing so nor are you living up to fulfill the requirements of good-heartedness inherent to friendship. Can one ever attain the path of virtue by giving up one's parents? Giving up of one's duties as a master or proprietor and of one's devotees has been censured in all Śāstras. By leaving us all alone in the forest to fend for ourselves, you have disregarded the duties called upon a hero."

Prahlāda said:

59-65. After hearing the lamented words of the Gopīs, the foster son of Nanda (i.e. Kṛṣṇa) learning their feelings for him as well as their seeking his resort pacified and cajoled them (i.e. the women of Braja) with his sweet words. The Lord then gave them lessons on spirituality. The gracious God said, "My separation from you all can never be for ever. I stay perpetually in the hearts of everything in existence in particular. My power pervades all including insane and the gods besides Indra. The Sun, Vasu, Rudra, Sādhyā and Maruts are all my followers. So also are Brahmā, Rudra, Viṣṇu, Sanaka and all the great sages. The senses, the mind, the intellect, the existence and even for that matter qualities like desire, anger, greed, infatuation and pride pervading the material substances, O Gopīs! have been caused by me. Hence, after learning all this, you—the greatly fortunate ones, do not grieve in your minds. I am always there in everyone's body. Hence you all—the sinless, try to act towards the welfare of all for my sake."

Prahlāda said:

66-68. After hearing these words of Kṛṣṇa, all the Gopīs who were earlier tied up with their destructive thoughts became free from doubt and difficulties in their minds. They got flooded with happiness resulting from the sight of Kṛṣṇa. With their minds clear of doubts the Gopa brides said, "Our birth has become successful today. So also our eyes by having a sight of yours who is dear to the city-bred women. The meritless do not bother to have a look of Kṛṣṇa—the Supreme Puruṣa. Though by appropriate words conjoined with commensurate deeds you—Madhūsudana has explained everything to us, the sense of deceit from our heart is not yet completely cut off."

69. Śrī Kṛṣṇa said, "O women of Braja! you will be free from the remaining part of your bondage by having a sight of this lake here and by touching its water. A bath in this lake fulfills all desires."

70. The Gopīs said, "Citations have been made regarding the miraculous effect of this pool. O Lord of the world and offspring of Vṛṣṇi lineage! Please narrate in details of the ways of going about this (i.e. a bath here)."

71-80. Śrī Kṛṣṇa said, "Yours taking a look of this pool has effected here in my presence. Hence, as per practice I need also to take a bath here as per proper procedure. One who takes a bath here with utmost faith on the twelfth day in the brighter period of moon in the month of Śrāvaṇa, i.e. August and thereafter offers libations of water to his forefathers with sincere intentions and makes charities as per his affordability for me and his forefathers, will obtain the abode of Viṣṇu taking along his forefathers with him. After coming to Maya *tīrtha* it is desirable to make offerings to me as part of worship by reciting a mantra and bearing the sacred grass (i.e. *kuśa*) and a fruit in hand. The mantra as prayer to recite is "Submerged in the dark well of life as a householder I am tied up being wrapped in hundreds of illusions. Hence, the Lord of the world, I am making offering as a part of worship by acceptance of which by you I may be salvaged. Please accept my offering with due obeissance of mine." Man needs to take bath here attended with utmost faith to offer libations of water to his forefathers. Then he has to perform the *śrāddha* with sincere devotion towards his forefathers. As a religious fee, he has to offer gold and silver. In particular, he has to offer an oblation made of rice, milk and sugar. One can also offer fresh butter, ghee, umbrella and deer-skin here. As I have equally taken a look of this reservoir of water beside you, hence I need also to come here regularly. The dear Gopīs, those who will take a bath here in this Maya lake, they will have the imperishable fruits like that of a bath in Gaṅgā and that of the abode of Viṣṇu. His forefathers belonging to three generations of his clan attain liberation. He will be added with sons and grand children. He will be embellished with wealth and riches. Blessed with life-long happiness, he will go to the city of Hari."

CHAPTER THIRTEEN

The eminence of Gopī lake as a pilgrim centre

Śrī Prahlāda said:

1. As Kṛṣṇa said so, the Gopīs became very delighted. Then they took bath in the lake and became free from their left-over bondages.

2-5. As it is, there was a profusion of pleasure with them following their having a look of Kṛṣṇa. So, sweetly they told Mādhava, "Fortunate is that prominent demon Maya who has made th is lake for it has made possible for you—the Lord of the world to come here with other gods. If you are pleased with us then you—the offspring of Vṛṣṇi lineage show us a favour and make another best of lakes here by our name. By getting an opportunity to have a look of yours and by meditating on you as well as singing your glory day and night we, in the mortal kingdom may be able to obtain the ultimate passage."

6. Śrī Kṛṣṇa said, "O noble ladies! I have accepted your love and devotion for me and I shall do that desirably dear to you all. I am always accessible through devotion and I shall grant you the same favour."

Prahlāda said:

7. After saying like this, the God then made another lake here (near the Maya lake) as desired by the Gopīs for their welfare.

8. The lake was deep and full of clean water. It was richly decorated with blooming lotuses and with flamingoes, Indian cranes and the gooses.

9. Different portions of it were decorated with white lilies, with blue lotuses and with assemblage of lotuses of varied colour. It was used to be served by prominent Brāhmaṇas and other semi-divine beings.

10. It used to serve the women as well as the youth belonging to the Yadu dynasty. People from all cities and towns used to frequent it day and night.

11-15. Seeing that water-body brimming with waves Kṛṣṇa became pleased enough to tell the Gopīs, "O Gopīs! take a look of this lake full of crystal water near the other lake, i.e. Maya lake. Clean water flows in this lake like the clean mind virtuous people have. It is due to you people that this lake has been formed here. Hence, it will have its fame associated by your name only. The word 'Go' means words/speech and I have had words with you people here. Hence, this place will acquire fame in the world by the name of 'Gopracāraka'. I have created this lake here to fulfill your loving wishes in this regard. Hence, it will be renowned in the world as Gopī lake."

16. The Gopīs said, "If you have created this lake by our name to oblige us then O Vārṣṇeya! give us an opportunity to put forward another request on our part."

17. Śrī Kṛṣṇa said, "You can ask for whatever that may be occupying your minds. I cannot deny the same as you people have come here guided by devotion."

18-25. The Gopīs said, "If the God is pleased not to deny us a boon, then let Kṛṣṇa alias Mādhava always come here in a palanquin carried by people. After coming here let him take a bath in the water (of the pool) here with due regard to laid down procedure. Let there be coexistence of gods, *yajñas* and *tīrthas* here as is usually associated with the presence of Keśava anywhere. As you are here, so also be there the conduct of charities and observance of any mental vow here as per rules as unavoidable with your presence anywhere. Let there be recital of the sacred syllable 'Om' as well as worship of gods and forefathers be inevitable here like your presence anywhere. The earth, the ocean, the light, the sacrifices, the people, truth, penance and the world beyond are the essential companions of you—the Kṛṣṇa. You also pervade the entire world—gods, the demons and human beings. Hence, Lord of the world and Janārdana, let there be no doubt that a bath here encompasses the three worlds together. Gaṅgā—the purifier of the three worlds is just the water of your feet. Lakṣmī stays on your breast and Sarasvatī on your face. You—Lord of the world, is integral to everything that breathes with life. Hence, O Lord of the world, be kind towards us and tell us what are you going to grant people in future in the Kaliyuga. Also tell us what fruits will devolve for those who after coming on a visit here stay back for six months as well as for those who will choose to put up here till they are alive."

26-44. Śrī Kṛṣṇa said, "O Gopīs! be pleased to listen from me without any doubt the fruits that will accrue to people after taking a bath here in this Gopikā lake. After arranging all ingredients meant for performance of worship, present a calf embellished with clothes and ornaments along with a cow to a householder Brāhmaṇa. That Brāhmaṇa should be of good character and conduct. He must neither be poor nor should he be pursuing well-being/welfare motivated by his own self-interest. Donation of cow to such a Brāhmaṇa results in attainment of the same fruits accruable by a bath here. The number of footsteps of Kṛṣṇa that a man takes look of here, his clan members get as many years of stay in the abode of Hari. Mothers of those men who happen to come here and walk together singing the glory of Kṛṣṇa at this Gopikā lake with accompanied instruments never have to suffer the pains of old age. These men also obtain the abode of Viṣṇu with all their desires fulfilled. One needs to make offerings as an associated part of the performance of worship after undergoing the bath skillfully here. Then with utmost faith one has to make the offerings attended on worship as per laid-down procedure and reciting the mantra saying, 'Obeisance to you—the Supreme Soul and bearing the appearance of cow. O Lord of the world! accept our offerings made as a part and parcel of worship here at the Gopracāraka Tīrtha and accept our reverence." After making the offering as per required procedure, one has then to apply mud on the body by one's own hands and take bath attended with utmost faith. After that one can make libations of water to gods and one's forefathers. With single-minded devotion one has to perform *śrāddha* here and donate gold and silver as part of the religious fee as has been stated to be. Specially, betel leaves and collyrium are to be offered here. Besides, one may donate garments made of silk and garments dyed with safflower here. Make donations of the apparel put on by a couple as well as their ornaments. Donate cows and strong bulls to Brāhmanas. Make charities to the poor, the blind and the miserly as per your abilities and affordability. A man attains the usual path of goodness by doing so. Along with him, three forthcoming generations of his clan also get enabled to attain that ultimate world. One fostering desire for son also gets blessed with a handsome son. Whatever desire a man nourishes, can attain the same besides attaining the final liberation through attainment of heaven by a bath in the Gopikā lake. The lake will be there as long as the human world remains and all of your fame in tandem with the lake will continue till the same lake persists. As long as men continue to celebrate the bath here in the lake, heaven will continue to revel in its greater, higher and exalted position. Becoming free from all sins, men will proceed in the direction of ultimate passage (by a bath here). The Gopī lake full of water forever will always hold merit. O Gopīs! all of you need to have a bath with me here in the lake by adhering to all rules in the month of Śrāvaṇa, i.e. August. By considering me as your husband or by imagining me as Brahma, all of you, the Gopīs can obtain the ultimate passage."

Prahlāda said:

45. Then the Gopīs, with due permission of God left in the same direction they had come from after paying their salutations to Govinda.
46. The God on his part after seeing off the Gopīs left for his own abode along with Uddhava and made his entry therein.

CHAPTER FOURTEEN

Eminence of Pañcanada Tīrtha

Śrī Prahlāda said:

1. There were many centres of pilgrimage in the world which was a matter of great wonder. But with the arrival of the severe *Kaliyuga* most of them got flooded with water.

2. The Brāhmaṇas, I am going to describe as to what purpose they all fulfilled. Try to understand. The prominent Brāhmaṇas, I shall tell in brief about their merits and the necessary formalities one has to fulfill to derive fruits out of them.
3. Seized of the burden of the earth and to restore the path of righteousness to the pious, Kṛṣṇa in association with the members of Vṛṣṇi lineage, arrived at Dvārāvat.
4. To have a look of Kṛṣṇa, Brahmā along with other gods and with Varuṇa, Kubera—the God of wealth, the Sun and the Moon had also come there at that time.
5. After giving shape to his mission in cooperation with Kṛṣṇa, Brahmā then founded a centre of pilgrimage there by his name.
6. That centre of pilgrimage was an auspicious one, a destroyer of all sins and was popularly known as Brahmakuṇda (i.e. a basin associated with the name of Brahmā). A foundation for the thousand-rayed Lord Sun was made on the shore of the same basin.
7. As the root cause of all gods, Brahmā is known as the grandfather of the world. As basically founded by him (i.e. Brahmā) this centre of pilgrimage is recounted with his name (as Brahma Tīrtha).
8. Seeing the Brahma Tīrtha, the moon then made a circular pond there. Named after moon, the same pool was equally a destroyer of all sins.
9-13. Seeing that the pool had an union of brightness with it, the virtuous God became happy and told the Creator (i.e. Brahmā), "Please listen to us. Those who after taking a bath here, offer libations of water in honour of their forefathers and worship this original place of the God of gods must get free from all sins. They must get equipped with wealth and riches." O Brāhmaṇas! they further said, "A man who takes a bath here with utmost devotion on the seventh day of the brighter period of moon in the month of Māgha (i.e. January), thereafter taking the sandal from the original place of Brahmā gets himself annointed with it and

worships the God with flowers, incense and makes offering of edible food, clothes and ornaments as per his ability, he should obtain the passage to the abode of Brahmā becoming relieved of all sins."

14. Then seeing Sāvitrī there Brahmā put up his idol there after giving it a brilliant form. He also gave a name to the same holy place.

15. One who takes a look of the Lord of the world Kṛṣṇa here with devotion and thereafter equally takes a look of Sāvitrī, he happens to enjoy life and becomes happy with fulfillment of all his desires.

16. By following it up with taking a look of the Creator, the same man gets blessed with long life free from diseases and with prosperity. He begets sons and children onto himself. Neither misfortune nor poverty and ignorance happens to him. He also does not have to fear ailment of any kind.

17-18. After going there, one needs to worship the Goddess with saffron, varieties of flowers and by making an offering of cloth as a covering for the Goddess. The visit there becomes successful by worship of the Goddess with intent devotion attended with making offerings of food, fruits, betel leaf and a necklace.

19. By her taking a look of the Creator neither widowhood nor sterility can happen to a woman. Misfortune never occurs to her nor her sons meet with untimely death. Her descendants keep growing and flourishing.

20. Hence with all efforts one needs to have a look of the Creator (i.e. Brahmā) with sincere intention. Kṛṣṇa gets pleased by this and a visit here becomes successful as a result.

Prahlāda said:

21. After seeing the richly decorated lake founded by Brahmā, the great soul Indra then made a relatively more beautiful lake named after him.

22. The ruler of gods (i.e. Indra) placed a Śivaliṅga of profound brightness on the shore of the same lake. By taking a bath here man can obtain the position similar to Indra.
23. As Indra had founded the worshipable Śivaliṅga here attended with genuine feelings, the holy place therefore, became very famous on the earth's surface as Indrapada. It is usually remembered as "Indreśvara".
24. The Brāhmaṇas, the fame of this place is due to the point that the Liṅga it holds is quite large and equally lifted up. A mere look of this relieves one of all sins.
25. The virtuous Brāhmaṇas, a man's bath here at Candrapada either on the eighth or the fourteenth day of a month results in imperishable satisfaction to his forefathers.
26. A man can attain that state of liberation by worshipping Indreśvara (i.e. the Liṅga) especially on that day when sun transits in the zodiac sign of Makara, i.e. capricorn.
27. Prepare a worshipable Liṅga here on that specific day of the month coinciding with the placement of the sun on the northern side of the equator and when the sun shifts its position with regard to its transit through the various zodiac signs. Then worship Śiva with Umā on the specific day earmarked for Śiva (i.e. on the fourteenth day of the darker half of Māgha, i.e. February). Stay up the entire night in conformity with the religious ceremony. By doing so, one can obtain the ultimate world.

Prahlāda said:

28. By seeing the Brahma Tīrtha as well as the Indra lake one can attain that form which is a unification of forms of Brahmā, Śiva and Indra with Viṣṇu.
29. Śiva—the husband of Pārvatī had also made a pond here full of clean water and decorated with varieties of lotuses.
30. Every part of the lake was covered with blue lotuses and it was decorated with Indian cranes. After seeing, that the lake has plenty of water, the bearer of trident who has the iconic bull on the flag-staff of his chariot (i.e. Lord Śiva) began to take bath there along with Brahmā and Viṣṇu.

31-43. Then becoming very pleased, all gods including Brahmā, Viṣṇu and other demons looking at the husband of Pārvatī (i.e. Śiva) said, "O God among gods! the great lake created by you here would be very famous by the name of Mahādeva lake. Anyone having a bath here and thereafter making libations of water to his forefathers and performing *śrāddha* with due devotion would obtain that ultimate passage. All gods would be very happy and that too beyond any doubt, by just having a look of this lake. Just a look of this Mahādeva lake would liberate one of all sins. After seeing this highly beautiful lake of Maheśa (an epithet of Śiva) Pārvatī did also make another lake here equally matchless in beauty. A destroyer of all sins, the same lake acquired its renown as Gaurī lake. A man has never to encounter bad circumstances by a bath in it with devotion. A woman taking bath here will never have to face misfortune and widowhood on her part. All desires get accomplished by a bath in this foremost Gaurī lake. After seeing the auspicious place, Varuṇa also made a holy lake there attended with devotion towards Viṣṇu. Named as Varuṇapada— the same lake on earth is also a decayer of sins. One has to make libations of water in honour of one's forefathers already attained to divinehood here on the full-moon day in the month of Bhādra, i.e. September. By doing *śrāddha* here for one's forefathers attended with faith, one goes to the virtuous world without any rethinking with regard to the same. One has to offer a jar filled with rice added with water and curd here. By donating cows, clothes and ornaments, one can ensure pleasure of Viṣṇu. Seeing the pool made by the God of water, the God of wealth made a pool on his own which became renowned on the surface of earth as Yakṣadhipa. Human beings can get all of their desires fulfilled by worshipping their forefathers obtained to divinehood with all devotion and by making charities of clothes to Brāhmaṇas here."

Prahlāda said:

44. After hearing that the sons of Brahmā who were (naturally) brothers amongst themselves to one another, had granted a favour to Viṣṇu, (the sage) Vasiṣṭha then brought down Mandākinī (an epithet of Gaṅgā) to the surface of earth.
45. Then Ambariṣa *et. al.* , of whom Kṛṣṇa was the guardian, hurried up and came to Dvārāvạt. There they happened to see Gomatī flowing into the sea.
46. Gods created a number of holy centres of pilgrimage and that is how the Pañcanada Tīrtha came on earth.
47. Gods had brought down the five rivers here through an earnest invocation. At that time Gomatī was there under the custody of Marica and Lakṣmaṇa.
48. To purify, Candrabhāgā went to Aṅgiraṣa, while Kuśāvatī went to Pulaha and Jāmbavatī to Kṛtra.
49. The great sons of Brahmā made them glorious by taking a bath in them. They attained their popularity through association with these ascetics.
50. Pañcanada Tīrtha is a reliever of all sins due to this. Human beings desirous of Heaven and liberation need to have a bath here.
51. O Brāhmaṇas! after going there observe self-restraint and then bearing a fruit in hand, recite the mantra (i.e. the sacred prayer) and make offering as part of the worship, as per laid down rule in this regard.
52. The mantra is: "The sons of Brahmā have brought these best five rivers here. O female deities! accept our offerings as part of worship to curtail and subdue our sins."
53. A man must take a bath here and thereafter may offer libations of water to his forefathers as per rule. Attended with earnest faith, he must perform *śrāddha* here as per rule.
54. He needs to give five jewels as well as seven types of grains to Brāhmaṇas. He also needs to give charities to the pitiable, the blind and the miserly as per his own capability.

55. (By doing so) with fulfillment of all desires, he goes to the abode of Viṣṇu. Besides, blessed with children and grandchildren, he gets entitled to happiness of the highest order.
56. Those who might have gone to the state of ghostly spirits or those who might have gone to insecthood in a particular clan and even the forthcoming descendants spanning three generations in a family—all attain liberation (by doing so).
57. Even by listening to this holy account and by continuously concentrating the mind on this account, one gets entitled to the blissful abode of Śiva. He attains that ultimate position becoming free from all sins.

CHAPTER FIFTEEN

Ruṣi Tīrtha: The eminence of Siddheśvara

Prahlāda said:

1. Hearing about the advent of Brahmā there Sanaka, etc. got prompted to follow. They came there and offered their salutations to the great grandfather of the gods (i.e. Brahmā).
2. Seeing the young prince (i.e. Sanaka) falling down on his feet to offer obeisance, Brahmā then held him up in his arms and embraced him.
3. Then Brahmā enquired about his health and everything about his welfare. He in turn, replied saying that he as well as others were fortunate enough to worship him (i.e. Brahmā) and other gods.
4-6. (Brahmā said) "You people have already attained complete accomplishment by virtue of a look of God. But my son, due to being young, your understanding is yet to be fully grown and you all continue to be ignorant. Keśava cannot

be pleased without worshipping Mahādeva. Hari does not accept prayers if Nīlakaṇṭha (an epithet of Śiva) remains unworshipped before hand. Hence with all efforts try to worship the dark-blue (Nīlalohita) God (i.e. Śiva). By this only, the worship of Kṛṣṇa obtains a completion." The sons of Brahmā then left after hearing these words of him.

7. The sages accomplished in yoga then proceeded towards the God's (i.e. Śiva's) temple and honoured by their devotion to Śiva, founded a Śivaliṅga there.

8. The virtuous sages! after placing the Śivaliṅga, all the sages then began to keep themselves unwaveringly engaged in a vow in their minds to create a well there for taking bath.

9. Then seeing the well full of clean and nectar-like water, the sages became very happy and said "well done, well done".

10-28. O Brāhmaṇas! seeing the Śivaliṅga as founded by his sons, the grandfather of gods (i.e. Brahmā) became pleased and then told them, "As the foundation of the Śivaliṅga here has been possible by all of your persistent yoga, it will acquire fame in the world by the name of Siddheśvara. As you have built up a well near the God having a dark-coloured neck (i.e. Śiva), it will therefore have its fame in the world as Ruṣi Tīrtha. O the foremost Brāhmaṇas! one can be free from debts to his forefathers by simply taking a bath here devotedly even without performance of *śrāddha* or making libations of water to them or giving charities. Even the liars and those having a constant habit of reproaching others will get purified beyond doubt by a mere bath at the Ruṣi Tīrtha. O the virtuous Brāhmaṇas! it will be auspicious to have a bath here on the equinox day (i.e. when the sun enters the zodiac signs of Aries or Librā) on the day of Manwa and in the month of Māgha (i.e. January-February) on the specific day considered as belonging to Kṛtayuga. What to speak about him who remains here on the forefront of the Śivaliṅga on that particular fourteenth day of the dark period of the moon in the month of Māgha, considered dearer to Lord Śiva and takes a bath in the Ruṣi Tīrtha. The Brāhmaṇas, he will attain that position of accomplishment which is given the name as Supreme. The greatly fortunate ones! therefore go there and after that carrying a fruit as well as the sacred grass (i.e. Kuśa) in hand, offer the same as per prescribed procedure while worshipping and saying "Please accept the offerings made as part of the worship." After making the same offerings as part of worship at Siddheśvara that snatches away all sins and in the contiguity of which is situated the Ruṣi Tīrtha, get your bodies annointed with mud and take a bath there with all earnestness. Then make libations of water to forefathers, gods and other human beings as per sequential order. Then perform *śrāddha* for forefathers attended with due regard and faith. Make donations especially of wealth there without the slightest sense of deceit. Offer juicy fruits in particular. Donate mattresses, rice grown on fields without specially being cultivated for that purpose and flour made of seven grains and added with jaggery. A man can be gratified by offering perfumes, garlands, betel leaves, clothes as well as drinks all-together. The mortal life becomes successful by worshipping the Siddheśvara Mahādeva and the husband of Umā. Even life taking shape in the germinating stage of foetus remains in tact. The father as well as the grandfather of one remain pleased by his taking a bath at Ruṣi Tīrtha and thereafter, following it up with taking a look of Siddheśvara Śiva. By prayers made for Siddheśvara and the resultant grace of him, men without children get blessed with the same while those having children get grandchildren. Even the poor become wealthy and rich. Evil deeds meet with destruction while good deeds tend to grow. The love of the leader of accomplishment (i.e. Siddheśvara) results in fulfillment of all desires of the mind. All desires of a man fructify by taking a bath at Ruṣi Tīrtha followed up with having a look of Siddheśvara Hara. Hence there is no need for deliberating on any other means towards realization of one's aspirations and desires. One has to worship Siddheśa (i.e. Siddheśvara) on that fourteenth day coinciding the darker period of moon in the month of Māgha, i.e. January-February in particular which is dearer to Śiva. This grants without any doubt the fulfillment of those desires that the mind specifically desires for. By this a man becomes like a Lord of Cintāmaṇi (i.e. the possessor of that specific jewel which fulfills the desires asked from it) and gets bestowed with inexhaustible wealth. By listening to this account as eclipser of all sins or by keeping one's mind unflinchingly occupied with this account within with earnest faith, a man can make a move towards the ultimate position.

CHAPTER SIXTEEN

The group of Tīrthas and their eminence

Prahlāda said:

1. Then O the foremost Brāhmaṇas! go to the good place of pilgrimage called Gadā Tīrtha. By a bath here with devotion, a man can obtain the same fruits resulting from making donation of land.
2. Make libations of water to forefathers, gods and sages as per the prescribed order in this regard. A *śrāddha* here ensures satisfaction/pleasure of one's forefathers.
3. By worshipping Viṣṇu present in his appearance as boar at Gadā Tīrtha with earnest devotion, a man can attain the superior world of Viṣṇu.
4. Then go to the richly decorated Nāga Tīrtha. By a bath here with all earnestness, a man can attain the abode of Nāga.
5. Then go to the Bhadra Tīrtha, which is worshipped across the three worlds. By only a bath here, a man can get the results same as that of donating a spotted cow.
6. Then go to the very beautiful Chitrā Tīrtha. By a bath here only, a man can obtain the same fruits as that accrue from donating a cow, the milk of which is a repository of abundant ghee.

7. O Brāhmaṇas! when Dvārāvat got flooded with sea water, many auspicious centres of pilgrimage there got submerged under the mighty water.
8. While most of them got extinct, some were still visible. O master Brāhmaṇas! I shall now speak all about them.
9. Go to Candrabhāgā there which is a reliever of all sins. By a bath here with devotion a man can obtain the fruits of Vājapeya i.e. a sacrifcial fire conducted with offering of clarified butter to the fire.
10. Candrā—the daughter of Nanda and Yaśodā is worshipped. She is a virgin and carries a spear, a sword and a shield in her hands.
11. She had subjugated demons like Keśī, etc. She happens to be the sister of Kṛṣṇa and Balarāma. All desires get fulfilled by having a look of hers.
12. Then the master Brāhmaṇas, go to the centre of pilgrimage called Mahiṣa Tīrtha. By taking look of it only, one can be free from all sins.
13. Then visit the Mukti Dwāra (i.e. the centre of pilgrimage acting as a door to liberation) which is a reliever of sins.
14. The sage Vasiṣṭha had brought the (river) Gomatī here. A bath here engenders the same fruits as if one has taken a bath in Gaṅgā in the Kaliyuga.
15. Flowing further down, Gomatī has met with the sea here. By a bath here with devotion, a man can attain the fruits of Asvamedha Yajña (i.e. the sacrificial fire involving sacrifices of horses).
16. By his austere penance Bhṛgu had also founded (the idol of) Ambikā here. Hence, in the world, it has been heard to have acquired fame in conjunction with its being worshipped by Bhṛgu in the first instance.
17. Man can attain that stage of ultimate accomplishment by remembering the Goddess. On the plains of earth here, there are a good number of Śivaliṅgas.

18. Then O the uppermost Brāhmaṇas! proceed to the meritorious Kālindī pool. Kālindī—the daughter of Sun had created this auspicious pool.
19. A man has never to face any difficult situation by a bath with devotion here. Then (the Brāhmaṇas) head towards the Sāmba Tīrtha—an abater of all sins.
20. By doing śrāddha here with all love and application as per prescribed procedure, one can derive the same fruits that result from charities of cow.
21. Then go to the Śaṁkara Tīrtha that is stated to purify the three worlds. By taking a bath here with devotion, a man obtains abundant gold in his life.
22. After this go to the reliever of all sins, i.e. the Nāga lake Tīrtha. Offer of libations of water in honour of one's forefathers as per prescribed procedure here entitles one to the abode of Nāga.
23. Then proceed towards the Lakṣmī river on its flow ahead towards the sea. A mere look of it takes away all sins.
24. O the master Brāhmaṇas! by performing *śrāddha* here one's forefathers obtain liberation. Making charities here results in fulfillment of all desires of the mind beyond doubt.
25. Then go to the centre of pilgrimage which destroys sins and is known as the Kambu lake. Making of libations here to one's forefathers as well as performance of *śrāddha* here in their honour yields the fruits of Agniṣṭoma yajña.
26. After this go to the Kuśa Tīrtha and offer libations of water to forefathers. Charities here as per one's abilities yields one the sacred world.
27. The reliever of all sins Druma Tīrtha is there in its vicinity. By performing *śrāddha* here, one can obtain the fruits of Vājimedha yajña (an epithet of the sacrificial fire enjoining upon one to make sacrifice of horses).
28. After this go to the Kuśa Tīrtha for the purpose of promoting and preserving contentment of one's forefathers. Making libations of water to one's forefathers as well as performance of *śrāddha* here ensures the same beyond doubt.

29. Then go to the auspicious and reliever of all sins Jāla Tīrtha. Durvāsā happened to curse the Yadu princes here out of anger.

30. Then Lord Śiva—the husband of Umā—created the Jaḷeśvara there. Man instantly gets free from sins by just having a look of Jaleśvara.

31. By devoted worship of Lord Śiva here, one also attains the world of Śiva.

32. Then human beings need to go to that beautiful Tīrtha known as Cakraswāmī Tīrtha. One attains the world of Viṣṇu by taking a bath here first and then following it up with making libations of water to his forefathers.

33. Then the foremost Brāhmaṇas! go to centre of pilgrimage formed by the sage Jagatkāru. O the best of Brāhmaṇas! by a bath here, a man never encounters difficult situations in life.

34-35. Then O the best of Brāhmaṇas! go to the place of pilgrimage named Khañjanaka. There was a powerful demon named Khañjạnaka. It has been heard that the same centre of pilgrimage had been named after the same demon. By a bath there men go to the world of Soma beyond any doubt.

36. O the good Brāhmaṇas! there have been many centres of pilgrimage here lying undisclosed/uncovered. One can raise oneself above all sins by going there.

37. Then O the best Brāhmaṇas! go to the place of pilgrimage known as Dundubhi. A visit here needs to be followed by a visit to the supreme Śiva Tīrtha and Gadā Tīrtha.

38. There is the Gaonlagā and tīrtha of the great soul Akrura here. There are also the tīrthas respectively of Balarāma and Ugrasena here.

39. There is also tīrtha of Arjuna as well as of Subhadrā here. There are also a Devakī Tīrtha and a Rohiṇī Tīrtha here.

40. The Uddhava Tīrtha as well as the Sāraṅga Tīrtha are also there. Satyabhāmā and Bhadrā have also made prominent tīrthas here.

41. The great soul Paraśurāma has also made a tīrtha here for (his father) Jāmadagnya. Prominent places of pilgrimage like Bhāsa Tīrtha and Śuka Tīrtha are also there.
42. Tīrthas for Kardama and the great soul Kapila are also there. There are also Soma Tīrtha and Rohiṇī Tīrtha.
43. In this way, I have made a mention of the other centres of pilgrimage here in brief. These also remove all sins and yield liberation for one without any doubt.
44. O the chief Brāhmaṇas! most of the centres of pilgrimage have receded to background with the advent of Kaliyuga. Either they have been innundated by the sea water or have got buried underneath the sand of the sea.
45. O Brāhmaṇas! this is the detailed account of the centres of pilgrimage which I have described to you in brief and based on my self-awareness and imagination. What more do you all desire to listen from me?
46. By listening to the accounts about them with due faith and by undertaking visits to such centres with all earnestness, O Brāhmaṇas, one goes to the abode of Viṣṇu becoming free from all sins.

CHAPTER SEVENTEEN

The breaking of ego of Rukmi and the servants of God

Prahlāda said:

1. So get yourselves sprinkled with the water or have a bath at tīrthas and make donations/charities as stated. Worship the God Kṛṣṇa who is the ultimate/supreme manifestation of masculinity.

The Sages said:

2-4. "The virtuous demon! we desire to hear about the ways of worshipping Kṛṣṇa in the whole. Please tell us about the ways to adopt. Who are the door-keepers there to the abode of Kṛṣṇa? Who are there on the front as well as in the rear? O demon king! Who is it that protecting and defending the palace (of Kṛṣṇa) from all sides? Please tell us the details to be followed and as per prescribed procedure with regard to worship of Kṛṣṇa? In any case, you are so fond of the feet of Kṛṣṇa. Hence, you are aware of the ways of worshipping him. Therefore, please tell us."

Śrī Prahlāda said:

5. O Brāhmaṇas! you all must have heard about ways of worshipping Kṛṣṇa as have been spoken about before. I shall describe you the procedure regarding the same in the Kaliyuga.
6. Listen carefully about the God situated at the door on the Eastern side of the Kṛṣṇa temple. He is Jayanta and is to be worshipped at the first instance. He is auspicious as far as doing away with the sins is concerned.
7. O the virtuous Brāhmaṇas! Indra at the first instance founded the idol of Jayanta for the purpose of worship of Keśava. I am going to describe about his followers.
8-9. Bajranābha, Sunābha, Bajrabāhu, Mahāhanu, Bajradraṣta, Bajradhārī, Bajraha, Bajralocana, Śveta murdhā, Śvetamālī are all the followers of Jayanta. Bearing arms in their hands, they all defend him day and night.
10. They assist Jayanta in compliance of his directions at the door on the eastern side of his palace. Vināyaka is their master on the same side supervising Jayanta's security needs.
11-12. The Sun with its ever-manifest bright rays, the seven-mother Goddess, Iśvara, Durvāsā, Takṣaka—the king of Nāgas are placed there. Senānī, Kārtikeya and the demons Mahāhanu as well as the Dīrgha Nakho are also well-placed there.
13. Viśvavasu, Gandharva, divine beauties including Menakā and the sage of Gods Vasiṣṭha are also present there along with Sanaka.

14. On the East, one has to worship all of them. After this as one heads ahead, he will come across a big banyan tree. Now listen from me about the Āgneya direction, i.e. the South-east.

15. Here Kṛṣṇa is visible in a form with face emitting excessive brightness and eyes red and bloodshot. Eating meat and drinking blood, Kṛṣṇa here bears black matted hair and his abode is stated to be a cemetery.

16. Excessively fearsome tormentors are placed in the Āgneya (i.e. South-east) direction. Now listen about them bearing arms in hands and defending the Southern direction.

17-24. Dandapāṇi, Mahānāda, Pāśahasta, Sulocana, Anibatyakrama as well as Dundubhi and Niswana are there in the Southern direction. Kharswana, Ghangharvāk, Mounapriya and Mallikākṣa are the efficient door-keepers here. There are Dundubhi, Vināyaka, the radiant Mahiṣa, the sun, Bhuṣana and Iśvara to efficiently defend the Southern front. The Goddess Caṇḍīkā, the demon Padmākṣa, the Kṣetrapāla and the Nāga Aśvastasa are also there. The Gandharvas named Citrāṅgadā and Urvaśī—the best of the divine beauties are there. The great among the trees and their king, the tall and stately Śāla is also there. The eternal and best of the sages Agastya known for his austerity is also there and all of them together and with due care and caution, protect and defend the Southern front. There are singing and dancing belles there making movements with their eyes, eyelids with all pleasure. At the same time they appear as if making a mockery of themselves appearing like naked, i.e. skinned hens to be dearly offered to the fire to get burnt. O Brāhmaṇas! with abundance of maces and arms in their hands, the God's security is strongly entrenched there. They also equally defend the South-west direction with all promptness. Next comes the Western front.

25-29. Svāstika, Saṅkhamurdhā, Nīlavāsā, Śubhānana, Pāśahasta, Śūlahasta and Ekpādekalocana are visible here. Vināyaka having flowers on his denticle is also there on the

Western direction. There are also Uddhava, the sun with its bright rays, Indra and the invincible God Śiva are also there. The Gandharva named Tumbarū, the prominent divine beauty named Ghṛtācī, the king of the Nāgas called Mahodara and the demon Ghaṭotkaca are also there. The demon named Pañcajana and the sage Kāśyapa are there. The Goddess named Kapālinī and the great holy Aswattha, i.e. the fig tree are also there. Kapila and Kṣetrapāla always eager to retaliate defend the same direction. After saluting one has to worship (all of them). Now listen about the Vāyavya, i.e. the North-West quarter.

30-36. One can see Bhanjana, Bhairava, Kālika, Ghaṭodara, Jhanjhakāmardana, Pingo, Ruru and Vraṇī here equipped with arms in hands to retaliate. In this way surrounded well from sides the God is guarded and protected. O the master Brāhmaṇas! Vināyaka Śyāmala is on the northern quarters. Besides, the Lord is guarded on the northern front by Manwantaka, Vīrupākṣa, Golaka, Śveta Sampluta and Unmatta. In the centre, the sun, Maheśvara—the Lord of Indra, the Goddess Kanṭheśvarī and the bird Khañjana are the defenders. Besides Vāsukī—the king of Nāgas, the foremost sage Sanaka and the demons, viz. Karmapṛstho and Golako are there in this quarter. The Gandharva named Nārada, the divine beauty Rambhā and the great banyan tree are also there. One has to worship all of them with due care. The Lord of Yakṣa—Savitā is there. Worship Śyāmā there with due efforts. O the master Brāhmaṇas! now I am going to tell you about all those placed in the north-east direction.

37-45. Durdhara, Bhairavrāva, the very strong Kinkiṇīka, Karāla, Vikaṭa, Mula, Balibhukta and Balapriya are there (in the north-eastern side). O Brāhmaṇas! alongwith all these guardians of the region accompanied by their wives, there is their leader, their lord and overall guardian Jayanta also present there. They help in checking/subduing the invaders and that way protect the inhabitants of the city. Following the commands of Jayanta they strike down the wicked and the vicious. Jayanta is always their master and protector with the place occupied by Nāgas. Surrounded by Nāga kings he is worthy of worship with all care and endeavour. As carnivorous, they are fond of meat. They defend the North-east quarter. The thousand-headed celestial being Śeṣanāga is present here in the place occupied by Nāgas. The eternal Vāsukī, Takṣaka and Padma are also present here in this direction. Śaṅkha, Kambalaka, the Nāga Aśvatara as well as Muktaka and Kāliya are present here. Besides Janaka and Aparājita are there. There are also thousands of Nāgas here having faces similar to cucumber. They are all worshipable with perfume, flowers, sacrifices as well as with lighting of incense sticks and earthen lamps. Worship them by offering rice cooked with milk and sugar. Offer meat, varieties of grains and intoxicating beverages. After them worship Jayanta—the leader of them as defenders by perfume, flowers, by lighting incense sticks and by making presents of clothes as well as ornaments. O the foremost Brāhmaṇas! after this go near Kṛṣṇa whom Devakī happened to rear up as her son. Before this, worship the chief of his followers named Rukmi first of all.

46. The sages said, "How could that wicked and king of the demons Rukmi be possible? And for that matter how could he be positioned before the door of the God evoking worship of humans every time?"

Śrī Prahlāda said:

47-50. When the king Bhiṣmaka tied up Rukmiṇī in a marital bond with Kṛṣṇa, then Caiddya (i.e. Śiśupāla) got angry and took Rukmiṇī away somewhere else. Then the God seized Rukmiṇī from the abode of Ambikā and retaliating through battle he made all including the sovereign Jarāsandha to flee. Then the powerful son of Bhīṣmaka, i.e. Rukmi resolved in his mind that he would not return till he killed the Yādava in a battle. Then O Brāhmaṇas! after making all the kings apprised of such a vow of him, he then stepped out, equipped with arms and weapons to fight. With a well-equipped army he then fought with Kṛṣṇa, but got defeated and killed by Kṛṣṇa. After killing him, the God made him to have an ugly appearance. But then Balarāma released him from the bondage. After that he made up his mind to die. Seeing her brother determined to die, Rukmiṇī—the daughter of the king of Vaidarbha (i.e. Vaidarbhī) asked Kṛṣṇa to get her brother back. Then after cajoling his dear Rukmiṇī, Janārdana made one of his best followers as Vighnanāśaka (i.e. destroyer of all impediments). O Brāhmaṇas! it is due to this reason that he is worshipped at the outset. His pleasure can be earned by worshipping him with offerings of perfume, unbroken grains, laddoos and with lighting of incense sticks. There is no other way than this to please the Lord of world.

CHAPTER EIGHTEEN

Humiliation of Durvāsā by demons

Śrī Prahlāda said:

1. Worship Rukmi—the leader of all followers and decorated with gold. With due devotion also worship Durvāsā, Kṛṣṇa and Balabhadra.
2. One may involve oneself in austere *yajña* accompanied by making the religious fee in a holistic manner to derive the desired boon. Comparable fruits to this can equally be obtained by simply having a look of Kṛṣṇa.
3. To fulfill one's devotion towards gods, one makes or digs up a well or a little bigger water reservoir or even a pond. But the fruits accruing to such activities can be yielded by taking a look of Kṛṣṇa just once.
4. One donates cows, sesame, land and gold for days together. But one gets comparable fruits of such donations by just having a look of the God Kṛṣṇa.

5. Attended with *prāṇāyama* one takes the name of any particular God repeatedly in mind and concentrates the mind on God with all sincerity. But comparable fruits to all these can also be had by having a look of Kṛṣṇa.
6. One takes a bath in Jāhnavī (an epithet of Gaṅgā) including other places of pilgrimage with all earnestness. But similar fruits can be had by just having a look of the God Kṛṣṇa.
7. By just three steps, the Trivikrama (an epithet of Viṣṇu) had encompassed the three worlds. By having a look of Trivikrama a man gets himself free from the sins of the three worlds.

8-9. The sages said, "How could the idol of Trivikrama come up on the earth's surface? When did it acquire the impression of Kṛṣṇa onto it? O demon king! please dispell our doubt in this regard. How could there be togetherness of Kṛṣṇa and Durvāsā? Please explain all this to us."

Prahlāda said:

10-51. O the foremost Brāhmaṇas! listen as to how could it be possible that the idol of Trivikrama and Durvāsā appeared beside each other on earth. Earlier, as the Kṛtayuga came to an end, Bali defeated Indra—the king of gods and as a result both Indra and Madhusūdana had to desert heaven. But then to restore heaven to Indra, Trivikrama appeared in his dwarf incarnation through the *yajña* of Kaśyapa and measured the three worlds by just three steps of his. The God then sent Bali to the nether world and made him to remain content as a king of the subjects there. By his as well as the devotion of others, the demon Bali satisfied Kṛṣṇa. Then the God on his own remained stationed there in exchange of Bali's devotion. To grant him a favour, the God placed himself there as a watchman at his door. Roaming here and there about the centres of pilgrimage in quest for liberation, Durvāsā—the celebrated sage then reached there and began to consider it fit for emancipation. Thinking like this from the angle of knowledge, the great sage then arrived at the confluence of Gomatī with the sea known as Cakratīrtha at present. Thinking that the same place would serve the purpose of liberation for him, he made up his mind to go there and headed towards it crossing through villages, cities, gardens and forests. After arriving at his desired region, he entered into the land of the demon known as Anarta. But muttering or sayings of the Veda or its study was prohibited in that region. Kuśa, the king of demons had reigned over the region and the subjects were thus served and looked after by him. The people in his kingdom were mostly and used to live by unrighteous means. But aware of the presence of Cakratīrtha in its immediate vicinity Durvāsā decided to take a bath there at the auspicious spot of confluence of Gomatī with the sea and to comply with his daily chore of religious ritual as a practice with an eye for liberation. Deciding like this the sage then thought for himself that it would be better for him to have a bath there fast and leave the land of the demon. Resolving like this, he then moved ahead fast on his pathway and happened to see the meritorious place where Gomatī met with the sea as he proceeded ahead. Then he put off his clothes and got his body annointed with cowdung and mud. Then after tying up the tuft of hair on the crown of his head and with the sacred grass *kuśa* in hand he got himself almost prepared to take a bath there as per prescribed procedure. But when the Brāhmaṇa was taking a bath there the notorious demons happened to see him and shouted, "Who is this man? Who is he? Let's go and slay him. In this region of ours looked after by us who is this man foolish enough to have a bath?" Saying like this, they all then took hold of him by his hips and knees and began to strike him with their clenched fists. The Brāhmaṇa as he was suffering from pain, began to tell them, "I am a Brāhmaṇa, hence not fit to be killed." After hearing these words of him and after noticing that the wicked demons were out to kill the Brahmaṇa, a great demon among them named Rūrū, prevented them from doing so. Taking hold of the clothes of the Brāhmaṇa left on the shore as well as the sacred grass *kuśa*, the demons in any case threw him into the water. Dragging him by feet and making him swear not to come back, the wicked demons made him forcibly out of the boundary of their territory. Seeing the Brāhmaṇa about to faint, the demons got angry again and told him, "If you happen to come here again, we shall kill you beyond any doubt. Do not look at the Anarta kingdom and the pond there in." Sensing that his life was in danger, Durvāsā began to worry excessively and thought what would be the use of his energies expended on penance if he, at all, cursed the demons. He told himself within that the rules of austerity on his part had already been violated and moreover his body had happened to decay. Hence the best course on his part would be to part with the body. In any case, who, taking his side, would impart him life at that juncture? He told himself, "Who could help him to have a bath at Cakratīrtha? And for that matter except for the lotus-eyed, i.e. Viṣṇu who could win this group of powerful demons in a fight and make the devotees free from fear? Except for the God bearing the discus in hands and happening to be the leader of gods like Brahmā, etc. and equally fond of all taking refuge under him, who else could protect him?" After deliberating in this manner for considerably a long duration and learning that the God Viṣṇu was there in the nether world, the celebrated sage then went into the region under the surface of earth to take refuge of Viṣṇu. His body had become lean due to fasting and in that pitiable condition he entered the palace full of Gandharvas and beautiful women of the demon king Bali. Viṣṇu, the chief of the gods was radiating there. Excessively elated within Durvāsā made his entry there. Seeing Durvāsā coming, the master of demons then got up to welcome the respectable man and offered him a seat. He offered him *Madhuparka* (i.e. a mixture containing equal parts of five substances, viz. milk, curd, ghee, honey and sugar) and a cow. Then placing himself on his side, he asked him with all politeness, "O Brāhmaṇa! please speak out the reason behind your coming here." Happily seated, the sage saw Trivikrama on the doorway of the demon king. He (i.e. Trivikrama) was without any fear. Seeing the four-armed bearing the mark of Śrīvatsa (i.e. curly hair) on his chest and the God of gods (Viṣṇu) there the best of the sages began to cry and said, "Save me and protect me. O Janārdana! O Keśava! you provide refuge to all afflicted with fear and distress in society. You also give refuge to the enemies as well as the humiliated. My sorrows had been due to tormentation by the enemies as well as their dragging me. I had been humiliated by them. Afflicted with hunger my condition had become pitiable. I could not complete my daily religious rituals due to the hurdles posed by the demons. O God Keśava! having good feelings for Brāhmaṇas be a resort for this Brāhmaṇa (i.e. me)." After saying like this Durvāsā then showed the marks of torture on his body by the demons to the God. Witnessing so and then realizing the humiliation on the part of Brāhmaṇa, the dwarf-incarnate God became very angry. He asked the Brāhmaṇa to speak by whom had he been humiliated and who put blocks on his pursuit of peseverance as per laid down procedure and as a Brāhmaṇa. Addressing him as a great fortunate soul, the God told him as to how could that be possible in the face of His presence as the upholder of Dharma. Durvāsā said, " O Madhusūdana, getting through self-perception that the Cakratīrtha would yield liberation for one, I visited the same place and was taking a bath there accompanied by all happiness. But before I could complete the bath, the bad and wicked demons happened to see me. Kṛṣṇa! holding me by neck, they striked me with their clenched fists. Taking hold of my clothes by force they threw the same into water along with the *kuśa* (i.e. the sacred grass) and the unbroken whole grains. They dragged me up along the way holding my feet. Throwing me out of their territorial boundary the stupid demons threatened me saying I would be killed beyond any doubt if spotted there again. Hence the God, help me to have a complete bath at Cakratīrtha and also give me some food. By this, Govinda! my perseverance would succeed as per the pescribed rules. By your favour, I could have a bath here and having the food, I would be satisfied mentally. This way by making my vow successful, I would continue to make visits of centres of pilgrimage on the earth's surface."

CHAPTER NINETEEN

Durvāsā's daily ritual of bath and the advent of Kṛṣṇa, Balarāma and Durvāsā

Prahlāda said:

1-3. The God thought once and again about what Durvāsā told him. Then the God told the virtuous and sinless Durvāsā, "O master Brāhmaṇa, I have lost my freedom and become subservient to the devotion of Bali for me. I have come thoroughly under Bali and I cannot do anything other than the commands of Bali. Hence, make a request to the demon and son of Vairocani Bali first. I shall comply with the wishes desired at the moment in your mind as per his commands."
4-8. After hearing these words, the Brāhmaṇa then hurried up, went to Bali and told him, "You are pre-eminent among those who conduct religious rituals involving sacrifices (i.e. *yajña*) and counted among the best known for giving charities. O great reservoir of benevolence! please show kindness towards me by sending the God to subdue the demons. By your favour in this way, I can complete the religious rite of taking a bath as per rule." The demon (i.e. Bali) would not be so pleased to hear these words. He told Durvāsā, "That will not be possible. The master Brāhmaṇa may therefore put forward any other request revolving in

his mind. He is prepared to oblige him by granting that without any doubt even if that may be difficult to obtain. On his part he may give himself in, but can never part with or lose Hari under any circumstances, for how could he think of losing Keśava whom he had got by dint of innumerable good deeds."

9. Durvāsā said, "Do not think that I am bound up with greed. O demon! just send Janārdana to protect my life."

10-14. Bali said, "O Brāhmaṇa! you must be aware that the God had assumed the incarnation as a strong boar to kill Hiranakṣya. Similarly the omnipresent Lord had assumed the incarnation of Nṛsinha (i.e. appearance having a man's body with a lion's head) to kill the pre-eminent Hiraṇyakaśipu among the demons. The virtuous God had also killed the demons named Vṛtra and Namuci and the Lord of Laṅkā (i.e. Rāvaṇa) through trick for the sake of gods. Assuming the form of dwarf, he first asked for land measuring his three steps. But then assuming the form of Trivikrama, Viṣṇu showed the world to comply with measurement of land amounting to three limitless steps of him. I have somehow obtained Viṣṇu by virtue of my meritorious deeds. Under no circumstances can I lose the God and Lord of the world who has been obtained by me in his magical shape of dwarf."

15. Durvāsā said, "I shall not eat without having a bath in the confluence of Gomatī with sea. If you do not send Hari, I shall put my body on its path of decay, i.e. I shall give up my body."

16. Bali said, "Whatever is destined, let it happen. The Brāhmaṇa! as you know, so you act. I cannot afford to lose the two steps to which Brahmā, Rudra and Indra equally salute."

17-18. Seeing both arguing with each other in this way, the Lord of the world known to have sympathy for Brāhmaṇas said mercifully to the Brāhmaṇa, "Be happy the foremost Brāhmaṇa. There can be no doubt that you need to have a bath as a part of your penance and perseverance. I have to kill all these demons assembled at the confluence of Gomatī with the sea."

Prahlāda said:

19-25. After hearing these words of the God to the Brāhmaṇa, the demon Bali then fell flat at the feet of God tightly holding both of his legs together. Then the Lord made Bali fortunate by giving him both of his feet and bearing the conch, the discus and mace in hands, he left taking Durvāsā along. Seeing Janārdana leaving along with Durvāsā, Halāyudha (an epithet of Balarāma)—the eternal power of masculinity followed them with his mace in hand. Balarāma holding his mace in hand was walking in the front. Behind him was Viṣṇu—the Trivikrama. Coming out of the nether world, the Brāhmaṇa Durvāsā was following both of them from behind. They all swiftly pierced out of the region under the surface of earth and appeared on the place where Gomatī had its confluence with the sea. Holding their bow firmly in hands and after fixing the arrows onto them both Kṛṣṇa and Balarāma then told the Brāhmaṇa to take a bath to the extent of his sweet will. After hearing both, the Brāhmaṇa then hurried up, took a bath and completed the necessary rites.

CHAPTER TWENTY

The war between demon Kuśa and Viṣṇu and the placing of Śivaliṅga over and above the demon

Prahlāda said:

1-3a. The demon Durmukha happened to hear the sounds of recital of Veda (i.e. Brahmaghoṣa) at that juncture. He got highly enraged and with eyes blood-shot in anger, he told Durvāsā, "We had beaten you up, but had left you free.

So why did you the wicked soul come here again to get killed?" After saying so the stupid demon then came to hit him with blows after clenching his fists.

3b-4a. Seeing him running towards him the virtuous sage Durvāsā then told him, "You, the sinner, do not touch me, i.e. a Brāhmaṇa engaged in performance of his daily religious rites."

4b-5. Seeing the demon excited enough to kill a Brāhmaṇa, Viṣṇu—the Lord of world then took out his sharp-edged discus and cut off the head of the demon to save Durvāsā.

Prahlāda said:

6-7. Seeing Durmukha to be dead, the demons became intolerant. Crying, they called out for one another saying, "all the demons hurry up and come together to go to that place where Durmukha has been killed." All the demons heard that Durmukha had been killed and Durvāsā had again been saved by Viṣṇu.

8-9. With their eyes blood-shot with anger and with varieties of weapons in their hands they began to curse the Brāhmaṇa Durvāsā as well as Kṛṣṇa using abusive language condemning Kṛṣṇa as one with a tortoise-like back, an illegitimate son of a widow, an angry man and Durvāsā as a polluter of Veda, a person with all inclination to deprive one of *yajña*, a destroyer of *yajña* and as one sounding the death-knell of dharma.

10. Armed with varieties of weapons they began to scatter the celebrated sage, Viṣṇu and Samkarṣaṇa (an epithet of Balarāma) with clubs, javelins, maces and missiles.

11. Having lost their senses in anger, they were fighting with several weapons. Viṣṇu was surrounded from all sides by the ferocious looking demons.

12. It appeared as if Viṣṇu had been surrounded by the moon, the sun and the cloud besides Balarāma on his side. Then both of them hurriedly fixed the arrow to their respective tidy and strong bows.

13. In the ensuing great battle they killed most of the demons. Fearing death many demons were also driven away.
14. After seeing that the demons were either killed or made to flu away by him (i.e. Viṣṇu) Kūrmapṛṣtha (an incarnation of Viṣṇu with a back resembling a tortoise), after giving his regards to Golaka made a retreat thinking his mission to be accomplished.
15. Golaka then striked Samkarṣaṇa (i.e. Balarāma) with three arrows. Seeing the eternal Balarāma wounded, Golaka then lost his senses with anger.
16. Swiftly rushing towards Durvāsā, he then attacked him on his forehead. Injured by the striking of fist, he fell down on the ground and began to shout.
17. After seeing Samkarṣaṇa lying on the ground and Durvāsā tormented with the injury on his forehead, he then said, "O God! do wait, do hold on. I have already killed the two heroes and my enemies by mace in the battle."
18-19. After seeing the Brāhmaṇa to be lying on the ground and crying, Golaka then made up his mind to kill Kūrmapṛṣṭha (i.e. Viṣṇu). Taking out a sharp-edged arrow made of iron, he then aimed at the chest of the enemy (i.e. Viṣṇu).
20. As soon as the arrow was released from his hands, the same flew away after wounding Viṣṇu. The body of Kūrmapṛṣṭha got dismembered by the force of the weapon. This way humiliated all the forces of the Lord then began to flee in different directions.
21. Seeing the dismantling as well as vanquishing of all the forces including Golaka, the doorkeeper then went and conveyed the same to Kuśa—the king of demons.
22. Hearing about the death of Golaka, the king of the demons (i.e. Kuśa) then commanded all the demons to come together and prepare themselves fittingly for the battle.
23. Getting the order of Kuśa, all the demons including Pañcajana, et. al. then headed for the battle seated on chariots and elephants.

24. Kūrmapṛṣtha stepped out with a collection of army comprising ten thousand soldiers, twenty thousand chariots and ten thousand elephants.
25. Accompanied by a large army and consisting of one lakh horse-riders and the same number of camel-riders, Vaka—the demon moved ahead.
26. Dīrghanakha—the able bodied commander moved ahead followed by his streams of army. Mahāmāya—the son of the minister of Kuśa was also there. The very strong and powerful demons, viz. Vighasa and Praghasa were also there.
27-29. The demons Urdhabāhu, Bakrasira, Kañcuka, Śivoluka, Brahmāghna, Yajnaha, Rāhu and Varvaraka were there. The intelligent Sunāmā, the minister named Vasunāmā, the commander Ugradamṣtra and his brother named Mahāhanu were there. Besides them, there were also a good number of other demons equally enraged. With the trumpeting sounds of chariots they all began to move ahead with all eagerness to fight.
30. Taking bath and thereafter putting on white clothes and getting himself adorned with a garland made of white flowers Kuśa went into a deep sense of meditation on Bhuteśa (i.e. Śiva) to worship Śambhu—the husband of Bhavānī.
31. He bathed the idol of Śiva with *Pañcāmṛta* (i.e. a mixture containing equal proportions of five ingredients, viz. milk, curd, ghee, honey and sugar) and massaged it with scented oil. He decorated the same with diamonds, jewels and a crown on its head bright like the rays of sun.
32. With singing and chanting of auspicious mantras he worshipped Mahādeva and then made the Brāhmaṇas to declare that "Let everything fare well."
33. Then he put on dress studded with ornaments. His protective guard on the chest was decorated with gems. His copper-coloured crown on the head was illuminating like the bright sun.
34. He was also adorned with an excessively beautiful necklace. Decorated in this manner and as such shining

brilliantly equipped with weapons the strong and powerful demon king looked up for his charioteer.

35. Then he asked Sunāmā and his minister Vasu to enquire was about the person and his purpose of killing all the demons.

36-38. Another demon Rūrū said, "Yesterday, a Brāhmaṇa had come here with all determination to take a bath at this place of confluence of Gomatī with the sea. O king! when we the demons stopped him from doing so, he retreated but came back again accompanied by Viṣṇu and Samkarṣaṇa (i.e. Balarāma). O great king! the Lord of the world, a great sympathizer of the Brāhmaṇas, had been on a killing spree of the demons since then. Many demons had been killed by him while some had fled away."

39. Sunāmā added, "Supported and accompanied by Vāsudeva, the Brāhmaṇa came here for bath. O king! tell us what option could we have except getting into the futility of a war?"

40. Kuśa became furious hearing such words of him. He then said, "Why should not I kill Keśava—the killer of Golaka?"

41. Saying so, the enraged master of the demons then got onto his horse to the loud beating of drums simultaneously.

42. He then saw the thousand-headed, the Lord of the gods and the bearer of discus in hand—Viṣṇu. Besides, he also happened to see the sinless Durvāsā.

43. Learning that Durvāsā happened to be a part and parcel of Lord Śiva, he decided not to kill him. On the other hand, he sent all the demons together to attack Viṣṇu.

44. With elephants similar in size like mountains, with chariots similar in size to clouds and with horses excessively active and swift, those demons encircled Viṣṇu completely from all sides.

45. The war of demons with both Kṛṣṇa and Balarāma appeared almost imminent. The other gods happened to

witness both Kṛṣṇa and Balarāma to be completely encircled by the demons.

46. Then picking up his mace and plough, the powerful Balarāma killed the pre-eminent among demons comparable to Kālānala and Yama.

47. Getting themselves either vanquished or killed by the powerful Balarāma, the demons fled hither and thither.

48-49. With their eyes blood-shot with anger the best and the pre-eminent demons like Baka, Yajñakopa, Brahmaghna, Vedadūṣaka, Mahāmakhaghna, Jambha, Rāhu and Vakraśira as well as other demons then began to strike at Janārdana to tear him apart into pieces.

50. Then getting enraged both Janārdana and Samkarṣaṇa began to strike the strong demons with their respective discus and plough.

51. The head of Baka got severed from his body by the discus of Kṛṣṇa while the demon known as destroyer of yajñas got shattered completely by the mace of Balarāma.

52. Rāhu got killed by the discus while others by the mace. Witnessing their killing and thinking that they had been defeated completely, the remaining demons began to flee in all directions.

53-54. After seeing his troops getting killed and running hither and thither, Kuśa, the demon king got enraged and with his eyes blood-shot with anger told the charioteer, "Let us go there". Then after going near him (i.e. Kṛṣṇa) he declared his own name by which he had earned his fame and then addressing him as Gadādhara (i.e. the bearer of the mace) asked him to give him a hearing as to why was he killing his demons?

55. Śrī Vāsudeva said, "These wicked souls are acting as hurdles to this meritorious spot of confluence of Gomatī with the sea which bestows liberation. Due to sin on their part from this angle, they have been killed by me."

56. Kuśa said, "Don't you know my presence here? So how can you leave this place remaining alive? If you get into

a continuous fight with me, that will be your end and you will definitely not remain alive."

57. After having said so, he then after assembling twenty weapons together, struck at Keśava. Assembling another eight weapons together, he struck the eternal Balarāma. After doing so he looked at the celebrated sage Durvāsā. But then realizing him to be a part and parcel of the God (Śiva) he asked him to leave the place without any delay.

58. But at the same time Śārṅga (i.e. an epithet of Viṣṇu) the best and foremost among the bearers of bow and arrow made all parts of the body of the demon Kuśa separate by striking his best of arrows. Then striking four arrows, he killed the four horses pulling the chariot of Kuśa.

59. By application of his half-moon shaped weapon, he separated the head of the charioteer. Before this he made his arrow defunct by his arrow and cut down the banner on the flag-staff of the chariot by another.

60-62a. With himself wounded and unseated from the chariot and his charioteer killed, Kuśa bacame disheartened. But then lifting up his heavy sword in hand he said, "If I kill you, my name will be considered for weighing in the scale of fame. Otherwise, if killed by a hero like you, I shall attain the ultimate passage. So Hari! please hold on and remain in the place you are in. I have forever taken refuge in the Lord Śiva."

62b. (However) Seeing him running in the height of anger with sword in hand, Viṣṇu then sportively cut his head from the body by his sharp-edged Sudarśana discus.

63. Seeing the severed head of Kuśa lying on the ground, the demon Khañjanaka then carried it back in the chariot.

64. With the retreat of the demon Kuśa, Viṣṇu and Samkarṣaṇa then became relieved and with all happiness withdrew from the battle and returned along with Durvāsā.

65. (However) to compensate, they put the demon Kuśa in the temple of Śiva and tried to appease him by bathing and worshipping him with perfume, lighting incense sticks and by singing accompanied by beating of drums.

66. The demon suddenly, got back life by the grace of Śaṁkara and then getting up began to utter Śiva, Śiva.
67. After seeing the demon getting back life again, the demons considering that as something auspicious, with good feelings began to say, "Let you have long life."
68. They further said, "What shall you reap by getting into the futility of war, if the Brāhmaṇa (i.e. Durvāsā) takes a bath there again and then proceeds on the direction of his own will?"
69. After hearing these words of them Kuśa said, "Hurry up and send the two who happen to protect the Brāhmaṇa."
70-72. The virtuous sages! so ordered by the king (i.e. Kuśa), Sumanā (i.e. his minister) then proceeded ahead and after paying his respects to Viṣṇu and the bearer of plough (i.e. Balarāma) told them, "Janārdana! Kuśa has sent me to you. His excellency wants to know as to what harm has he done that you have been killing the demons? You are free to leave after making Durvāsā to have a bath here. You must be aware that blessed by Mahādeva, Kuśa has already obtained immortality."
73-75. Śrī Viṣṇu said, "You—the sinners, always engaged in evil deeds are posing as obstacles on the road to this centre of pilgrimage which is a giver of liberation. Hence, you all demons will have to be killed without any doubt. Bring back the sacred *kuśa* grass, the sesame and the unbroken whole grains which Durvāsā carried along to use in the very activity of performance of worship and which, all of you threw into the water. All of you, leave this meritorious place of pilgrimage along with your carriers, your family members and with all the members of Kuśa lineage as per your awareness and enter into the region under the surface of earth."
76. With his eyes reddened with anger after hearing such words Sumanā said, "Keep fighting. This won't be possible."
77. Sumanā then conveyed all that Viṣṇu told him to Kuśa. Kuśa got angry and became fully flared up after hearing him.

78. He got onto his chariot fast and then proceeded ahead to encourage the fighters. He remembered Pināki (an epithet of Śiva) identifiable by the bull on the flag-staff of his carrier, in his mind.

79. Subsequently, the horripillating war of Keśava with Kuśa and other demons followed.

80. Yajñaghna hit at the head of Samkarṣaṇa with a heavy mace. But he fell on the ground getting hit in turn by Samkarṣaṇa on his head.

81. God Hari killed Kañcuka by his discus. Ullukaśva and Brahmaghna also got killed by him.

82. Besides them, many other demons got killed by Keśava. Kuśa got into the top of highest anger after witnessing his demon folks lying dead on the ground.

83. The ferocious Kuśa then attacked Keśava with the ultimate best weapon at his disposal. But the God enjoined with anger cut off the head of Kuśa.

84. Keśava saw his cut-off head falling down on the ground. With his sword, he then cut off his hands and feet into pieces.

85. Seeing Kuśa turned into pieces as a result of injuries inflicted upon him by Keśava, the demons then began to gather pieces of his body and thereafter taking them along went to Śiva's temple.

86. The demon got back life instantaneously by the gracious favour of the bearer of trident (i.e. Śiva) and then getting up immediately he uttered, "Where is Viṣṇu?"

87-89a. Lifting up his mace and with anger he began to make advances to fight with Janārdana (i.e. Viṣṇu). Then seeing the already dead one to regain life and manifestedly speaking, Viṣṇu asked Durvāsā, "How is it that he (i.e. the demon) is not dying. As it is, I had separated the head from his body and had made his body into pieces. How is he getting back life again? What could be the reason behind it? Please tell me."

89b. After the God's saying like this the virtuous sage then began to think and meditate.

90-91. Then becoming aware of the sole reason behind the same he told Madhusūdana that getting pleased with him Mahādeva had made Kuśa immortal. Hence, despite turning him into pieces, life-force was not being taken away from him. Then getting himself fully surprised, the God began to deliberate as to how could he kill him.

92. The God kept on telling himself that he had to devise a way by which the demon could not gain back life again as per the blessing of Śaṁkara. When the God was contemplating like this, the demon got up with a shield and sword in hands saying, "Wait, wait and remain where you were".

93. Seeing Kuśa, happening to be a part and parcel of Śiva, advancing once again with a mace in his hands, the God killed him by his mace.

94-95. With the attack of God, the head of Kuśa got separated from the body and he fell down on the ground. But Hari then swiftly took up the body of Kuśa lying on the ground. Putting it into a ditch, he then covered it completely with earth. Janārdana then placed the worshippable Sivaliṅga there (upon the covered ditch).

96. Subsequently as the son of Danu (i.e. Kuśa) regained consciousness, he saw the Śiva Liṅga placed above his head and began to think about it anxiously in an intense manner.

CHAPTER TWENTY-ONE

Importance of Viṣṇu worship at Gomatī Tīrtha

Śrī Prahlāda said:

1. The son of Danu said, "O Kṛṣṇa! you have killed me fraudulently and quite cunningly. I cannot overstep or disregard the Śivaliṅga ."

2. Śrī Viṣṇu said, "O demon! I have been quite pleased with your might obtained under the protection of Śiva. O great mind! you may gracefully solicit the boon as desired in your mind."
3-5a. Kuśa said, "As I worship Mahādeva so do I intend to worship Hari. Let there be an idol combining both these forms which would be a boon for me. O Lord! you have already placed the Śivaliṅga on top of my body. Let it be named after me and remembered as Kuśeśvara. If you have to favour me with your grace, let my fame actuate in this way."
5b. After this, the celebrated God said, "It will be like that." Then the demon stayed put there.
6. Then Mādhava sent some of the demons to region below the surface of earth. Some of the demons also went back accompanied by Viṣṇu.
7. The eternal Viṣṇu remained placed there since then. Durvāsā—the foremost of the sages did also acknowledge it as a centre of pilgrimage conferring liberation on one.
8. Considering that the God Trivikrama (i.e. Viṣṇu) would be present there at Cakratīrtha on the banks of Gomatī, Durvāsā got convinced that the same place of pilgrimage would therefore be a giver of liberation. Hence, he also placed himself there.
9. In this way the Lord Trivikrama has been present there since then. And this is how the Lord has descended on the earth in the Kaliyuga again inhering part and portion of his essential character of Kṛṣṇa.

Prahlāda said:

10. O Brāhmaṇas! now listen with attention to the ways Hari needs to be worshipped. Worship of Hari here in the months of Caitra (i.e. March) and Vaiśākha (i.e. April) has been said to yield fruits in particular.
11-14. A man who after making an idol of Madhusūdana at Dvārāvat undergoes such rituals like taking a bath, then

applying perfume on the idol to worship the God Kṛṣṇa and then decorates it with clothes, lights up incense sticks and earthen lamps, offers ornaments, betel leaves, fruits and other offerings associated with the very act of worship, and then conforms to the practice of staying up for the night reciting the name of God, lighting up an earthen lamp full of ghee and then falls flat on the ground to make his obeisance as well as sings accompanied by beating of drums and reads out religious books, he gets all his desires fulfilled by worship with such procedure and with due faith.

15. By putting on the sacred thread on body and worshipping (Viṣṇu) in the month of Śrāvaṇa (i.e. July-August) one can ensure undecaying happiness of one's forefathers along with successful attainment of one's desires in mind.

16. The virtuous Brāhmaṇas, by worshipping the Lord Kṛṣṇa on the eleventh day of the brighter period of Moon in the month of Kārtika (i.e October-November) one can obtain that ultimate passage.

17. Besides, by bearing the sacred thread on the body and worshipping Viṣṇu in the month of Śrāvaṇa (i.e. July-August) one can obtain the abode of Viṣṇu with accomplishment of all desires.

18. Worship Lord Viṣṇu on that special day which is considered to be above all the auspicious moments transcending the four yugas and falls on the twelfth day in the months of Aṣāḍha (i.e. June-July), Jyeṣṭha (i.e. May-June), Pouṣa (i.e. December) and Māgha (i.e. January) when the sun is usually placed in the Southern hemisphere of the earth.

19. By worshipping Kṛṣṇa at the confluence of Gomatī with the sea in the Kaliyuga, one can attain that divine and sacred world. There can be no doubt to rethink about this.

CHAPTER TWENTY-TWO

Importance of worshipping Rukmiṇī

Śrī Prahlāda said:

1. O adorable Brāhmaṇas, now listen to the way the activity of worship has to be complied with, which I am describing. After bathing the idol of Lord of the universe apply perfumed ointments onto it. Then worship it with basil leaves after decorating the idol with ornaments.
2. Make offerings of edible items and then lighting up a lamp and holding it in hand move it around before the God. Worship Durvāsā as well while worshipping the lotus-eyed (i.e. Viṣṇu).
3. Human being needs to worship Gaṇeśa and Garuḍa with devotion. He has to make donations as per ability and affordability being free from any sense of deceit.
4. Also give alms to the poor, the blind, the miserly and all those who come seeking refuge under you.
5. Then man has to go to the temple having the deity of the daughter of king of Vidarbha, i.e. Rukmiṇī. Worship her by lighting earthen lamps, incense sticks and by making sacrifices as well as of gifts.
6. A man remains aff ected with afflictions by diseases as well as retrogade planetary movements in the Kaliyuga till he does not worship the beloved of Kṛṣṇa with necessary faith.
7. Fear of diseases, sorrows and losses will continue for a man in his material life till he does not worship the beloved of Kṛṣṇa with devotion in the Kaliyuga.
8. Man will continue to be poor, unhappy and fight shy of strangers till he does not worship the beloved of Kṛṣṇa in the Kaliyuga.
9. A woman will continue to be attended with the sorrows and misfortune of having dead children till she does not get a look (in other words worship) of the beloved of Kṛṣṇa.

10. The male species will continue to be plagued with the fear of enemies, disruptions in family life and idiocy in the Kaliyuga till they do not have a look of the beloved of Kṛṣṇa with faith.

11-57. (Hence) it is desirable to worship Kṛṣṇa and Rukmiṇī as per settled procedure. One needs to bathe both of their idols with a mixture made up of milk, curd, honey and sugar. Offer different kinds of perfume as well as the juice of sugarcane. Bathing of the idols with water collected from different centres of pilgrimage ensures realization of all desires on one's part. For him, who bathes Rukmiṇī—the favourite of Kṛṣṇa in this manner, nothing in this as well as the next world appears difficult to obtain. By applying the paste made up of sandalwood, turmeric and musk on the idol of Rukmiṇī, a son begets a son for himself definitely. By worshipping her with the Mālatī flower (i.e. a scented-flower white in colour) and the lotus having one hundred petals, one earns honour of everyone getting blessed with beautiful appearance and tends to enjoy life forever. The Goddess needs to be worshipped specially with flowers like Kaner, Jasmine, Champak (i.e. a fragrant flower predominantly seen of yellow colour) lotuses particularly blooming in water bodies, Ketakī (i.e. a flower of plant called Ketaka) and flowers of pink colour. She has to be worshipped with vapours of the fragrant powder known as Aguru and with fragrant gum resin. While worshipping her, she has to be offered with soft and tender white clothes distinctively found in different regions of the world. As a dress for her covering, one needs to offer Rukmiṇī—the favourite of Kṛṣṇa a robe adorned with ornaments and jewels and especially with pearls. One who worships Rukmiṇī in this manner will never encounter unhappiness, preponderance of unrighteousness and lack of wealth in his family. He will not be childless. He will also not have to serve under people engaged in undesirable and lowly activities having pointers towards deceit. In this way the mother Goddess of the world, Rukmiṇī has to be worshipped by human beings in the Kaliyuga. The

Goddess can be pleased through the offer of all edible foods. One can plead the Goddess by offering betel leaves and worshipping her with all faith by vapours of camphor before her after lighting up the same. So the Brāhmaṇas, bearing a fresh fruit with a piece of sugarcane in hand make your offering as a part of the worship as per laid-down procedure and saying a mantra like, "O daughter of ruler of Vidarbha and the beloved of Kṛṣṇa! We bow down to you. O Goddess and giver of all wishes! please accept our offerings of worship and we pay our obeisance to you."Then guided by sincere feelings light a lamp for the purpose of waving before the idol (i.e. for āratī of the Goddess). It is desirable to do the waving of lights before the Goddess by lighting camphor in particular. Then carrying some water in a conch-shell move it around the idol attended with the requisite feeling. After that put the same conch bearing the purified water on your head. Then O Brāhmaṇas! falling flat on the ground give your reverence to the beloved of Kṛṣṇa. Do also worship other Brāhmaṇas and their wives as per your capacity. Make offering of necklace, vermillion, clothes and stoles. Worship by fragrant flowers and by applying saffron paint on the idol. Please the Goddess with safflower, collyrium and betel leaves. Offer her eatables like sweetmeats, sugarcane, honey and butter. Along with Rukmiṇī, Keśava gets pleased by this. O best of Brāhmaṇas! Keśava specially gets pleased by offering of fruits. Then Unmattaka—the doorkeeper (of the Goddess) is to be worshipped. After bathing his idol with fragrant substances apply saffron on it. Light up incense sticks and then worship it with flowers. With regard to eatables offer him meat and alcoholic beverages. After making enough of such different kinds of offerings offer the idol grounded rice. Then worship sixty-four female ascetics placed behind his idol. Then worship the bearer of all accomplishment who is also the Kṣetrapāla, i.e. the protector of territory everywhere (i.e. Śiva). Worship the proprietress of embodiment of various forms and the seven female ascetics there. Behind them are seated the eight wives of Kṛṣṇa, viz.

Rukmiṇī, Satyabhāmā, the auspicious Jāmbavatī, Mitrabindā, Kālindī, Bhadrā, Nāgnajito and Lakṣmaṇā who are favourites of Kṛṣṇa. Worship all of them there. They are all worshipable as per desirable procedure by offering of curd and *kheer* (i.e. a preparation made of rice and milk added with sugar). One needs to stay up for the entire night as a religious duty after lighting earthen lamps accompanied by songs with beating of drums for this purpose. Besides, one also needs to repeatedly proclaim their names while doing this. One who worships these eight wives of Kṛṣṇa in this way gets blessed with children, grandchildren and with wealth as well as good fortune. He also happens to realise all his wishes by the grace of Viṣṇu. So what is the need of making a great number of donations or for that matter of observance of any religious vow with all strictness for him as everything gets attainable for him by having a look of and worship of Rukmiṇī— the mother Goddess of the world and the favourite of Kṛṣṇa. Again, why does he have to conduct a good number of *yajñas* and comply with the practice of making paramount religious fees for the same as he has already taken a look of and pleased Rukmiṇī—the mother Goddess of the world and the dearest of Kṛṣṇa. He who has taken a look of Rukmiṇī—the mother Goddess of the world and the dearest of Kṛṣṇa can be considered to have made all donations, *havans* and the repeated utterances of name any God within forever on his part. That individual can be considered to have acquired those eight aspects of perfection/accomplishment without any difficulty who has happened to have had a sight of the favourite of Kṛṣṇa — by visiting Dvārāvat. His life can be assumed to have become successful as well as all wishes of his mind to have actuated in reality who has happened to have taken a look of the darling of Mādhava (i.e. Rukmiṇī) after visiting the abode of Kṛṣṇa in Kaliyuga (i.e. Dwārkā). What value, winning a kingdom or for that matter attainment of liberation can have for him who is yet to have a look of Rukmiṇī—the mother Goddess of the world and the dearest of Kṛṣṇa? Hence with all efforts men must worship and take a look of Rukmiṇī—the beloved of Kṛṣṇa as the same grants fulfillment of all desires. She in particular, is always to be worshipped during the first nine days of the month of Aśvina (i.e. September) which are considered sacred for the Goddess Durgā. People who worship the beloved of Hari on the ninth day of the same period by bathing her idol, by offering perfumes as well as adequate edible substances and stay up a night by lighting earthen lamps accompanied by singing religious discourses in her honour to the accompaniments of drums and attempt to proclaim her name loudly, can happen to please her—the daughter of Bhiṣmaka, resulting in accomplishment of all of their desires. Besides, a sincere worship of her on the fourteenth day of the month of Kārtika, i.e. October/November on Deepawali as per the injunctions of Śāstra results in attainment of all that have been specifically aspired for or willed. Those who worship the mother of Kandarpa (i.e Kāmadeva and Rukmiṇī) with fragrant flowers on the eighth day of the brighter period of moon in the month of Māgha (i.e. January) and present before her idol many gifts can be understood to have made their lives including their wishes successful. Men happening to have a look at the dearest to Mādhava, i.e. the Goddess Rukmiṇī on the twelfth day of the month of Chaitra, i.e March can be understood to have made their material life fortunate. They get blessed with children and grand-children. They get embellished with wealth and fortune. In life, they get free from diseases. This way, they happen to get that position of good health. Men who worship the beloved of Kṛṣṇa on the eighth day of the month of Jyeṣṭha (i.e. May) get all their wishes fulfilled beyond any doubt. Alternatively by worshipping the Mother in the month of Bhādra (i.e. September) men get free from all sins and attain the passage to the world of Viṣṇu. Those who take a look of Rukmiṇī along with Kṛṣṇa on the twelfth day in the month of Kārtika, i.e. November there will be no room for fear of anything at any time for such people. One who takes a look of Rukmiṇī and Kṛṣṇa present here together in their mutual company can be considered to have made his/her life successful. He/she gets blessed with sons and children having a relatively longer life. He/she happens to get blessed with undecaying wealth and fortune. Poverty/misery hardly ever occur for him/her. As it is, he who takes a look of Rukmiṇī and worships her—the beloved of Kṛṣṇa, goes to the world of Viṣṇu getting free from all sins. It is said that the meritorious fruits attended with taking a bath as well as making donations at all the centres of pilgrimage endure well into the Kaliyuga due to the abiding presence of Kṛṣṇa. O Brāhmaṇas! there can be no scope for liberation in the Kaliyuga without a visit to Dvārāvat. Kṛṣṇa had devised it in ancient times to tie down Bali. O great and foremost Brāhmaṇas! the God by his grace had also granted him that (i.e. liberation). The best of Brāhmaṇas, the great soul Mārkaṇḍeya had happened to say so to Pradyumna in olden times keeping in view his efforts in this direction (i.e. of attaining liberation).

CHAPTER TWENTY-THREE

Significance of Dvārakā visit and bearing of basil garland

Mārkaṇḍeya said:

1-96. O Indradyumna! try to understand the greatness of Dvārakā. The husband of Rukmiṇī (i.e. Kṛṣṇa) stays here in the Kaliyuga to drive away all hardships and difficulties. Those who read and listen to the greatness of Kṛṣṇa in the Kaliyuga cannot have residence for themselves in the abode of Yama for eight *yugas* in succession. Nothing in this as well as the other world will be difficult for him/her to obtain for whom the story of Kṛṣṇa is always held higher/greater in importance than his/her own life. The fruits accruable to inhabitation of thousands of years of Manu's count at Kāśī, can be obtained through just a stay for five days at Dvārakā. If an outcaste stays in Dvārakā in the Kaliyuga he obtains the passage realisable for the ascetics. The founder of creation, i.e. Prajāpati has said so. A man nurturing a desire to always visit Dvārakā can reap the same fruits emerging out of a visit to Kurukṣetra. The fruits which accrue to a bath at Somanāyaka during the time of eclipse in Soma planet have been stated to result equally by having a look of Janārdana at Dvārāvat. The fruits that can be earned by staying at the Puṣkara pilgrim centre and by undergoing the practice of making donations for a substantial number of years (i.e. a crore of years) can be earned by just having habitation at Dvārakā for a single day. Having a look of the son of Devakī at Dvārakā for a single day is understood as a foundation for reaping hundreds and lakhs of fruits. O king! a living being in the Kaliyuga can make his life fortunate by simply nurturing a constant desire in mind to visit Dvārakā for the purpose of having a sight of Kṛṣṇa. The foremost king, now listen to the fruits that accrue to one by staying for the entire day of the eleventh day of a month in the vicinity of Kṛṣṇa at Dvārakā. Such people may consider themselves to be fortunate enough for by having a look of the purifying face of Kṛṣṇa, they get themselves free from crore of sins. The fruits which can be earned by observance of vow attended with worship of Kṛṣṇa and by conducting of *Yajñas* as well as by making of greater donations, can be had by just having look of Kṛṣṇa once at Dvārakā. Those men who bathe the head of Kṛṣṇa with milk can reap the results of each drop of milk equalling one hundred Aśvamedha *Yajñas*. This is how it is remembered. Ten times the fruits of milk-bath is obtainable by curd-bath. Ten times of the fruits of curd-bath is obtainable by bath with ghee. Ten times of the fruits of ghee-bath is attainable by honey-bath. Ten times of all these fruits are obtainable by bathing the head of Kṛṣṇa after combining all these four with water. Fruits multiply ten times by making offering of flowers growing near the shore of water bodies. So is also the case of offering jewels of superior quality. The virtuous king, similar is also the case of offering water and perfume with mantras (i.e. consecration). Bathing the idol with the juice of sugarcane qualifies for results equivalent to conduct of one hundred yajñas involving sacrifice of horses. So is also the result, O king! of bathing the idol with water of centres of pilgrimage. Those who rub the water off the idol of Kṛṣṇa with a cloth after bathing the same get themselves cleansed off about a lakh of their sins earned through evil deeds. After bathing the Lord of the world, one has to put a garland of flowers onto the idol. By doing so one gets entitled to the fruit of one gold coin corresponding to each flower on the garland. By blowing the conch, etc. at the time of bathing the God, one gets the opportunity of residence in the Brahmaloka. One who reads the treatise containing one thousand names of Kṛṣṇa (i.e. Viṣṇu) at the time of bathing the idol, he can earn the fruits equivalent to making donation of one hundred Kapilā cows per each letter of the same name. O king! such fruits can be obtained by reciting verses of the Gītā. Eulogies through Gajendramokṣa as well as the most prominent of hymns also bring in similar results. The king, the God gets pleased even through recitation of hymns composed by other sages and all desires get fulfilled. So what to specially speak about the recitation of Veda at the time of bathing the idol of God. O king! the merits of such rites cannot be described. Those who dance before the idol of Kṛṣṇa at the time of bathing it, sing as well as recite the Vedic hymns, make conscious sounds proclaiming the victory of Kṛṣṇa, sing and dance with harmony of their clappings and either laugh or proclaim the magical deeds of Kṛṣṇa, can be presumed to have become free giving up the cycle of birth through a mother's womb. O king! he who recites the glory of Kṛṣṇa at the time of the ritual of bathing his idol, does not happen to remain in his mother's lap with face upward and raised. One who makes a mixture of sandalwood, the fragrant powder Agurū, saffron, camphor and musk of the deer and applies the same on the idol of Kṛṣṇa, is presumed to have fulfilled the religious procedure to earn for himself a place in the abode of Viṣṇu along with his forefathers till the subsistence of the Creation. Indradyumna, any individual who applies paste of sandalwood on the idol of Kṛṣṇa everyday without fail and worships it by lighting incense sticks as well as by other fragrant substances, gets eligible for a habitation of as many years in the abode of Hari as per the calculation of number of years in a yuga christened with the name of the famous Manu. One can adorn the God with ornaments as per one's capability. These may be of gold as well as of pearls of superior quality and brightness. Fruits attended with such activity is already acknowledged by the group of gods called Rūdra as well as Indra. Except Mādhava himself, even the sages are not aware of this. O king! those who worship Kṛṣṇa—the Lord of the world and destroyer of all impurities in the Kaliyuga, offer basil leaves and the Ketakī flowers, a garland made of jasmine flowers and with such flowers blooming forth in their respective lands—the fruit of each of such flowers has been declared to be equalling that of the Rājasūya *yajña.* Men who worship the Lord (i.e. the husband) of Rukmiṇī (with all adoration and faith) as per their capacity and affordability get entitled to merriments in the abode of Viṣṇu for as many years constituting one hundred times of the age as per estimation of Manu. Again such meritorious fruit is also obtainable by worshipping the son of Devakī with all faith by basil leaves with tender flower stalks. The fortune that awaits upon getting yoked to yoga or by becoming an accomplished yoga practitioner or by exceeding liberality in making gifts and donations or by serving centres of pilgrimage or by faithful devotion to mother or by observing the religious vow on that specific twelfth day of a month considered to be free from negative effects of Hell and the fruits usually waiting upon observance of the religious ritual of staying awake for a night and dancing and singing to the glory of Viṣṇu before his idol or by being a devotee of Viṣṇu or by reciting the Veda or by the Vaiṣṇavites by their recital of the Viṣṇu Śāstra or by worshipping Kṛṣṇa—the husband of Rukmiṇī by a garland made of basil leaves all such fruits, O king! are similar in their merit. As the beloved Lakṣmī is to Viṣṇu, so is basil relatively more dear to him and especially the basil available and sprouting up at Dvārakā comparatively give fruits. Even the very activity of worship in the temples meant for Viṣṇu outside Dvārakā with whatever fragments of basil available in the Kaliyuga can result in merits comparable to Dwārakā. Even worshipping of Kṛṣṇa—the annihilator of impurities of the Kaliyuga with the leaves of Ketaka plant, O king! results in reaping of the fruits of Aśvamedha *yajña* per each of the same leaf offered in worshipping. There can be no doubt that by worshipping Kṛṣṇa—the God of the three worlds with jasmine flowers one gets even that fruit most difficult to obtain and under no circumstances can one be deprived of it. O king! worship of the Lord (i.e. the husband) of Rukmiṇī by seasonal flowers results in realization of all wishes of men including the difficult ones also. O Indra-like king! those who light incense by mixing the black Agurū powder with camphor before Kṛṣṇa, they happen to attain the position comparable to Kṛṣṇa. Men by making a perfumed substance with a mixture of ghee and gum and by worshipping the Janārdana by lighting it up attain the fortunate state of bliss. Lighting up earthen lamps before Kṛṣṇa, O king! makes one to bury all sins and attain that position of radiance. He who lights up a chain of earthen lamps on the doorways of the Kṛṣṇa temple obtains kingdoms measuring up to seven islands per each lamp in the chain so set up. One who puts forth his wishful pleadings before Kṛṣṇa by offering his favourite eatables while worshipping ensures everlasting appeasement of his forefathers till the subsistence of Creation. One who submits himself before the God, O foremost king! with all sincerety within, all his wishes of mind reap actuation till the endurance of Creation. The leader of men! one who offers camphor and betel leaves along with betel nuts to Kṛṣṇa gets fortunate enough to obtain the position of God of fire. After adding camphor to water in a pitcher, one who places the same before Kṛṣṇa will never have to face scarcity of water for himself including his grandfathers till the subsistence of creation. One who protects the Lord from heat by waving a fan or any other thing like a cloth near him (i.e. his idol) then the chief of kings, there will hardly be any sinner in his family to head towards the abode of Yama. There will be no motion left for him, O great king! except for his remaining in the atmosphere. One who makes an altar of flowers in the temple of Kṛṣṇa, lights up incense and perfumes to create a fragrant atmosphere, he happens to roam around playfully in the sky seated on a chariot decked up with crores of flowers. One who pleases Kṛṣṇa while moving in the air, the God happens to bless him by kissing on his forehead while he is in motion. One who decorates the mansion (i.e. the temple of Kṛṣṇa) by placing the stems of plantain tree, he happens to stay in the world of Sun till the earth subsists. One who lights up incense sticks as well as puts a string made of beads of sandalwood in the temple of Kṛṣṇa, he gets served by divine nymphs as well as the leader of gods (i.e. Indra). With devotion, one who hoists a flag on the top of the mansion (temple) of Kṛṣṇa, he gets entitled to play with Brahmā following his obtaining the status of Brahmā. He, who makes a beautiful shape on the floor of the Kṛṣṇa temple having the *svastika* symbol integral to it, gets entitled to the sportive pastimes in the three worlds. He, who puts up heaps of flowers on the altar of the temple of husband of Rukmiṇī, gets an opportunity to roam merrily about all the heavenly gardens as well as in the company of foremost of men. He, who makes/spreads out coloured paintings in the mansion of the God of gods (i.e. Kṛṣṇa) gets eligible to put up in the world of Rūdra (i.e. Śiva) till the subsistence of seas. The great king, he, who makes a bright sign like that of rays of the moon on top of Kṛṣṇa and side by side continues to put up at Dvārakā, gets entitled to reside in the immortal Soma world. One who offers umbrella consisting of many spokes as well as decorated with sewn coloured clothes, decked up with beautiful jewels and having its handle to hold made of gold, for the purpose of Kṛṣṇa, he happens to engage himself in sportive pastimes with his forefathers surrounded by lakhs of immortal gods. The leader of men! he who gifts an aeroplane-like carrier made by humans, i.e. a palanquin to Kṛṣṇa—such a good deed on his part gets rewarded with his making wealth and he, getting entitled to the status of Brahmā. He stays and breathes in for a period making one day of Brahmā. The king, by worshipping and waving lighted lamps before Kṛṣṇa he gets entitled to experience a sense of pleasure by getting nearness to Kṛṣṇa. By further brightening up the lights with addition of camphor to wave before the God, a man can happen to reside in the exclusive world of Kṛṣṇa (i.e. Vaikuṇṭha) for a period of seven *kalpas*, i.e. till the time of dissolution of seven creations. By putting water into conch and then by waving the same before Kṛṣṇa, one happens to stay in the ocean of milk in the vicinity of Kṛṣṇa till the subsistence of Creation. After doing like this, O king! if one takes a round of the idol of Kṛṣṇa from left to right with all faith, then reads out the treatise containing his one thousand names as well as other hymns in his honour, he gets rewarded with lands measuring upto the size of seven islands according to the steps taken by him while making a round of the idol. Paying one's obeisance to Kṛṣṇa by falling flat on the ground is equivalent in results to that of the *Aśvamedha yajña.* Appeasement of Kṛṣṇa by good songs with a melodious voice gives the same results as that of the recitation of the Sāma Veda beyond any doubt. By dancing before the God accompanied by utmost happiness as well as attended with earnest devotion one happens to get rid of sins committed in periods constituting a number of ages as per estimation of famous Manu. Religious discourses before Kṛṣṇa with devotion of the highest order induces the same results per letter of the discourse as that accrue from making donation of one hundred Kapilā cows. By appeasing Kṛṣṇa by reading out the Ṛg Veda, Yajur Veda and Sāma Veda, the noble Brāhmaṇas can stay in the world of Brahmā till the dissolution of Creation. Those who read out the Yoga Śāstras and the Vedantic Purāṇas in the close proximity of Kṛṣṇa, piercing the sun rays, they happen to proceed to the abode of Hari. Śrīmad Bhāgvad Gitā, the treatise containing thousand names of Viṣṇu, the treatise called *Bhiṣma Stava rāja, the Anusmṛti* and the *Gajendramokṣa* are also very much loved by Kṛṣṇa. Those who read out the Śrīmad Bhāgavat near Kṛṣṇa can always have sportive pastimes with ascetics carrying along hundreds and crores of their clan members. O king! those who read out the Rāmāyaṇa, Vyāsa's Mahābhārata and the Purāṇas attain liberation beyond any doubt. One can reap hundreds and thousands of merits by reading out the Gitā etc., before Kṛṣṇa on the twelfth day of a month. O king! the merits get multiplied by crore of times by staying awake the entire night on the twelfth day of the month to conform to the religious ritual. Similar fruits can also be obtained by regularly putting up at Dvārakā. Sins earned through evil deeds of hundred years get wiped out by having a bath at Gomatī and following it up with a look of the face of Kṛṣṇa. Fortunate are those men who can make libations in memory of their forefathers with the water of Gomatī in its confluence with the sea at Dvārakā during the Kaliyuga. The king, a sight of Gomatī gives the same satisfaction like taking a bath at the mouth of Gaṅgā at Haridwār, at Prayāga, in Gaṅgā itself, at Kurukṣetra, at Prabhāsa, at Śukla Tīrtha, at Śrī Sthala and in the Puṣkara and then following it up with making libations of water as well as offering balls of cooked rice in honour and memory of one's forefathers. Even by taking the name of Gomatī within oneself with all sincerity and earnestness, the fruits of Cāndrāyaṇa (i.e. the religious observance of a penance connected with the Moon's age) can be obtained by one despite the fact of his/her staying far away from Gomatī. Fortunate is the region Dvārāvat as Gomatī flows there. Even the beloved of Rukmiṇī (i.e. Kṛṣṇa) stays there for ever on his own. How can there be the loosening of the bondage of sins on them in the Kaliyuga who are already stupefied by evils without their having a bath on the shore of Gomatī. Kṛṣṇa has made Gomatī in the Kaliyuga as a ladder to Heaven. It creates love in the minds of animals including goodness in humans. The stair to heaven may not be visible. A sight of Gomatī is just like having a sight of Heaven. As a grinder of sins it is a giver of happiness to the sinners. Just a bath in it induces liberation. The sea roars here with its water coming in touch with that of Gomatī. The powerful king, one has to go there where Kṛṣṇa is equally present. There are impressions of the circular discus on stones here in the confluence of Gomatī with the sea. As worshipping them results in liberation, so who will not like to adopt this place to serve? O king! the imprints of the circular disc of Kṛṣṇa are quite clear here.So who, for the purpose of killing sins, will not like to serve this place in the Kaliyuga? Since olden times, the Gods had taken resort to this place for its remaining largely out of sight and contact of the demons. So who'll not like to serve this place? As Kṛṣṇa — the son of Devakī did not give up the city of Dvārakā even in the Kaliyuga, so who would not like to serve the city by words and deeds with full application of mind?

Mārkaṇḍeya said:

97-189. O king! now listen to the account of this place/ city as a destroyer of sins which I am narrating. You shall definitely be free from the sorrows integral to bondage of society and family by listening to this. In ancient times, O king! there was a Brāhmaṇa by name Candra Śarmā in the kingdom of Avantī. Always a devotee of Śiva, he was a master of Vedas. Always bearing Śiva in mind, his words and actions never reflected anything other than his allegiance to Śiva. O king! his religious observance of any vow or penance had no other connection than Śiva. He was not observing fasting on the specific day considered auspicious for Hari nor was he undergoing any other religious penance for the same purpose. Except observing religiously the fourteenth day of a month considered auspicious for Śiva, he was not observing religious penance for any other God. O King! he used to visit all places exclusively demarcated for Śiva or used to go to centres of pilgrimage meant for Lord Śaṁkara. He never visited the centres of pilgrimage of the Vaiṣṇavas. Every year he used to visit Somanātha. O Lord of the men (i.e. the King)! he never used to desist from performing *yajñas* specially for Soma (i.e. Śiva). Of course, eighty-nine years passed in this way in his discharge of duties of devotion to Śiva. Once, during the festival earmarked for Soma, kings in large number, from various regions as well as the people equally in vast numbers under their governance assembled at Somanātha to take a look of Lord Śiva. After having a look of the Lord Someśvara, they then went to the city of Kṛṣṇa (i.e. Dvārakā). Despite their offering invitation to Candra Śarmā to accompany them, Candra Śarmā did not go to the city of Dvārakā. Instead he said, "I do not consider any other centre of pilgrimage in the three worlds to be above that of Śiva. As per my knowledge there is no other God than Śiva to be the master lord". So leaving Candra Śarmā behind, they all went to the city of Dvārakā. The next day, when Candra Śarmā left for his own home, suddenly he happened to see his grandfathers, as if, he was in a dream. With huge bodies the ghostly spirits appeared ferocious to him in dream. Simultaneously, some of them also equally appeared in lean and emaciated bodies with bouts of sneezing. He began to tremble out of fear after seeing such an excessively terrible dream. Candra Śarmā said, "Wherefrom have you all such ugly-shaped and ferocious animals hail? I have never happened to see such animals in the course of evolution on the surface of earth nor have I ever heard about them before." The ghosts said, "O foremost Brāhmaṇa! do not be fearful of us. We are all your ancestral grandfathers. Afflicted with great sorrows, we have come to you." Candra Śarmā said, "My grandfathers had reaped the fruits agreeable to the penance on their part. My only point of wonder is what could be the reason behind your becoming ghosts." The ghosts said, "Our son, listen to the reason behind our becoming ghosts, which we are narrating to you. We had always opposed and violated the observance of religious practices in the past specified for that particular day considered auspicious for Vāsudeva. In particular, we acted as hurdles before the religious practice of staying awake for the night observed in adoration of Hari. Our son, be apprised that it was due to this that we have become ghosts. Our downfall to the terrible hell will happen without any doubt. Hence, we shall remain here with you till the unprecedented submersion of existence." Candra Śarmā said, "Ruination by ghosthood will not be there for those who have relinquished faith in Kṛṣṇa and have given up the observance of religious vows on the twelfth day of the month specifically dedicated to Kṛṣṇa and by worship of Śaṁkara, etc. Such fate in any case, awaits those who fail to please the annihilator of the three worlds (i.e. Śiva) by their devotion. Otherwise, with the God's blessing of agreeable situation for them, they shall never attain the state of ghosthood." The ghosts said, "O son! the sins attended with creating barriers on the pathways of the religious observance of the twelfth day dedicated to Kṛṣṇa cannot be mitigated without atonement. The misfortune of ghosthood therefore will not go away certainly. The son, one who does not atone persistently has to suffer the sins of killing cows, despite the fact of his worshipping Śaṁkara and without worshipping Keśava. First of all, Keśava needs to be worshipped. After that one may worship Maheśvara. Then the remaining gods are to be worshipped with all devotion. Like the branches of a tree spread out of the main, i.e. the root branch, the entire existence comprising the mobile and the immobile has been born out of Vāsudeva. (Hence) the learned never worship the branches keeping aside the root. Hari—the Lord of the universe and the sovereign of the three worlds, is (therefore) worshipable in particular. (Those who worship Hari) deeply on the particular day meant for him, they get fortune. If due to some reason or other that day is afflicted, their forefathers get into the degraded stage of entry in the wombs of ghosts. The God does not accept offerings to the sacrificial fire made in his honour on such day. Similar is also the case with their forefathers who do not accept the oblation of food made in their memory on such day. (So the crux of the matter is) When the Sun does not acknowledge the worship of him, how will the forefathers accept the same? As the conduct of *havan* is prohibited when the period of full moon falls on two consecutive days so is the worship of Hari on the particular day meant for him but which is afflicted with abuses and leading one to obtain the status of ghosthood. The full-moon day in the month of Vaiśākha (i.e. April) is specially recommended for conduct of religious activities like *śrāddha* etc. It has been an established matter having longstanding validity that neither the God accepts the offerings made to the sacrificial fire in his favour nor do one's grandfathers acknowledge the oblations of food made in their memory on the third day of the month of Vaiśākha (i.e. April). (Hence again the validity of assertion that) where God himself does not accept his worship, how shall the grandfather do the same? Therefore, learned men must refrain from performing any such activity on the third day of Vaiśākha which has been a longstanding forbidden day in this regard. If one does so out of certain infatuation he continues to remain in the ghostly state almost forever. Even his strive towards meritorious deeds through service of large number of centres of pilgrimage fail to do away such predicament. (Similarly) if one observes the monthly sacrifice meant for the full-moon day on the tenth day of a month which has been a long-established forbidden practice or observes the annual *śrāddha* for his forefathers on the day before the annual day which again is forbidden, he can be understood to have made a beginning on the path to Hell. (Equally) one does not have to perform the *Agnihotra* (i.e. the oblation to fire conducted with recitation of a specific mantra) meant for the full-moon day on the tenth day of a month which again has been forbidden with longstanding importance. Prajāpati (i.e. Brahmā) has stated not to do so. Similar such thing has also been stated with regard to the conduct of *śrāddha* during the dark fortnight of moon (i.e. the declining phase of moon) as fittingly suitable in the frame of one's own time. The benefits of *śrāddha* conducted in this manner neither increase nor decrease. O son! all such things have been stated by Manu as well as the commentators of Vedānta. This is the proof behind such actions leading to nothing other than ghosthood. In these ways animals attain ghosthood in the reality of existence. One must therefore, decide as to what actions are fit/desirable on his /her part with due regard to the decrees of Dharmaśāstras. After paying your reverence to Somanātha you did not proceed ahead in your journey to have a look of Kṛṣṇa. So what fruits would you, at all, derive? It is said that both Hari and Hara are present in the highest image of God. Hence, differentiation that this is Śambhu and that is Hari cannot be the criterion as to what is ought to be done as duty. The difference between Kṛṣṇa and Somanāth is hardly ever visible. The visit to Somanātha becomes complete by taking a look of Kṛṣṇa. Hence, the son, both the places have to be visited without any doubt. A look of Someśvara implies visit to Dvārakā. On way to the worshippable Liṅga at Somanāth is situated Prabhāsa where the pure soul Keśava is present accepting the offerings of eatables by devotees as a part of worship. If after taking a look of the God Someśvara, a man does not visit Dvārakā, all his paternal ancestors will fall down to the terrible hell. The son, you, in particular, have not observed the religious duty laid down for the specific twelfth day in a month meant for Kṛṣṇa. We have observed the religious duty with adherence to the compliance of good deeds on our part. But as the day on which we observed the same was attended with abuses and negativities, we do not visualize any sign of our exit/ coming out of the abode of Yama." Candra Śarmā said, "The grandfathers, if, due to ignorance I did not comply with the religious observance meant for the twelfth day of the month specifically for Kṛṣṇa, why did you all observe the same on the day marked with stake? The ghosts said, "Tempted by the tricks of some wicked Brāhmaṇas, fortune tellers and Śukrācārya as well as due to their cruelty that we have got entry in the wombs of ghosts. All our actions inclusive of making donations, undergoing of penance, conducting of sacrificial fire and the observance of repeatedly taking names of God have gone futile. We have come in the wombs of ghosts due to the religious observance of the twelfth day specified for Kṛṣṇa on that day involving stake. Due to the religious observance on the prohibited day which, obviously, is not the day favourite to Kṛṣṇa, the son! your grandfathers have degraded themselves from heaven to ghosthooḍ" Candra Śarmā said, "(Dear) grandfathers, how could the ruination of ghosthood be obtained? By which actions would that be actuated? I shall do all that as desirable." The ghosts said, "Centres of pilgrimage like Gayā, Prayāga, Puṣkara, Kurukṣetra, Ayodhyā, Avantī, Mathurā, Arbuda and lakhs of such pilgrim centres cannot do away with this (sin) except Gomatī. (Like Puṣkara) Gaṅgā, Sarasvatī and Narmadā also do not qualify for the same. Obliteration of ghosthood is visible on the shore of Gomatī in the Kaliyuga. This is possible by making oblation with the water of Gomatī followed with a look of the face of Kṛṣṇa. Sins committed extending a crore of birth also get obsolete by this. Embracing the virtue of asceticism and retiring to forests appear to be vain in face of this. Son, if you have committed the religious observance meant for Viṣṇu on the day so forbidden, then go and take a look of the full moon- like face of the God (i.e. Viṣṇu). By going to Dvārakā of Kṛṣṇa you can create the ground for nullification of the fate that has happened to us. Not doing so will render the merits earned, so far, on your part, meaningless. Everything that you claim to have made for, has become vain in the absence of worship of Keśava. Whatever virtue you may presume to have attained by dint of worship of Śaṁkara, has become futile without the worship of Keśava. Your (re)birth will happen in the womb of ghosts. The fruits of well-being which you have earned for yourself will be complete by having a look of Kṛṣṇa. This will be so and without any doubt by coming in proximity with the place where Gomatī has its confluence with the sea. If the sight of Someśvara is not followed by having a look of the God Kṛṣṇa, the fruits of the pilgrimage cannot be appropriated. Śiva himself has said so. Śiva has said, "One who has happened to have a look of Kṛṣṇa, has undoubtedly taken a look of mine for both of us have one image beyond any doubt and there is no difference between me and Kṛṣṇa. (Hence) it is the duty of one to visit Dvārakā for the purpose of taking a look of Kṛṣṇa after having a look of mine. A look of Kṛṣṇa following a look of mine results in superior fruits. If a human soul purified by having a look of Kṛṣṇa takes a look of mine, that human being can never re-enter the cycle of rebirth with his retreat from the heavenly world of Viṣṇu." Somapati—the God of gods, has on his own stated so earlier. We have happened to hear so from the mouths of the Brāhmaṇaṣ in the course of religious discourses at Puṣkara. Hence, undertake a visit with an eye towards getting a look of Kṛṣṇa. Otherwise, the sinful entry into the wombs of ghosts awaits you. When people having committed crimes take a look of Kṛṣṇa, they get freed from sins committed since birth without any doubt. By worshipping Kṛṣṇa—the son of Devakī—all gods including Brahmā, Rūdra and the Sun get worshipped. O son! without worshipping Kṛṣṇa as well as Gods like Rūdra, etc. your grandfathers will never be pleased. Hence, go to Dvārāvat and take a look of Kṛṣṇa. By this we will be released from the womb of ghosts and obtain the ultmate passage. O son! the sages have never encountered anyone who had happened to wash parts of his body in the water of Gomatī in the Kaliyuga to have gone into any other womb. By simply striking the water of Gomatī with both the feet even the ineligible and incompetent people open the gateways for passage towards a sin-free world. The advocates of Brahmahood have stated so. Again by performing *śrāddha* at the confluence of Gomatī with the sea, one ensures unprecedented satisfaction of one's forefathers which endures till the final deluge (i.e. annihilation) of the world/ creation. All fruits of merit which are earned through baths at the various centres of pilgrimage located at the spots of confluence of different rivers with the sea, can be had by a bath for just a day at the confluence of Gomatī with the sea at Dvārakā having proximity to Kṛṣṇa. Fruits of *śrāddhas* conducted at thousands and crores of centres of pilgrimage can be had by making libations of sesame in honour of forefathers at Gomatī. By feeding ascetics in the Kṛṣṇa temple, satisfaction of forefathers can be ensured for the number of yugas equal to the each grain of cooked rice in the food so offered. The donations of underpants, clothes, small metallic pitchers (usually carried in hands by ascetics) umbrellas and footwear to ascetics (at Gomatī) ensure fruits having lasting effect till the subsistence of seven creations (i.e. Kalpas). Even the outcastes, O son! get fortunate by coming and putting up at Dvārakā in the proximity of ascetics. Those who take a look of the face of Hari everyday extended over the three time zones of the day, viz. morning, noon and evening, never get rebirth spanning endurance of creation for hundreds and crores of years. Subsequent to widowhood falling upon a woman, if she takes refuge at Dvārakā, she can uplift ten thousand members of her clan to the ultimate sacred position. What is the use of having a son who does not visit Dvārakā? That particular woman is far better than having one hundred sons if she happens to inhabit the Kṛṣṇapuri, i.e. Dvārakā. Those who after going to Kṛṣṇapurī worship Kṛṣṇa with basil leaves they not only obtain fruits of their own life but also enable cross-over of their forefathers and great grandfathers from bondages accompanying the deeds of their respective life-times. If one bears onto himself/herself the garland made of basil leaves (after taking it off the idol) of Kṛṣṇa, he/she gets ten times the fruits of Aśvamedha *yajña* per leaf on the same garland. If a man puts on the garland made of the wood of basil plant (after taking it off the idol) of Kṛṣṇa, the Lord Viṣṇu blesses him with the same fruits accruable to one by a visit to Dvārakā. A man who prays to Lord Viṣṇu through offer of garland made of wood of basil plant and thereafter bear the same on his body with all faith, sins do not come near him due to his getting the pleasure of Kṛṣṇa—the son of Devakī, forever. The God Himself resides in the body of that mortal being who wears ornaments made of wood of the basil plant on his head as well as on the arms of his body. One who executes his actions after putting on a garland made of basil leaves can be said to earn crores of merits for his forefathers as well as gods in the Kaliyuga. The messengers of the king of ghosts, i.e. Yama get overpowered by seeing an individual wearing the garland made of wood of basil plant from a considerable distance like houses getting uprooted by storm. "Sins never spread in those houses which are decorated with garlands made of basil wood and leaves." This is an age-old saying of the advocates of Brahmā—which we have heard. Hence, bearing of garland made of wood of basil plant is desirable for you. There can be no doubt that it takes away the sins of both this as well as the next world. If one moves around with the garland made of basil wood or of basil leaves the fear of nightmares or happening of anything ominous or even of enemies will rarely occur to him/her. It is understood that the ascetics, women and widows who happen to spend their life in this centre of pilgrimage in this Kaliyuga have obtained freedom from rebirth along with crores of their clan members. Those who do not wear such garland (i.e. of basil wood or of basil leaves) due to some reason or other, they remain under the overwhelming influence of sins and continuing to be burnt by the anger of Hari, they never return from hell. For you—the son, observance of the religious vows called Unmīlinī, Vanjulinī, Trisprusapakṣa-vardhinī, Jayā as well as Vijayā is mandatory on the eleventh day of a month. The eighth day of a month which is a destroyer of sins is favourite to Kṛṣṇa. The son, religious observance on this day at Dvārakā grants one with liberation. This has been so stated by Kṛṣṇa Himself.

CHAPTER TWENTY-FOUR

Dvārakā's greatness : Kṛṣṇa's boon and the account of Candra Śarmā

Śrī Mārkaṇḍeya said:

1. O king! after the forefathers in the appearance of ghosts made such statements, Candra Śarmā—the best of Brāhmaṇas then went to Dvārakā.
2. The foremost Brāhmaṇa visited regularly that particular spot at Dvārakā where Kṛṣṇa happened to be present along with Rukmiṇī. He also visited other centres of pilgrimage there.
3. The gods always remain there, where *yajñas* are performed regularly. The sages and ascetics adept in yoga also put up there.
4. Dvārakā is such a city which grants wishes of all and the city is served by all—the accomplished, the divine singers, the divine beauties and men including those having deformed bodies.
5. Dvārakā is the city where Gomatī—one of the stepping stones to heaven flows. The prominent Brāhmaṇa happened to have a sight of the same city which grants liberation to human beings.
6. One gets rid of sins like Brahmicide by entering into its territory. So, who will not like to serve this city repositing such power of remittances by a mere sight only?
7. After going to the city of Kṛṣṇa, i.e. Dvārakā, Candra Śarmā had a sight of both the Gomatī and the sea. Thinking within to have become self-fulfilled he considered his youthful life to be quite fortunate.
8. After seeing the beautiful city of Kṛṣṇa as well as the lotus-like face of Kṛṣṇa, the Brāhmaṇa felt gratified enough to consider himself fortunate on earth.
9. After seeing the face of Kṛṣṇa and the attractive idol of Rukmiṇī as well as the city of Dvārakā, the Brāhmaṇa thought

to himself, "What use, crore of centres of pilgrimage are left with for him to serve?"

10. The Brāhmaṇa told himself that he got the opportunity to have a look of the auspicious Dvārāvat by virtue of thousands and lakhs of meritorious deeds on his part. It was indeed a matter of his great fortune that he had availed the same opportunity on the twelfth day of the brighter period of moon in the month of Vaiśākha (i.e. April) implying observance of religious rites for the sake of Madhusūdana (i.e. Kṛṣṇa).

11. The twelfth day of the month of Vaiśākha (i.e. April) demarcated for religious observance in respect of Madhusūdana and known as *Trispruśo* is a destroyer of hundreds and crores of sins. Those human beings who religiously observe this day may be considered as fortunate.

12. If the day meant for religious observance called *Trispruśo* falls on a Wednesday, by worshipping Lord Viṣṇu at Dwārākā with performance of *yajña* men can attain those fruits which may not be possible even through service of crores of centres of pilgrimage.

13. Telling himself within like this that best of Brāhmaṇas (i.e. Candra Śarmā) took resort to the shore of Gomatī. He took a bath there as per the decrees of Śāstras and followed it up with the observance of prescribed religious rituals.

14. After bathing he made libations in honour of his divine forefathers as per stated procedure. Then the king, after obtaining the auspicious stone having the imprint / image of discus of Kṛṣṇa on it from Cakratīrtha he did the religious duty of worship of the same as per laid down procedure in the Puruṣa hymn of Ṛg Veda.

15. After this, remembering words of his forefathers, he worshipped Śiva and made offering of balls of cooked rice in honour of his forefathers as per laid down procedure.

16. He offered masseuse, clothes, flowers, incense sticks and lighted earthen lamps. Fully aware in mind, he offered sweet potato as food to the deity.

17. He made offering of betel leaves (to the God). Then he lighted lamps and thereafter adding camphor to the flame of the same lamp, paid homage to the God reciting hymns repeatedly. While moving the lighted lamp before the deity as a functional need of worship, he made round of the circumference of deity again and again.

18-39. He stayed up the entire night as a matter of religious observance and pleaded for God's pardon while making round of the deity. In the process, the three broad divisions of the day as per the time framework of eight hours per each division passed. Then Candra Śarmā said, "O Kṛṣṇa! listen to the words of mine—the pitiable and helpless. Keśava! please rescue me as I have been deeply affected with the fear of worldly existence. Even the devotees who might have committed sins in their lives, do not put up with sorrows by service at your lotus-feet. So what to speak of men who are sinless and who comply with the religious observance meant for the twelfth day of the month of Vaiśākha (i.e. April) specifically demarcated for your worship? My ancestor forefathers told me that they had been afflicted with sins for committing religious observance on the forbidden tenth day of a month. Janārdana! I have come to you seeking your favour/kindness so as to do away with the effects on them as part of their bad/unconducive/unfavourable deeds on that count. O Kṛṣṇa! they stayed awake for the entire night as part of the religious observance meant for the twelfth day of the month on that day which as it is, was a forbidden day. Let their sins get nullified like dissolution of salt in water. Due to their religious observance on that forbidden day, my grandfathers have got into the highly sorrowful state of ghosthood. O Lord of the world! please tell me as to how could I liberate my ancestor grandfathers from their state of ghosthood? I shall try my best to comply with the same for the sake of their release. O foremost of the Yadus (i.e. Kṛṣṇa)! shower your grace on them. Infatuated with ignorance, they could not worship you. Me the sinner, has taken complete refuge in the faithful devotion for Śiva. Neither have I shown devotion towards you nor have I complied with the religious observance of that particular day meant exclusively for you. O Kṛṣṇa! neither had I visited Dvārakā ever before nor had I have a bath in the waters of Gomatī. I did not also take a look of this lotus-feet of yours which is a giver of liberation. All the good fruits earned by my having a look of the Lord Someśvara had become futile by my not undertaking a visit to Dvārakā. O chief of the Gods! my ancestral forefathers have already told all this minutely to me. Hence, O Keśava! let you grace me so that the merits earned by me before by my good deeds do not go in vain. O son of Devakī! I have seen your face which is difficult to have in the three worlds and about which I did not hear in the Purāṇas. I may remember that even though Śiśupāla, etc. tried to harm you and invited your anger, they attained liberation by getting killed in your hands. Since today, it will be my earnest duty to worship you every day. I shall continue to do so even on the day forbidden specially for your worship and shall have food after observing ritual for half of a day. It will be my avowed duty to observe the religious activities meant for the twelfth day of a month which you are quite fond of. Besides, due regard of those having faith in Bhāgavat (i.e. cult espousing faith in Viṣṇu) will be my averred duty superior to life and wealth. I shall always read out the book containing your one thousand names. It will be my duty to regularly worship you with your favourite basil leaves. On the advent of the day meant for religious observance by staying up the entire night in your reverence, I shall bear the garland made of basil wood onto myself and engage in dancing and singing. Visit to Dvārakā everyday will be my duty. I shall listen to the sayings in books on you to be conversant with your varied accounts. Every day, with all devotion, I shall touch my head to the water of your feet. I shall also eat the food which I offer as a matter of worship with all devotion. With due regard, I shall bear on my head the flowers left over after offering to you. I shall always offer you eatables of which you are fond of. Like this, all that by virtue of which your pleasure may be induced, will be my duty in the most significant manner. In this way, O Kṛṣṇa! I have put forth before you, my desirable pursuit of devotion/faith in you.

Śrī Kṛṣṇa said:

40-41. Let there be your welfare Candra Śarmā—the good Brāhmaṇa. Along with you, your grandfathers will come to my world. Look at your ancestral grandfathers being seated on Garuḍa, i.e the Golden eagle. The good Brāhmaṇa, they have become free from ghosthood by my grace."

The grandfathers said:

42-70. O son! we have obtained liberation undoubtedly by your grace. We have got release from the ghost wombs by having a look of the face of Kṛṣṇa. Fortunate are the human beings in the world as well as their sons, grandsons and great grandsons who after having a look of Somanātha have taken a look of Kṛṣṇa at Dvārakā. Fortunate is that widow who has undergone a visit for the sake of having a look of Kṛṣṇa (at Dvārakā). Such action on her part rescues a hundred members of her clan besides her from the Hell. The outcaste who undertakes such a conjugated visit (i.e. visit to have a look of Śaṁkara followed up by a visit to have a look of Hari), he obtains the ultimate liberation and he gets accompanied by his forefathers in such attainment. After undergoing repeated pilgrimage to the same place, i.e. Dvārakā, one who stays there as a follow-up to asceticism he never returns from the abode of Viṣṇu for hundreds and crores of years of the subsistence of creation. What use of earning merits for one by visiting crores of centres of pilgrimage located on the shores of water bodies if after having a look of the Lord Someśvara, he neither takes a look of the face of Kṛṣṇa nor does he take a bath in the waters of Gomatī? He definitely deprives himself (by doing so). His forefathers in the divine kingdom reprobate him for such sinful action of not visiting Dvārakā after having a sight of Someśvara. The merit that is derived from a hundred pilgrimages is implied in just having a look of Kṛṣṇa following a look of Someśvara, i.e. Śiva. Soupernya, i.e. the Garuḍa Purāṇa states so. All his deeds in worldly existence have gone in vain under the tutelage of infatuation/ignorance who has not taken a look of the God Kṛṣṇa after having a look of Someśvara. By coming to Prabhāsa and having a sincere look of Kṛṣṇa, a man can earn fruits amounting to ten thousand visits to Prabhāsa. This is because all pilgrimages, all gods and all *yajñas* materialize by remaining present before or in proximty of Kṛṣṇa and having a look of him—the embodiment of *yajñas* in the three time durations of the day. So the son! what is the use of visiting various centres of pilgrimage or for that matter of choosing to stay in many places of pilgrimage? The fruits of all centres of pilgrimage can be acquired by a sight of Dvārāvat. After killing Kaṅsa, Jarāsandha and the demon Naraka, Kṛṣṇa—the son of Devakī had relieved the Earth of the burden of their sinful deeds. Then he set up the beautiful city of Dvārāvat near the sea. With an exalted mind Kṛṣṇa put up there seeking the pleasure of company of beautiful women. Brahmā, Agni (i.e. Fire God) Vāyu (i.e. Air God) Sun God, Vāsava (i.e. Indra), the rising day, mortals, Brāhmaṇas, kings, the king of Nāgas from Hell remain there. Rivers, rivulets, mountains, natural forests as well as implanted forests and big forests, cities, villages, seas as well as streams remain present there. Yakṣa, demons, Gandharva, the accomplished, Vidyādhara, Rambhā including other divine beauties, sons of Diti like Prahlāda etc., demons like Bibhiṣaṇa, the wealth-giver and the leader of Yakṣa, i.e. Kubera, sages, saints, the accomplished (i.e. Siddhas) yogis like Sanaka, etc., planets and stars like Dhruva and whatever mobile and inert objects present on earth, always stay there in proximity of Kṛṣṇa. They do not give up the auspicious city of Dvārakā which Kṛṣṇa has made his own. O son! as you have served the city and equally had a sight of Kṛṣṇa, we shall be free from the wombs of ghosts and attain the ultimate passage. Our existing state has been the result of sin of religious observance meant for the twelfth day of a month in honour of Kṛṣṇa on a prohibited day other than this. O son! you have undoubtedly dissipated the same and we shall obtain the ultimate position. The sins incurred on your part for observance of the religious vow meant for the twelfth day on that day marked with debilitations have got minimised by your taking a look of Kṛṣṇa. (Hence, in future) continue the religious observance of the twelfth day of the month meant for Kṛṣṇa. You must always protect yourself from the debilitating effect associated with the religious observance in honour of Kṛṣṇa meant for the twelfth day or the tenth day of the month. Otherwise, you shall again return to the womb of ghost without any doubt. The son! sins as far as possible in the three worlds can equally happen to occur on the earth's surface by religious observance laid down for the twelfth day of the month in the name of Kṛṣṇa on some other forbidden day. There is no room for atonement of religious observance of the day meant for Hari on the day marked with poignancy/stake. Those who do so cannot go to heaven even after passing out of one hundred ages of creation as per calculation of Manu. O son! ghosthood is intolerable. More intolerable than this are the torments inflicted upon by Yama. Hence, the son! one can never be called upon to observe the religious vow of twelfth day implicated with poignancy. Those who do so, do it out of ignorance and motivated by fraud or some elements of roguism. They all along with their fathers get into the wombs of ghosts. Observance of the religious vow meant for the twelfth day on the stakeful tenth day is destructive for children. Besides, it destroys all good deeds of the past as well as the reposing of faith in Kṛṣṇa. Let there be your welfare (O son!). We shall head to the abode of Viṣṇu following our obtaining His position. We shall not come back again to the denomination of life and rebirth.

Śrī Kṛṣṇa said:

71-91. O Candra Śarmā—the best of Brāhmaṇas! I have been pleased with your devotion. Though a Śaiva, you have become a Vaiṣṇava. Though you have not religiously observed the day of mine for seventy-nine years, the same has become complete beyond doubt by my grace. Through your heart-touching observance of fasting on the day meant for me and called *Trispruśo* and by the grace of Dvārakā as well as by your having a look of mine, this has become possible. You did not worship me due to your ignorance and due to your infatuation under devotion towards Śiva. I have however actuated the same by my grace. The best of Brāhmaṇas! those who take a look of mine at Dvārakā in the month of Vaiśākha (i.e. April) or otherwise do the same on the specific day meant for me and known as Trispruśo and on the day called *Banjula,* i.e. the day when cows give maximum milk and during the period when days begin to open up and extend in duration and during the fortnight showing rising or growing period of the moon, no crime including the crime of Brahmicide committed by them will even continue to have any validity for them. Even a man who by his natural disposition continues to do good deeds since his birth like a learned one can have his share of fruits by taking a sight of my city (i.e. Dvārakā). Fruits resulting from visit to all centres of pilgrimage on the surface of earth including Prabhāsa can equally be had by having a look of my city and listening to its accounts. By reading out – wherever it may be — the eminence of the city of Dvārakā on my birth day (i.e. the eighth day of the dark period of the fortnight of Śrāvaṇa i.e. month of August) one can earn merits by my grace. The virtues one earns by residing in my city (i.e. Dvārakā) and by taking a look of mine without fail for three times a day, i.e. during morning, noon and evening, can be had equally in the Kaliyuga by reading its (i.e. the city's) account. In this Kaliyuga, O the best of Brāhmaṇas! Kāśi, Mathurā, Avantī, Ayodhyā, Māyā (i.e., Gayā), Kāncī, my city (i.e. Dvārakā), the beautiful Śāligrāma, the prolific Badarī, sites denomitated as auspicious like Kurukṣetra, Bhṛgukṣetra and Puṣkara, Prayāga, Prabhāsa, Hātakeśvara, Gaṅgādvāra, the place of confluence of Gaṅgā with the sea where elephants throw water by their trunks, the forests such as Naimiśa, Dandaka and Vṛndāvana, places of pilgrimage on the shores of Sindhu, i.e. Indus as well as all the temples on Arbuda—are all similar to Dvārakā. O the best of Brāhmaṇas! even all (auspicious) forests, (meritorious places in) Magadha, various pools of water, the foremost mountain Himālaya including its snow-capped peaks, all rivers flowing on the earth's surface like Gaṅgā, etc. and all centres of pilgrimage encompassing three time zones are equal to the city of Dvārakā. The exception of my city in the Kaliyuga is that it holds together all these places of pilgrimage. O Brāhmaṇa! access to my city as well as an enabling look of mine can only be possible for you by putting in efforts of one hundred years. The virtuous soul! your death will occur by my grace on my day named as *Trispruśo* during the brighter fortnight of the month of Vaiśākha, i.e. April. Life-force will leave your body before me passing through the tenth door of my land here, i.e. Dvārakā on Wednesday. And the learned soul! this will happen undoubtedly by my grace. (Now) the Brāhmaṇa, go back to your own place. All of your desires will be fulfilled. My devotees do not get destroyed even at the final end of creation. My human devotees never get carried away by anything ominus. Indeed nothing ominus can really exist for crore of their clan members.

Mārkaṇḍeya said:

92-95. Then as one hundred years passed out, in the process of the Brāhmaṇa, i.e. Candra Śarmā's regular visits to Dvārāvat, he gave up life as per the advice of Kṛṣṇa and attained liberation. Indradyumna! I have thus narrated to you the greatness of Dvārakā and how it happened. I shall describe you again if there is any question or inquisitiveness (arising) in your mind. By listening to or reading about the magnificient greatness of Dvārakā one can obtain all fruits. Kṛṣṇa has said so. By propagating about the abode of Kṛṣṇa here, i.e. Dvārakā through writing, one can derive the same virtues attended with an actual visit to Dvārakā invoking Kṛṣṇa's grace.

CHAPTER TWENTY-FIVE

Greatness of Dvārakā, Gaṅgā, Gayā, Gomatī, Gītā, etc.

Indradyumna said:

1. O the foremost sage! please narrate in details about this sacred centre of pilgrimage which destroys sins. I have some curiosity.

Mārkaṇḍeya said:

2-66. O king! there are three cities in the time of Kali which are favourites of Hari and which grant the wishes of those desiring to earn religious virtue as well as (the ultimate) liberation. They are Mathurā, Dvārakā and Ayodhyā. People serve these cities considering that the Kālindī, i.e. Yamunā at Mathurā, Gomatī in the proximity of Kṛṣṇa (i.e. Dvārakā) and Sarayu at Ayodhyā grant liberation. Worship of Kṛṣṇa at Dvārāvat and of Rāma at Ayodhyā grants and induces goodness and well-being. Liberation can be obtained by remembering Hari or Viṣṇu at Mathurā. It is fortunate enough to have Mathurā in this world where Hari himself appeared in his incarnated form. It is fruitful for the world to have Dvārakā where Viṣṇu engages himself in playful sportive activities. Ayodhyā - a giver of all desires, is equally fortunate amidst these three cities, which God Rāma himself promoted with an eye for preservation of religious righteousness. In Kaliyuga serving Mathurā by staying there for a single day yields the same fruits which are obtainable by serving Kāśī for as many years that Creation has been stated to thrive. Fruits that accrue to service at Prayāga for thousand of years beyond the estimation of Manu's period of Creation can be appropriated by a stay and service at Dvārakā for half a moment of the blinking of eyes. The fruits that are obtainable by staying for one hundred years at Prabhāsa and Kurukṣetra can be obtained through a prayer lasting for half a moment of the blinking of eyes. Getting an opportunity to sing the glory of Rāma—the sovereign of Ayodhyā or of Keśava at Mathurā or of Kṛṣṇa having his abode at Dvārakā is quite difficult to have. By singing the glory of God at Mathurā, by listening to God's glorified activities at Dvārakā and by taking a look of Ayodhyā, one gets that culminated position which is attainable through undergoing three stages of purification. Kṛṣṇa appeared in his incarnation at Dvārakā and these three places are comparable to heaven on earth. By listening to the glory of these (centres of pilgrimage) or by having a look of them one gets free from the stream of the ever-decaying life. By listening to the accounts of the three cities of Ayodhyā, Mathurā and Dvārakā or by making pictures of these or simply by having a sight of these, men can have remittances of their sins accumulated through ages. (The tired mind) in Kaliyuga gets rested by remembering the God Kṛṣṇa or Hari or Viṣṇu. By staying up for the night to religiously observe the twelfth day in honour of the God, one reaps the fruits of *yajña* involving sacrifice of horses, i.e. Aśvamedha *yajña.* O virtuous king! those who regularly recount the childhood sporting activities of God in these places, they earn tutelage over golden mountain. O king and the foremost among men! people are fortunate to have the opportunity to swim and take bath in the confluence of Gomatī with the sea. By taking bath on the western front of the confluence and thereafter joining palms of both hands together to make a cavity and then by holding water in it and remembering Dvārakā people can reap crore times the fruits. By contemplating within about the city of Dvārakā in the Kaliyuga, a man derives easily the same fruits attending upon making donation of Kapilā cows. O superintendent of men, i.e. the king! by visiting Dvārakā in Kaliyuga, a man reaps the same fruits yielded from a visit of the Gaṅgā sea, i.e. the Bay of Bengal and of the gateway of Gaṅgā i.e. Haridwār. O ruler! I, Mārkaṅḍeya who holds memory of creation in seven time-zones can tell this that there is no other auspicious place like Dvārakā. O king! there is no other fortunate sage like Durvāsā who could obtain Hari by rendering the glory of Dvārakā in words. (Hence) the king! there is no need for you to visit Kāśī, Kurukṣetra, Prabhāsa or Puṣkara. Visit Dvārakā and take a look of the auspicious face of Kṛṣṇa. Fruits of a thousand of Aśvamedha Yajñas, i.e. the sacrificial rite to fire making sacrifice of horses as well as of a hundred Rājasūya Yajñas, (i.e. the sacrificial rite to fire conducted by a monarch in commemoration of his or retention of his undisputed sovereignty) can be had on every progressive step that a man takes towards Dvārakā. The chief and best of kings! the lives of those individuals, whose minds never deviate from visiting Dvārakā, can be considered as fruitful in the Kaliyuga. The son who offers balls of cooked rice at Gomatī having proximity to Kṛṣṇa, his mother, father and grandfather get blessed. That land/region in a country gets purified where a man moves about with an impression of sandalwood paste on his body which the Gopīs, i.e. consorts of Kṛṣṇa are fond of. So, what is the need of making any description of that place specially again? By holding the leaf of the basil plant indigenous to the city of Dvārakā and which is used in the worship of Kṛṣṇa on head, one becomes like the manifest Indra on the surface of earth. That particular day when Lord Viṣṇu won victory over the demons, residence in the city of Kāśī, the basil leaves and the Amalaka fruit are favourites of Kṛṣṇa. Reading out of Bhāgavat Śāstra as well as of Rāmāyaṇa, visit to Dvārakā, garland made of jasmine flowers and religious observance of staying up for the night by singing favourite hymns are very much dear to Kṛṣṇa. In the Kaliyuga, Kṛṣṇa along with the city of Dvārakā happens to remain present in an individual's home where the very fragrant sandalwood which the Gopīs, i.e. the consorts of Kṛṣṇa used to apply on him, is always available. All sins committed by causing injuries to cows or by killing them get immediately repulsed through the purificatory touch of sandalwood, the paste of which the Gopīs used to apply on Kṛṣṇa. By offering one piece of sandalwood—the paste of which the Gopīs used to apply on Kṛṣṇa—to the Vaiṣṇavas one can facilitate one hundred and one members of his clan to successfully tide over the ocean of worldly existence. Yama including his orderlies feign from showing their might in the houses of those having temple with the basil plant indigenous to Dvārakā. The son of Vyāsa, i.e. Śuka is said to have made hundreds and crores of meritorious deeds by singing the glory of Kṛṣṇa with the basil leaves produced on the soil of Dvārakā. O king! through a survey and churning of all Śāstras and Purāṇas once and again that I found no other city to be like Dvārakā. After going to Dvārakā one who has made kīrtans singing the glory of Kṛṣṇa can be presumed to have wishfully completed bath in thousands of centres of pilgrimage including performance of *yajñas*. What will one do by subduing the senses of organs of the body or for that matter by studying the Śāṃkhya if one has not visited Dvārakā? Those people are undoubtedly like asses who have not visited the city of Dvārakā and taken a look of the face of Kṛṣṇa. They can only consider themselves to be gratified and fortunate enough to religiously observe the twelfth day so specified in honour of Hari by staying up the whole night and by continuously dancing with devotion as a matter of complying with such religious observance. By going to Gomatī and thereafter by visiting the Kṛṣṇa temple, one by making offering of balls of cooked rice as per his/her ability can ensure liberation for his/her grandfathers. That embodied soul who has already visited the city of Dvārakā can hardly ever be a ghost or a Satanic spirit. O king! merits that await parting with the body at Prayāga after observing fasting can be reaped in a fraction of moment by religious observance of the twelfth day near Kṛṣṇa. O king! in the Kaliyuga, you can make the same fruits from making donations of a crore of cows on the day of Solar eclipse by uninterrupted inhabitation at Dvārakā. The fruits attended with donations of a crore karat of gold on the solar and lunar eclipses can be had by taking a look of Kṛṣṇa. The children as well as grandchildren, grandmothers as well as grandfathers, the maternal in-laws as well as servants including the pet animals of those, O best of men, i.e. the king! who happen to have a look of the happy Mādhava, i.e. Kṛṣṇa on a swing (this is possible during the month of Caitra i.e. March) can have a life of play and pastimes with Viṣṇu till the creation remains afloat (i.e. subsists). Or else the king! you can go near Kṛṣṇa on any twelfth day. Having a look of Kṛṣṇa during any time of Kaliyuga especially will not cause any difference (in yielding fruits). Religious observance always of the twelfth day so demarcated in honour of Kṛṣṇa near him amounts to (as if) one has remained in the proximity of Kṛṣṇa for ages together. Serving Dvārāvat during the Kaliyuga is known to induce virtue in particular. It is easy to get at the six auspicious cities (viz. Ayodhyā, Mathurā, Kāśī, Gayā, Kāñhī, Avantikā) during Kaliyuga, but very difficult to obtain Dvārakā. By simply remembering it or by singing its glory in chorus, the city of Dvārakā blesses men with all enjoyments of luxury besides liberation. The standing of the city is due to the protection of the sages like Durvāsā. Passage through Kaliyuga cannot be possible for one without invoking Kṛṣṇa's favour. (In this yuga) even gods like Rūdra, etc. come to have a look of Kṛṣṇa. The lord of men (i.e. the King)! by taking a look of Rukmiṇī for three times a day (i.e. during morning, noon and evening) while repeatedly uttering the word Kṛṣṇa and Kṛṣṇa within oneself, one can make one's life fruitful. Seeing their descendants heading towards Dvārakā, the forefathers of a clan get free from hell and moving in the space on their way towards heaven they happily and smilingly keep singing. By simply remembering and singing its glory in chorus, a man's evil deeds committed clandestinely get washed away. So what to speak of the fruits yielded through a bath at Gomatī? What more is left for one to do after witnessing the God blowing the conch with

Rukmiṇī at the gateway bearing signs of conch and after having a look of the four-armed, i.e. Viṣṇu at the place of pilgrimage called Pindāraka? Rukmiṇī, the son of Devakī, the sandalwood—the paste of which were the Gopīs, i.e. the consorts of Kṛṣṇa so fond of and the basil leaves are difficult to obtain in the world during Kaliyuga. More difficult than all these remitters of sins on earth are considered the religious observance of offer of balls of cooked rice at Gayā, having a look of Kṛṣṇa at Dvārakā and to rear/nurture an Aśoka tree in one's residential premises as Kaliyuga approaches. Having an Aśoka tree and Dvārakā are equal to each other in meteing out fruits of virtue. There is no question of any one of them having more or less fruits. Viṣṇu himself has stated so. O king! I am describing to you as to how or by virtue of which having an Aśoka tree can produce relatively more results? This is by fasting on the twelfth day and then having food after completing the religious duties associated with the observance of the twelfth day. By doing this one can definitely attain the supreme position as of Viṣṇu. Rearing up an Aśoka tree in one's residential premises means, in the stage of life as a householder, his house has turned into a place of pilgrimage and penance and source of liberation. Service of Aśoka tree, Dvārakā, Gaṅgā, Gomatī, Gokula, singing the glory of Govinda in chorus, obtaining the sandalwood of which the Gopīs were so fond of and study of Gītā are rare to encounter/obtain. Man who listens to the accounts of Kṛṣṇa with devotion for Keśava in mind happens to reap fruits equal to conduct of a thousand Aśvamedha *Yajñas* (i.e. sacrificial rites involving sacrifices of horses). One who listens to the accounts of Keśava reflecting his greatness by staying up for a night, attains the position of Viṣṇu which is free from all sins. By reading or listening to the great accounts of Kṛṣṇa with faith men obtain the fruits that donation of cotton equalling a man's weight yields. O king! even donations made in lesser amount during the religious observance in honour of Kṛṣṇa also grow into crore times. The learned say so. Sins earned by a false sense of pride, by chcating in weighing and by buying of girls as well as cows get buried by the religious observance of the twelfth day in honour of Kṛṣṇa by staying up for the night (in the worship of God).

CHAPTER TWENTY-SIX

Worship of Hari on the twelfth day

Śrī Mārkaṇḍeya said:

1-2. After seeing the Vaiṣṇava Prahlāda—a learned in all religions, a master in the Vedic *Śāstras,* a keen devotee of Bhāgvad, to have come and settled in Gomatī with all happiness, the highly enlightened Sages having knowledge of the essence of all *Śāstras* and guardians of all religions came near him and asked:

The sages said:

3-5. Without attempting to acquire knowledge, without contemplation and without controlling the organs of senses, how could you acquire such a masterly position? Please tell us in brief, in a friendly manner as to the acquisition of such fruits on your part which have so far been only partly seen and mostly unseen. As a distinguished person of all religions, please tell us everything in a conclusive manner. After the highly fortunate souls said so, the devotee of Nārāyaṇa began to say in brief for everyone's welfare:

Śrī Prahlāda said:

6-8. Listen to this greatly mysterious matter which I am narrating. All sins get destroyed by listening to it. The essence of this matter is inherent to Aṣṭādaśa Purāṇa. I am going to tell you that which is equally a giver of enjoyment and liberation. Mahādeva was seated in a happy position when Ṣaṇmukha, i.e. Kārtikeya for the sake of everyone's welfare asked him with due devotion:

Skanda said:

9. O God! what is the remedy for this sorrow/strife-stricken world? Be kind enough to tell about the means of happiness and ways of liberation.

Iśwara said:

10-54. Four kinds of sins committed through crores of birth in the Kaliyuga can go away by religiously staying up for a night and giving discourses on the Vaiṣṇava *Śāstra.* Anyone staying up for the night and giving lectures on the Vaiṣṇava *Śāstra* in honour of Hari can be considered as a devotee of mine whether he is poor or otherwise. My devotees must consciously practise the religious observance of staying up for the night in honor of Hari. Otherwise, by nurturing antagonism towards Janārdana they shall be relegated as sinners. O Ṣaṇmukha! fruits of Agniṣṭoma *yajña* are ensured in a twinkling of eyes for those who stay up for the night and sing the glory of Hari on the specific day so allocated for him. While observing the religious ritual of staying up for the night if one takes a look of the face of Viṣṇu once and again and does so with all delight and exaltation, members of his clan obtain the divine passage and get entitled to proximity of Hari. With attainment of liberation from crores of sins, people get free from the pathways leading to the abode of Yama because they have entertained their minds by singing the glory of Kṛṣṇa and by studying the *Śāstras* dealing with him while staying up for night for the observation of the twelfth day meant for the God. The nights for those people turn around as good mornings and they become fortunate like people having good deeds who undergo the religious rite of staying up the night to worship Hari even while on the face of death.

Endowed with children those men get blessed with wealth, earn name and fame for themselves and thereby add meaning to their manhood in whose family the sons so born observe the religious duty of staying up for night for the sake of Hari. They can be construed to have desirably performed *Yajñas,* offered balls of cooked rice to their forefathers at the primary spots at Gayā and have taken a bath regularly at Prayāga by the religious observance of staying up for the night in worship of Hari. O Ṣadānana, i.e. Skanda! the devotees of Viṣṇu are always dear to me for they observe religiously to stay up for the night in worship of Viṣṇu— the giver of well-being. Even a man who after listening to the accounts of Kṛṣṇa does not get happy or who even does not attempt to stay up for the night to worship Kṛṣṇa, he happens to bring disrepute to his mother. All these point to bad deeds on his part. Even the merits germinated out of good deeds of a hundred years on one's part go in vain if he/she does not stay up for the night to conform to the religious practice of worship of Viṣṇu as the specific day meant for Him approaches. When a son as well as his children and a daughter as well as her children observe the religious rite of staying up for the night to worship Hari, they liberate their forefathers dragged to Hell by the attendants of Yama. The forefathers themselves have happened to say this eloquently. In other words, in spite of conducting one hundred *yajñas,* one cannot attain liberation. One can never have respite from the human world without the religious observance of staying up for a night in the worship of Kṛṣṇa. Hence, it is the duty of everyone to observe the ritual of staying up for a night in the worship of Kṛṣṇa for the sake of welfare of his forefathers. One's entry into the world in embodied form will not occur again by sheer devotion of Bhāgvad as well as by singing the glory of Govinda through prayers. If one's religious observance of staying up for the night conjoins with the Vijayā day, i.e. the tenth day of the brighter period of moon in the month of Aświna, i.e. September-October, it can be taken for granted that he / she has burnt up on his/

her own the chances of getting birth again in bodily form. There can be no doubt that one gets completely united into the body of Keśava by staying up for the night with all earnestness in His worship on the *Trispruśo* day, i.e. the twelfth day of the month specially demarcated for His worship. Sins—both minor and larger can never affect him who with all earnestness keeps his eyes wide open while doing the ritual of staying up for the night in worship of Kṛṣṇa. Now let me tell you the merits waiting upon the great devotee of Bhāgvad who observes the twelfth day of the month meant for worship of the God by singing along with harmonious rhythm of drums while staying up for the night together with making donation too. Such a devotee earns the same fruits that are derived from making offering of sesame measuring upto a thousand *prastha* (i.e. a unit of measurement) along with gold to Brāhmaṇas on that particular day of the month when the Sun or any planetary body passes from one zodiacs sign to another. By making presents of gold measuring upto one hundred *karats* along with a calf of the Kapilā cow on the twelfth day of the month meant for worship of Kṛṣṇa while going through the religious observance of staying up for the night required for the same day, one may happen to see the fruits resulting from that manifestedly in the Kaliyuga. O son! he who pleases Padmanābha (i.e. an epithet of Viṣṇu) on the specific day meant for Hari (i.e. the twelfth day) by reciting the hymns composed by the divine sages or by reciting the Vedic hymns addressed to Viṣṇu or the son! he who observes the same day by chanting the several mantras in the Ṛg, Sāma and Yajur Vedas addressed to Viṣṇu either in Sanskrit or Prakrit, get the love and affection of Lord Viṣṇu. Brahmā had said so to me. O Saṇmukha! a man can attain the same fruits as earned through taking twenty-one rounds of the three sacred places like Kāśī, Mathurā and Gayā by staying up for the night in connection with religious observance of worship of Kṛṣṇa on the twelfth day of the month meant for Him. The fruits accruable to making donations of one hundred cows along with their calves can equally be appropriated by incurring pleasure of Hari with recitation of hymns. Observance of the religious ritual of staying up for the night with recitation of Vedic mantras/hymns addressed to Hari gives ten times of the fruits. (Hence) one's pursuit of sitting up for the night in worship must bear this in mind. Reading out the Gītā and the Viṣṇu Sahasranāma (i.e. the book containing the one thousand names of Viṣṇu) is like reading out the same before Viṣṇu and near the Vaiṣṇavas on the twelfth day of the month addressed to God. I cannot describe the fruits of reading out during night of the holy Bhāgavad, the Skanda Purāṇa which are favourites of Hari and those of the books giving the sweet and graceful accounts of Kṛṣṇa as a child and his pastimes with the Gopīs or that of worship of Keśava. O pupil! Keśava only knows them. By lighting earthen lamp and then by sitting awake for the night he who worships Hari with chanting of hymns, his virtues never decline for a time-span of one hundred creations. By worshipping Hari devotedly by sitting awake throughout the night and as far as possible with bunches of basil buds as well as basil leaves, possibility of rebirth gets negated for one. Bathing the idol of Hari, then massaging it and thereafter worshipping it by sitting up for the entire night by lighting up earthen lamps, incense sticks with chanting of hymns and offer of food and betel leaves to the God never go to dogs. O Ṣadvakra (i.e. Skanda)! one intending to nurture a heightened sense of reverence for me can attempt so by observing the religious ritual of sitting up with eyes wide-open for the whole night to worship Hari with great devotion on the twelfth day. While sitting up for the night with eyes wide-open for the purpose of worshipping Vāsudeva on the day specially laid down, all gods come down and dwell in the bodies of beings undergoing the same religious observance. Those who read out the Mahābhārata imbibing the glory of Vāsudeva while sitting up for the night to worship, obtain beyond doubt, the same passage usually accessible to the yogis. Those who read out the accounts of life of God

Rāma as well as that of (his) killing of Rāvaṇa while doing the religious observance for Viṣṇu by staying up for the night, they obtain the ultimate passage. The virtues accruable to reading of the four Vedas, the worship of Hari and that of having a bath in all centres of pilgrimage are attainable by sitting up awake for a night and worshipping Hari. Fruits earned by donating ten thousand chariots, one thousand elephants and one lakh strong and stout horses can be had by sitting up awake for a night to worship Hari. As stated by the sages fruits that result from making donation of grains equalling weight of a thousand of mountains or that of crore of people can be had by sitting up awake for a night in the worship of Hari. The same fruits as accruable to giving a crore of virgin girls in marriage, of gold weighing hundreds of *karats* and of ten thousand gems can be obtained by sitting awake for a night in worship of Hari. One hundred thousand of the fruits of reading *Aṣṭādaśa* Purāṇa can be obtained by sitting awake for a night in worship of Hari. Fruits greater than that generally available to Brāhmaṇas by reading of Manusmṛti can be obtained by sitting awake for a night in worship of Hari. Fruits that result to men from making donation of rice during period of drought as well as by offering food to one thousand ascetics can be equally obtained in the Kaliyuga by sitting awake for a night in the worship of Hari.

CHAPTER TWENTY-SEVEN

Desirability of sitting awake on the twelfth day to worship

Īśvara (Śiva) said:

1. Staying awake in the night in worship of Hari on the twelfth day of the month is the best *yajña*. It is a celebration that takes away all sorrows and bestows virtues on one. During

the religious observance of this day men worship Hari and listen to the beautiful Bhāgvat. Such a good devotee reaps crore times the fruits of *Vājapeya yajña.* Cutting into pieces his chain of sins, he attains the temple of Kṛṣṇa.

2. One might have a collection of crimes onto oneself by committing murder. Similarly one might have indulged oneself in crores of petty/lowly enjoyments. One might have encircled himself by sins one lakh times by killing of teachers. However, if one listens to Bhāgvat and undergoes the religious observance of staying awake for nights in worship of Hari, one tears apart all his sins/misdeeds. Becoming free from all sins, he gets blessed with a pure body. Becoming like Indra, that man enters the solar kingdom.

3. If the occurrence of the twelfth day meant for sitting awake throughout the night to worship Hari coincides with the eleventh day of the month and further the same day has conjuncture of the *Śravaṇa* star—a usual happening in the month of Bhādra, i.e. August-September as well as that of the son of Soma, i.e. moon (an epithet of the mercury planet) the great grandfathers of the religious observers of eleventh day get liberated from Hell.

4. Nothing is considered greater than the donations made for Lord Viṣṇu as well as for one's forefathers on the auspicious twelfth day which is dear to Viṣṇu. Indeed such action on one's part is comparable to the uplifted Meru mountain.

5. He who goes to the river Mahānadī as the twelfth day meant for Viṣṇu approaches and offers libations to forefathers after holding water in hands by joining them together in the shape of a cup and thereafter performs *śrāddha,* thousands of desires of their forefathers get accomplished and they remain contented.

6. O son (i.e. Skanda)! listen, the fruits that result for one by his seeking refuge of Brāhmaṇas as well as by his offering credits to them can be acquired by sitting awake for a night in the worship of Viṣṇu.

7. The fruits that result from making donation of cow studded with gold, a milched cow, a honeyed cow, skin of black buck, Meru-mountain-like heaps of silver and gold and by offer of gifts/presents to Brāhmaṇas can be obtained equally by sitting awake for a night in the worship of Viṣṇu.
8. O Ṣaṇmukha! fruits attending pursuit of truth, observance of purity, upholding abstemious mind, inculcation of qualities like generousity, charitableness and forgiveness and the ten *Aśvamedha yajñas* involving high religious fees can be obtained by sitting awake for a night in the worship of Viṣṇu.
9. Fruits obtained by having a bath in the supremely worshipable river (i.e. Gaṅgā), by offering balls of cooked rice to one's forefathers at Gayā in the religious observance of *śrāddha* and by donating gold at Kurukṣetra can be had by sitting awake for a night in the worship of Viṣṇu.
10. One might have committed ten thousand murders or one might have stolen innumerable gold. But by reading out the song accounting the glory of God while sitting awake for a night in worship of the gracious God, one can sound the death-knell for all such sins.
11. O Ṣaṇmukha! those who have evicted sleep due to their being completely engrossed in the worship of God sitting awake throughout the night, dreams of road to the Yama world or his attendants or even of any other being never haunts them.
12. What is the use of repeated chanting of the wish-fulfilling Agnihotra mantra or any other such mantra wearing saffron robes and bearing a matted lock of hairs on the head by one when only sitting awake for a night in the worship of Kṛṣṇa on the twelfth day specifically laid down grants one with fulfillment of wealth, realisation of desires, a fully-awakened state of righteousness and the final liberation in the destructive Kaliyuga.
13. Nārada had stated all this earlier with all certainty to the son of Vinatā, i.e. Garuḍa as the most discernable object for one. He had said, "There is no other God greater than

Kṛṣṇa and there is no day other than that meant for the worship of Kṛṣṇa to be fittingly pursued as a matter of religious vow."

14. O gods! O Khagendra sage, O *siddhas* and other ascetics! Nārada has said so. Besides, with their hands raised up, the devotees have also stated that there is hardly any other day than the eleventh day so auspiciously meant for the worship of Kṛṣṇa to be followed as a matter of religious vow.

15. Addressing Garuḍa, Nārada has also said further that the sinners never pray to Hari and in the Kaliyuga, it is not possible to have people engaged in his devotion or in reading of the specific *śāstra* giving his accounts. The ignorants only observe the tenth day having the conjuncture of the eleventh day and foresake the auspicious day.

16. Those who follow such forbidden day to worship Murārī, always remain distressed, diseased, sinful and depressed. They act as the constant factor for ruination of their own clan. They invariably go to Hell.

CHAPTER TWENTY-EIGHT

Eminence of sitting awake on the twelfth day in worship of Viṣṇu

Mārkaṇḍeya said:

1-13. O king! after doing the religious observance of staying awake for the night for the purpose of worshipping Viṣṇu as per laid down procedure one causes/brings in welfare for one's forefathers. So then, what can Yama do? Whether one has taken food or has observed fasting or even if one has adopted purity onto the self or has remained unclean—by merely doing the religious observance of sitting awake for the night in the worship of Hari, men have been stated to have obtained liberation. Whether a man has bathed himself or not—his presence in the place where the religious observance of sitting awake for the night in the worship of Hari is being conducted—has been considered as his having taken a dip/immersion in all the centres of pilgrimage. Such a man is learnt to have had a divine vision and is on his way to heaven. Even the untouchables by observing the rite of sitting awake for the night in the worship of Hari happen to arrive on the path of salvation. So what to speak again of those born in respectable varṇa reclining upon the pursuit of good dealings? Like sleep going away with the sounds of a young woman reaching one's ears so is the case with the religious observance of sitting awake for a night in the worship of Kṛṣṇa by listening to the stories of Hari as well as by repeated chorus of prayer addressed to Hari. Brahmicide, drinking habits, theft, misbehaviour with a teacher's woman and the excessive occupation of mind with sins get cleansed with the religious observance of sitting awake for a night in the worship of Viṣṇu. Again by having a look of Hari, those having the tendency of libido have been stated to get freedom. Sins earned through words or by indulgence of mind or by any other ways go away in a fraction of a moment beyond doubt by sitting awake for a night in the worship of Hari. By joining the assembly of those engaged in the observance of sitting awake throughout the night in worship, one's sins get destroyed to the extent that those cannot be remembered again. O king! the learned view that the fruits of worship of the mother Goddess, *śrāddha* at Gayā and pilgrimage of auspicious centres are the same as that of religious observance of sitting awake throughout the night in the worship of Hari. O king! worship of mother is equal to that of performance of ten thousand *Aśvamedha yajñas*. A spring of water made to rise by digging the ground with the head of the sacred grass causes welfare for a full one hundred years. The fruits of drinking a cup of water collected from the centre of pilgrimage known as Puṣkara cannot even equal one-sixteenth portion of the fruits resulting from religious observance of sitting awake throughout the night in the worship of Hari. O king! the fruits that result from making donation of an earth full of gold can be obtained by sitting awake throughout the night in the worship of Hari. Actions resulting in bad deeds on the part of one's self get deactivated and become void, i.e. vanish away beyond doubt by performance of the religious ritual of sitting awake throughout the night in the worship of Hari.

14-47. O king! I shall once again describe in brief with regard to the fruits that result from sitting awake throughout the night in the worship of Padmanābha (i.e. an epithet of Viṣṇu) as pointed out by the learned. By doing the religious observance of sitting awake in the night in the worship of Hari, a yogi pierces the disc of Sun to reach that ultimate position which one obtains through arduous practice of *sāṇkhya yoga.* As in due course rivers and drains flow into the sea to find their final resting place so is the case with those who sit awake in the night to worship Hari to ultimately find togetherness with that supreme position. A man might have reached the height of sins by committing them in a gigantic proportion comparable to the size and height of mountains like Meru and Mandāra. But by sitting awake in the night in the worship of Hari, all his sins vanish away without any doubt. Lord Kṛṣṇa grants aspirations of men for royal authority and power, for heaven, for liberation or for any other thing desired for while they remain engaged in worshipping him by singing songs of his glory with their eyes wide-open throughout the night. O king! by sitting awake throughout the night in the worship of Hari, the outcastes even obtain that pious position. So what is the need to speak again about the wise and the Brāhmaṇas in this regard. Without *japa* and meditation, O king! even the singers doing the rite of sitting awake throughout the night in worship of Hari get benefitted. Individuals depraved in deeds have also been stated to obtain liberation by sitting awake throughout the night in the worship of Hari. O king! it is established that there is nothing holier for men in the three worlds than perseverance through the religious observance of sitting awake for a night in the worship of Hari. For you the king, it is of utmost duty to repeatedly remember the Garuḍadhvaja (i.e. the God sitting on the chariot having the insignia of Garuḍa on its flag-staff, in other words Viṣṇu). Your duty is always not to have food on the eleventh day and following it up with sitting awake in the night in the worship of Hari. It is the ever-present position that the outcastes avail the virtuous passage by the religious observance of sitting awake for the night in the worship of Hari. O king! what is need to say about other's place in the hierarchical *varna* system including the Vaiṣṇavas? O king! those who do not pass off to sleep while sitting awake throughout the night in the worship of Viṣṇu, their mothers do not face any pain/difficulty/hindrances in conceiving. Similarly the king! it is the duty of one to observe the religious ritual of sitting awake in the night in the worship of Hari to get away from the possibility of getting entry into the mother's womb again. Those who are fearful of getting that ultimate liberation and desire to keep off from all efforts towards attainment of happiness must also observe the religious duty of sitting awake in the night to worship Hari. O king! those who undergo the religious practice of sitting awake throughout the night in the worship of Hari with full devotion, get the fruits of *Aśvamedha yajña* as they pass through each and every moment in the entire process. O king! there is specially no difference between the time regarding whether the God is in bed or has already risen from sleep in respect to sitting awake throughout the night in the worship of Hari. Indeed religious observance of the same on both the occasions generate the same merit. Viṣṇu has said so before hand. Either they may be Brāhmaṇas, Kṣatriyas, Vaiśyas or Śūdras or they may be birds, worms, insects and any other creature—all of them who observe the religious duty of sitting awake in the night to worship Hari attain that supreme position which the yogis reach unstinted. Sins of any order including those same as Brahmicide, gets destroyed beyond doubt by the religious observance of sitting awake throughout the night in the worship of Kṛṣṇa. On one side, there are all centres of pilgrimage. On the other, there is the option to sit awake throughout the night in the worship of Kṛṣṇa which is dear to him. The former cannot be equal to the latter in yielding merits. Indeed worship of Kṛṣṇa by sitting awake throughout the night yields relatively more rewards in relation to the former. This is what the poets say. The sun, Indra and gods like Brahmā and Rūdra (i.e. the group of gods supposed to be inferior manifestations of Śiva) assemble without fail at the place where the observance of sitting awake in the worship of Kṛṣṇa which again is favourite of Kṛṣṇa is being conducted, i.e. in way. All the holy rivers like Gaṅgā, Sarasvatī, Revā, Yamunā, Satluja, Candrabhāgā, Vitastā, etc. (also) remain present there (i.e. at the place where the very religious observance of sitting awake for the night in the worship of Hari is being conducted). O best of kings! ponds, lakes, seas as well as all other streams of water apparently remain present where the religious observance of sitting awake for a night to worship Hari is being conducted especially on the eleventh day. Men nurturing the desire to earn the blessings of God (usually) sing, dance and play the *vīṇā* while worshipping Kṛṣṇa sitting awake throughout the night. Irrespective of the fact of one being attended with devotion or not or for that matter whether one has purified oneself by having a bath or not, the very activity of worshipping Viṣṇu by remaining awake throughout the night relieves one of crores of sins. One gets entitled to residence of thousands of years in heaven equalling the innumerable dust particles underneath his feet by worshipping Hari sitting awake throughout the night. Therefore, (O Skanda!) one needs to proceed for observing the religious ritual of sitting awake throughout the night to worship Mādhava on the twelfth day of every month throughout the year to do away with the pollution that generally characterises the Kaliyuga. Considerably a large number of sins committed on one's part extended over hundreds or a crore of years and which can be comparable to the Meru mountain in their height and magnitude get burnt out by sitting awake throughout the night in the worship of Hari. O king! now listen to the fruits, I am describing, of the religious observance of sitting throughout the night on the eleventh day of the month with eyes wide-open to worship Hari attended with faithful reverence in the Kaliyuga. Fruits as same as that are yielded by a man by remaining undeviatingly engaged in penance at Kāśi on the banks of Jāhnavī (an epithet of Gaṅgā) for a thousand of *yugas* can be obtained by the religious observance of sitting throughout the night with eyes wide-open in the worship of Kṛṣṇa on the eleventh day of the month. The fruits that a man obtains by observance of fasting for a thousand years can be appropriated by the religious observance of sitting in the worship of Hari throughout the night with eyes wide-open on the eleventh day of the month. It is very difficult to obtain the Vaiṣṇava position despite undergoing the religious practice of performing a hundred or for that matter even a crore of *yajñas*. But by religious observance of the twelfth day of month by sitting awake throughout the night in worship of Kṛṣṇa one definitely obtains the same position easily. One who does not observe the religious practice of sitting awake throughout the night in the worship of Viṣṇu with all earnestness, there is every possibility of him moving towards the sin of oppressing others. By their just observing fast for that occasion which requires sitting awake throughout the night to worship Hari, men having no feeling for Viṣṇu get accumulated sins on their part burnt up with an opportunity to roam about in the gardens of heaven. Hari himself goes there where there is Bhāgvat *śāstra*, where the religious observance of sitting awake throughout the night in his worship is held regularly and where the stone called *Śāligrāma* is available. In the Kaliyuga, the seven cities as well as the words in Veda do not hold that much holiness as the observance of the sitting up awake throughout the night in the worship of Viṣṇu on the holy day of Viṣṇu himself. The holy day meant for the worship of Viṣṇu advents. But those men and women who do not worship him by observing the ritual of sitting awake throughout the night with eyes wide-open, remain submerged in the dark and difficult hell beyond any doubt.

CHAPTER TWENTY-NINE

Assemblage of all tīrthas at Gomatī, the divine voice, impact of Dvārakā and eagerness to visit it

Prahlāda said:

1-15. O Brāhmaṇas! now I am going to describe you all something different. This is about the eminently great virtue of Dvārakā which is even higher in mystery. I am going to describe about the old and beautiful history of it. This has an impelling force to dispel the doubts of (even) gods and sages putting up at centres of pilgrimage. Coinciding with good fortune of a unique nature the planet Guru, i.e. Jupiter began to transit in the zodiacal sign of Leo. After seeing this, Nārada the best Brāhmaṇa for whom Bhāgāvat was always dear, came to the banks of Godāvarī. Seeing the assembly of all the centres of pilgrimage to be found in the three worlds as well as that of all streams of water on the banks of Gautamī, i.e. Godāvarī, he began to wonder. Centres of pilgrimage like Kāśī, Kurukṣetra, Ayodhyā, Mathurā, Māyāpurī, Kāñchī, Avantī were all present there (i.e. at the banks of Godāvarī) along with many forests having dwelling units in the shape of Āśramas, i.e. hermitages of ascetics. Harikṣetra, Gayā, Puruṣottam, Prabhāsa and many such other auspicious centres of pilgrimage which grant liberation to human beings were present there. Holy rivers like Jāhnavī, Yamunā, Revā,

Sarasvatī, Soumyā, Gaṇḍakī, Taptī, Payoṣṇī as well as the master of all rivers, viz. the ocean were present there. Prominentlly holy rivers like Kṛṣṇā, Bhīmarathī, Kāverī as well as most of the rivers to be found in heaven, the mortal world as well as in the nether world were present along with centres of pilgrimage on their banks. With its transit through the zodiacal sign of Leo, Guru, i.e. Jupiter was present there on the shore of Godāvarī. Lakes and ponds like Puṣkara and the seven Sindhus were also present there. The Meru mountain—a glimpse of which induces holiness and removes all sins as well as the eminent Prayāga which embodies within it the holiness of all centres of pilgrimage were present there. The sages—proficient in the Vedas as well as in writings subordinate to the Vedas as well as others like the divine sages, gods and forefathers were present there. With Bṛhaspati, i.e. the planet Jupiter's coming to transit through the zodiac sign of Leo, the Moon, Aditya, i.e. the sun as well as other gods came to remain present there on the shore of Godāvarī along with the paternal figure of planets. Holy centres of pilgrimage found to be in existence here and there in the three worlds began to remain present there on the shore of Gautamī. All got struck with wonder to witness such a happening. Being delighted on his part, the divine sage Nārada began to remain there along with other sages. And as the period of Jupiter's transit through the zodiac sign of Leo got over, all then began to retreat towards their own places. Along with other sages, Nārada came before the Goddess Gautamī seeking permission to take leave. But the Goddess on her turn got depressed after listening to all the Brāhmaṇas. Heated up with anger for Nārada's keeping bad company she then spoke with all sorrow.

Gautamī said:

16-22. (Nārada!) you have already seen the assemblage of all holy places of pilgrimage, rivers like Gaṅgā, etc. forming like a garland and the seas, mountains and Gayā which are holier from all the three directions to be on my shore. All these places, Nārada! are known to grant liberation in the three worlds. O great sage! the gods, ancestral fathers, the accomplished, the sages, a lot of human beings, Prayāga—the ruling pilgrim centre as well as an embodiment of the virtues of all places of pilgrimage are brightening up the three worlds by getting purified in my company. O master! they are all leaving for their respective places. And now, I am left tired and getting scorched day and night. O Lord! coming very much in the company of bad people and the sinners, I was getting burnt out. Nārada! now it is my good fortune to have company of the virtuous. Delighted, all have gone back to their respective places. It is being said that the merits/virtues on their part have been due to my favour. Now tell the way as to what I, as it is already unhappy should do for the purpose of getting peace.

Prahlāda said:

23. The divine soul Nārada after listening to the words of Godāvarī began to deliberate for a while with regard to the condition of the grief-stricken soul and then with doubts in mind began to say.

Nārada said/thought:

24-25. Oh! it is highly strange of the great misfortune of Gautamī. There is visibility beyond doubt of the gods, places of pilgrimage and the rivers on the one side to have accumulated virtue on their part as a result of their coming in company of hers, i.e. Godāvarī. But they have left leaving behind all their sins for Godāvarī to be scorched with. It is, therefore, to be thought out as to how to alleviate her from the fire of sins.

Śrī Prahlāda said:

26-31. When all the sages were thinking like this within themselves as to what could be chalked out, the divine soul Gautama came before them, i.e. the leading sages. After having a look of him, the sages and other gods made their fitting reverences. Jāhnavī, Yamunā, the holy Narmadā as well as Sarasvatī arrived there. Besides, the rest of the other rivers of the three worlds followed suit. Vārāṇasī with other hermitages descended on the earth's surface through ages also assembled there. They all worshiped him. After that the sages said, "O great sage! we have already had a bath in this river and got ourselves protected. We have got ourselves fully purified by your grace. You have quite kindly brought this Gaṅgā as Gautamī down onto the surface of earth. By having a bath in this river men have become divested off their sins and as a result, they have been gratefully benefitted. But what for is Gautamī being excessively tormented for her coming in contact with bad people? Hence, Gautama! please give your mind as to how could Gautamī be made free of sins and keep flowing remaining in an eternally blissful stage. How could she regain her earlier shining state?

Prahlāda said:

32-35. After the sages' saying like this, Gautama got worried in mind. Looking at the face of Nārada and with a smile. Gautama said, "This river Godāvarī snatches away all that severely unfavourable to the holy regions including the centres of pilgrimage. So, the question is how to relieve Gautamī of her torments? There is hardly any such centre of pilgrimage in the three worlds where after having a bath during the conjuncture of Guru, i.e. Jupiter's transit through the zodiacal sign of Leo, people do not come to Gautamī to have a dip in its waters for purification. The reign of some of the main centres of pilgrimage like Kāśī and Prayāga has been due to Gautamī's favour. So all of you—the ascetics who are equally dependent on centres of pilgrimage, please tell me as to what should I clearly and thoughtfully examine about the difficult situation that has come before us.

Prahlāda said:

36. After the sage's (i.e. Gautama's) saying so, the other sages however, could not say anything. As it is they got somewhat infatuated. So to know about the way Gautama then spoke to Gautamī.

Gautama said:

37-40. By my appeasing Śaṁkara through perseverance and worship, I have brought you—the Goddess here. So it is he, i.e. Śaṁkara who could devise/suggest the way of getting out of this difficulty. Gautama began to think like this. With all faith and devotion Gautama then began to meditate on the God stated to bear Gaṅgā on His head, i.e. Śiva. The ascetics having their minds purged off all dirt heard something unprecedentedly astonishing in the meantime. When the great soul Gautama was thus meditating on Mahādeva, a reverberating voice sounded from the space sending ripples of delight in the three worlds. O Brāhmaṇas! the various directions/regions of the world began to resonate with that voice. The voice had no form and it was not indicating anything. But it was ringing the auspicious bell of relieving distress all around.

The divine voice said:

41-48. It is a matter of great surprise that while this great region of Godāvarī engenders happiness and welfare of everyone, the learned are equally involved in a great ocean of sorrow in the same context. O preceptor Gautama and the sages like Nārada et al.! please be kind enough to listen to this message of mine regarding centres of pilgrimage. Look towards the western coast of the sea. There, on the north-western front is a growing and good centre of pilgrimage called Dvārakā. In its onward course, the virtuous Gomatī has met with the sea there. The great Viṣṇu is always present there with his face towards the west. It is the place known as bearing the fire to always burn up sins from the grave to the gravest order. The God himself had burnt up the worldly mischief of an unparallel kind to ashes here. Like the sun, he is always present there to annihilate sins in the three worlds. Thus to reward Godāvarī by helping her to burn up her sins, O greatly fortunate souls! all of you head towards Gomatī along with other centres of pilgrimage. O best Brāhmaṇas! all of you will reach the holy Dvārāvat with my favour. Then the truth will appear before you by the impact of Dvārakā.

Prahlāda said:

49-53. After the utterances of such words coming from the voice above all the sages got pleased and remained assured within their minds. Hearing about the best of the centres of pilgrimage, with offering of ghee to the sacrificial fire they began to take the names of Hari. They began to tell themselves that they had sensed victory and had become more fortunate among the fortunates. It is a stroke of luck that they did not go down under the trap of attachments. They had come to know of the best among the centres of pilgrimage. Then all the centres of pilgrimage along with holy regions, jungles and hermitages, Vārāṇasī, Prayāga, etc., rivers like Sindhu and the known seven rivers, Gayā, the pools of water commonly known to have been sprung forth by the gods, ancestral forefathers, the gods as well as men got very exalted hearing such words as per the divine voice and began to say 'Hail you' 'Hail you'. They said, "Oh! this is the best of the centres of pilgrimage which is the destroyer of everyone's sins. We bow down our heads in reverence to Dvārakā—the ruler of all centres of pilgrimage."

Śrī Prahlāda said:

54-58. Hearing about the best of the centres of pilgrimage or even to learn that such a centre of pilgrimage is even better than the best and this place of pilgrimage is for the best of the best gods, i.e. Kṛṣṇa, as well as the destroyer of all difficulties an element of eagerness crept into the all good centres of pilgrimage assembled there. With their voices raised, all those centres of pilgrimage descended through ages began to discuss amongst themselves. Ruṣi Tīrtha and gods said, "When shall we get to see that holy Dvārakā looked after by Kṛṣṇa. The divine idol of Śrī Kṛṣṇa as well as his discus beautify the same place. When will it happen for us to have a bath at Gomatī? When shall we get the opportunity to have a bath at Cakratīrtha and happen to see the Kṛṣṇa temple there? Getting an opportunity to have a perception of virtue of a high order, when shall we be able to make for that gate of liberation under wraps? Difficult is to obtain an opportunity to have a dwelling at Dvārakā. Equally difficult it is to have a look of Kṛṣṇa. Similarly the Brāhmaṇas! it is difficult to have a look of Rukmiṇī after a bath at Gomatī."

CHAPTER THIRTY

Celebratory visit of Godāvarī, places of pilgrimage, gods and great sages to Dvārakā

Śrī Prahlāda said:

1-5. Then all those good places of pilgrimage began to feel a sense of pleasure within. They all went to Dvārāvatī (i.e. Dvārakā) and earned virtue on all their parts. Seeing their procession towards Dvārakā both Nārada and Gautama began to think that this would result in an atmosphere of great celebration there which would be equally appealing to the mind. "All centres of pilgrimage need to undertake a visit for Kṛṣṇa." (Thinking like this) all sages, gods with all centres of pilgrimage, taking Gomatī along with an eye towards her getting rewarded in turn, went to Dvārāvatī with all pleasure. Since then all centres of pilgrimage, all holy regions on the land as well as sages and gods began to take rounds of Dvārakā with pleasure. Carried by faith, earnest devotion and an ardent longing for a look of Kṛṣṇa they on their way then told Nārada—the player of *Vīṇā* and the learned in truth.

The Sages said:

6-10. By virtue of our collection of virtues through worship, perseverance, donations at the altar of *yajñas*, observance of religious vows and visits of the great centres of pilgrimage on the earth's surface as well as with your blessings that we got to see this place abounding in the holy *kuśa* grasses (i.e. Dvārakā). Now we intend to ask from the highest teacher of the ascetics (i.e. Nārada) as to what is the procedure to visit Dvārakā as has been declared with all glorification. O sage! what rules have to be pursued on our part and what duties we need to abstain ourselves from? What should we listen to and which recitals of praise should we remember on our way? Please tell us also about the merriments worthwhile on the passage to Dvārakā. So also the great fortunate soul! we will like to know about each and every activity that further adds to the happiness of devotees on their way. O the great fortunate soul! kindly tell us about all these as has been recited with glory.

Śrī Nārada said:

11-26. Do shave and bathe before worshipping Hari with due faith. With all pleasure, do feed the Vaiṣṇavas as per your capacity. Then with the consent of those great Vaiṣṇavas have the offerings made at the time of worship as food for yourselves. Then lie down on the ground with all satisfaction to sleep. While lying down, remember Kṛṣṇa within your mind. Then as the morning breaks in do your routine purificatory jobs including having bath, etc. to worship the God of the world. Then make your fees to the great Vaiṣṇavas. After that pay your reverences and seek their permission before leaving. While making reverences to the Vaiṣṇavas do remember the older in your clan/family, Brāhmaṇas, other Vaiṣṇavas as well as all your dear ones in the back of your mind. After obtaining their permission, start your journey with great pleasure towards Dvārakā by singing accompanied with musical instruments and by reciting hymns. For the purpose of visiting Dvārakā, always maintain calmness in the mind, observe purity, adapt to *Brahmacarya*, i.e. celibacy and sleep on the ground having control on your senses. Read the book containing thousand names of Viṣṇu. Read the Purāṇa as well. Inculcate generosity in the mind and always serve the virtuous. A man can donate rice keeping in tune with his financial position. Even donations made in smaller quantity as per one's capacity grow into crore proportions. If one donates a small piece of land with devotion on the road leading to the centre of pilgrimage meant for Kṛṣṇa, that minor piece of land so donated becomes like an island and the contours of virtues earned on his part cannot be measured. Further by giving balls of boiled rice to one individual at the pilgrim centre of Dvārakā near Kṛṣṇa one derives fruits of ten thousand *Rājasūya Yajñas* (i.e. sacrificial fire usually conducted by a king in sustenance of his coronation based on the popular will). Fruits derivable through conduct of thousands of *śrāddhas* at Gayā can be obtained by men through offering of rice on the way to Dvārakā. By offering medicine, food and drinks as well as by donating blankets, footwear, clothes and wealth as per one's power and capability on the way to Dvārakā one kills the sins of illegitimate marriage. For that matter one raises oneself well above this and renders futile the statement of the learned in this regard. Donations on the way to Dvārakā kills one's inclination and desire to backbite and cause bad name to others and one's tendency to cheat or harm others and eye other's food. Indeed one gives up such a nature. The stigma of making wealth by petty means does no longer hold for one by one's listening to divine story of Viṣṇu as well as by making prayers containing his divine names. It is desirable to mutter Vedic mantras as well as the hymns of *Agama śāstra* on way to Dvārakā for they enhance the devotion of pilgrims. O the sages! I have described you the fruits of visit to the pilgrim centre exclusive to the worship of Śrī Kṛṣṇa in the Kaliyuga. I cannot be able to give a complete picture of the same covering all the yugas. O the foremost Brāhmaṇas! I have spoken all this in return of what you all asked. Hence, it is for you to bear in mind, to hurry up and make all efforts to have access to Viṣṇu.

Śrī Prahlāda said:

27-41. So told by the sage Nārada, all of them got encouraged and swiftly took to the path leading to the temple of Kṛṣṇa as if a pair of wheels got added to their feet. On way, some of them listened to the popularly known divine account of Viṣṇu, lending ears to which brings the God well into one's heart. O Brāhmaṇas! taking the names of Viṣṇu especially in the Kaliyuga always holifies. Prayers containing names of Viṣṇu yield great merits. Some ascetics sang the glory of the divine *Purāṇa saṁhitā.* It brings to light the greatness of Viṣṇu which grants well-being of a high order. At some times in the past Viṣṇu had done activities reflecting bravery and goodness. Some people listened to such activities of Viṣṇu in his magical form with happiness beyond limits. There were some devotees who listened to the auspicious accounts of Vāsudeva. With watery eyes, they spoke about them with devotion and happiness beyond any bound. Some remembered the God as primordial, as beyond death and as all powerful. Some ascetics muttered the names of God as well as recited hymns addressed to him with happiness beyond limits. Some ascetics muttered hundred names of the God on their way to Dvārakā while some others concentrated on one thousand names of God. Well above both these categories some (prefered to) muttered one lakh names of the God. Some on their way rejoiced by singing the customary songs bearing names of Hari. Some people carried the special flags addressed to the God and set out on their way towards Dvārakā in a celebratory mood. Some set their way by singing with beating of drums, by clapping and making proclamations addressed to the glory of God. There was hardly any more fortunate way than this in the three worlds. A sight of all this was good enough to generate the noble feeling of sighting good Vaiṣṇavas. Holy rivers like Jāhnavī, Yamunā, Sarasvatī, Revā and all others were proceeding on their way singing and dancing. Centres of pilgrimage like Prayāga, etc., seas and best of mountains were also there on the way. Vārāṇasī, Kurukṣetra as well as all other holy regions were also moving on the way. All the existing centres of pilgrimage as well as other holy regions in the three worlds with their leading worshipable gods were proceeding on the noble path to Dvārakā singing and dancing. On each step of theirs on the road to Dvārakā they were reaping thousands of merits amounting to the innumerable dust particles underneath their feet. In this way all the ascetics including Nārada, etc. accompanied with places of pilgrimage got to see the Kṛṣṇa temple from a distance.

CHAPTER THIRTY-ONE

Taking the look of Dvārāvat as an idol

Prahlāda said:

1-12. With its divine light, the temple of Dvārakā destroys the darkness surrounding birth in embodied form. Throwing fear away from the minds of devotees, it fills them with supreme bliss. The staff holding the flag atop the temple enhances its glory. With its divine and virtuous light, it flutters on the temple-top like on top of a mountain. Beholding Viṣṇu adorned with weapons, all of their sight got fixed and then keeping aside their footwear and umbrellas, all of them fell flat on the ground to pay their reverence. The lying on the ground of all the centres of pilgrimage offered one with something equally great but strange. It appeared as if all those leading Brāhmaṇas and the holy regions were on the way to their final liberation. Vārāṇasī, Kurukṣetra, Prayāga, Jāhnavī, Yamunā, Narmadā, the holy Prācī as well as Sarasvatī were amidst them. Godāvarī as well as the auspicious three holy regions similar to Gayā were there among them. The great holy region like Śāligrāma as well as the auspicious Cakra river were present among them. Rivers like Payoṣṇī, Tāptī, Kṛṣṇā, Kāverī which always grant one with holiness, places of pilgrimage like Puṣkara, etc., seas as well as the best of mountains, holy regions that give liberation like Ayodhyā, Mathurā, Māyāpurī, Avantī, eternal places like Śrī Raṅga and especially the Prabhāsa were present amidst them. The greatest of the holy regions called Puruṣottama, auspicious jungles as well as all centres of pilgrimage extant in the three worlds were present there. Seeing the holy Kṛṣṇa temple, happiness was continuously evident on their being. With utterances of words like "hail you" "hail you", they paid their homage to God. They were also taking aloud the name "Hari". With tears of pleasure and hearts brimming with love all the sages as well as centres of pilgrimage were reciting hymns in honour of the God. Witnessing all of them reciting hymns with their selves completely taken over with happiness the great sage Nārada then told them.

Śrī Nārada said:

13-24. You all—the good souls have accumulated virtues on your part. In this way, with merits earned over thousands of births that you all have succeeded in having a look of this Kṛṣṇa temple. In your minds (it is true that) all of you have nurtured the desire to visit Dvārakā for having a look of God Kṛṣṇa. But a look of Viṣṇu can be possible by firm devotion. Lesser penance on any count cannot yield such a result. All the ancestors in your clan have become gratified by your having a look of Kṛṣṇa. For you all, it is a matter of celebration to visit Dvārakā and to equally have a look of the beloved of Hari, i.e. Rukmiṇī. Blessed are the Gautamī alias Gaṅgā and the great sage Gautama known for his austerity and penance. It is by virtue of their grace that everyone's welfare has materialized. All of you— the ardent believers in and followers of pilgrimage have taken hold of the fruits that result from one's pursuit of studies, *yajñas*, donations, penance and observance of religious vows. As it is, all of you as centres of pilgrimage and as holy regions will remain present here for all times to come and along with all gods as per orders of Kṛṣṇa. Those who happen to put up here get blessed with great fortune. On my part, I have become holier. All of you in any case are (directly) seeing the well and the highly fortunate Godāvarī and the Jāhnavī here. As it is, the holy Dvārakā which is a favourite of Kṛṣṇa, always shines here. All can notice the presence of greatly fortunate and auspicious Vārāṇasī here. You, the lords can see the chief among the holy regions like Kurukṣetra at Dvārakā. Holy regions like Mathurā, Kāśī, Māyāpurī and Ayodhyā do also shine at Dvārakā in a similar way. Neither Avantī, nor Kāñcī, nor Puruṣottama nor even Kurukṣetra shine during solar eclipse. Similar is also the case with the Gayā centre of pilgrimage. But Dvārakā has its own distinct standing in this regard. As the sun reigns amidst planets and stars so is Dvārakā amidst all the ruling centres of pilgrimage.

Prahlāda said:

25-35. The Brāhmaṇas got very pleased after hearing words of Nārada. Deeming for themselves that as holy regions and centres of pilgrimage, they have already rewarded Gautama, leaving Gautamī behind, they then proceeded ahead. On her part Gautamī was equally and highly pleased. Giving her reverences to Śrī Kṛṣṇa then and there, she then followed them fast. Singing and dancing along with playing musical instruments, keeping their flags aloft and observing the religious ritual of reciting hymns all of them together then moved ahead in their strive towards making Dvārakā their resort. Keeping all centres of pilgrimage ahead before his eyes, and with Prayāga—the beautiful and master centre of pilgrimage in the middle of them, Nārada remained happy looking at it. The virtuous sage (i.e. Nārada) subsequently took bath in the river. All the rivers namely Jāhnavī, Gautamī, Revā, Yamunā, Sarasvatī flowing in the East, Sarayu, Gandakī, Tāptī, Payosṇī, Kṛṣṇā, Bhāgīrathī, Gaṅgā, Kāverī—the destroyer of all sins, the highly holy Mandākinī, the holy Bhogbatī including all those descended on earth through ages went ahead and had a look of the (holy) city of Dvārakā. Following them from behind were the seven seas along with their respective centres of pilgrimage. After them were the jungles and the holy hermitages. They were pursued by beautiful mountains like Meru, etc. They were all singing (in chorus) and dancing. The great sages were reciting hymns. Highly exalted in their minds, the sages and gods from all sides were moving on while singing, dancing and taking aloud the name of Hari. With the playing of musical instruments and sounds like 'hail you Kṛṣṇa' they all presented one with an atmosphere of heightened happiness. Along with all learned Brāhmaṇas in the art of conducting of *yajñas,* they came near the banks of Gomatī. Seeing all those great virtuous souls united in reverence and equally in a happy state of mind, Nārada said:

36-37. O Bhāgīrathī! O Revā! O Yamunā! O Gautamī! listen to me. The best and gracious Gautamī is like a goddess and has acquired fame for itself in the three worlds. A bath in its holy water emulates the knowledge of Brahma.

It is due to this reason that Gomatī is rated as the best among all centres of pilgrimage. One gets freedom through knowledge of Brahma or by meeting with death at Prayāga. By a bath only at Gomatī, one gets liberation along with one's ancestors.

Prahlāda said:

38-46. Thus getting informed about the highly wonderful greatness of the Gomatī as a centre of pilgrimage, they all then took bath at Gomatī with due faith and proceeded ahead in a celebratory mood. Thus to behold the beautiful Dvārakā, all the holy regions, centres of pilgrimage, rivers and seas, etc. arrived at the door to the temple consecrated to the deity Kṛṣṇa at Dvārakā. Adorned with pearls and golds the temple at Dvārakā appeared to be seated on a divine throne. Dressed up in beautiful white clothes it was emitting the same aura like that of Rūdra (i.e. the group of gods as inferior manifestations of Lord Śiva) and the sun. The temple appeared to be clothed in beautiful clothes with its premises emitting scent. It was adorned with jewellery and other ornaments. With a crown on its head, beautiful earrings and bracelets, it was shining. Bearing conch, the discus and mace in its hands, the deity was appearing to grant one with the boon of fearlessness. Painted with white leaves the ceiling of the temple was giving a look of pomp and grandeur. The breezy premises of the temple were giving impressions as if they were fitted with fans. With recitation of hymns by pilgrims as well as with their singing and playing of musical instruments, the entire environment of the temple was evoking an atmosphere of pleasure and happiness. Beholding the Dvārakā city at the backdrop of such a background was enough to give the impression as if the same city is seated on a throne. Everyone (i.e. the centres of pilgrimage and the holy centres descended through ages, the forests, mountains, the rivers as well as the gods and sages) was giving its homage to the city with well-founded devotion.

CHAPTER THIRTY-TWO

Eminence of Dvārakā—as per attendants of Viṣṇu

Prahlāda said:

1. To offer his homage to the favourite city of Hari, Nārada then went ahead and with all happiness and politeness made the following utterances in honour of the Dvārakā city.

Śrī Nārada said:

2-20. Look, the great fortunate soul! your brightness has further got added up with all centres of pilgrimage, gods as well as sages having come close to you. Look at Prayāga there before you with other centres of pilgimage. O Dvārakā! it has fallen flat at your feet on the ground showing faith of a wonderful kind. There is the Puṣkara centre of pilgrimage offering its homage which in itself is an auspicious sign. There is also the holy Gautamī to which all centres of pilgrimage have taken resort to. Coinciding with the transit of Guru, i.e. the planet Jupiter through the zodiac sign of Leo in the month of Bhādra, i.e. August-September, a great fortune has dawned on her, i.e. Gautamī. But due to her getting polluted through bad people having taken bath in her waters, she has been excessively burnt up with the fire of sins. Apprised of her way-out of this by the sages and as per their worthy words, she has come here with the noble wish to get relieved of her predicament. O Dvārakā! the divine and holy Gautamī is paying her reverence to you. You can also behold the highly holy and auspicious Bhāgīrathī before you. Showing their happiness once and again, they are offering reverences at your feet. You can also look at the beautiful Narmadā making salutation at your feet. Look at Yamunā, Candrabhāgā, Prācī, Sarasvatī, Sarayu and Gaṇḍakī. Also have a look at the rivers those flow on the eastern side of Gomatī which are present there at the same time. Rivers like Soṇa, Sindhu as well as other prominent rivers have remained present there equally. Kṛṣṇā, Bhimrathī and the holy Kāverī are among the other prominent rivers present there. Rivers like Sītā, Cakṣyu, Bhadrā are offering their salutations at your lotus-feet. O Dvārakā! even all those highly holier rivers stated to have originated in the seven islands are also keenly offering their salutations to you. The highly holy Mandākinī has come there before you along with Bhagavatī. You can also see Vārāṇasī—the giver of liberation to be present before you with all sobriety. With all devotion they have bowed down with their heads at your feet. The greatly holy Kurukṣetra has also been offering its salutation day and night to you. O Dvārakā! look at Mathurā offering reverence at your feet. Ayodhyā, Avantikā as well as Māyāpuri are offering their salutations at your lotus-feet. Kāñcī, Gayā, Viśālā as well as Virajā have fallen flat on the ground to offer their reverences to you. The great holy region like Śāligrāma is also there at your feet offering its obeisance. The sacred centres like Prabhāsa and Puruṣottama are present there before you. O beautiful Dvārakā! Bhārgavādi as well as all other holy regions awakened with devotion are offering their salutations to you repeatedly. See also the seven seas bowing down before you. Look also at all the forests, where the sages put up for a short while, making their salutations to the city, i.e. Dvārakā. Have a look that forests named Dhanuṣka, Daśāraṇya, Daṇḍakāraṇya and Arbuda, and the hermitage named Nārāyaṇāśrama are equally offering their reverences to Dvārakā. There are also thousands of mountains like Meru, Kailāsa, Mandāra, Himādri, Vindhya, Śrī Śaila, etc. present here with great happiness. All of these in the pursuit of their happiness are making salutations to you again and again. Gaṅgā, etc., the seas and the mountains are dancing in front of you. All the sages as well as gods are also taking your name aloud.

Śrī Prahlāda said:

21-28. After his (i.e. Nārada's) saying like this, Dvārakā got pleased in mind. Seeing all dancing in pleasure, Dvārakā embraced them quite lovingly. Then touching Gautamī by her hands she spoke to her quite endearingly. She also spoke to Bhāgīrathī, Prayāga and all other centres of pilgrimage. All got happy as a result of Dvārakā's sweet dialogue. In the meantime something quite unusually astonishing happened there which enhanced happiness of everyone. Reverberating sounds combining songs, music and resonances of "hail you" "hail you" from above the sky happened. Echoes with distinct utterances of the holy word "Hari" were made. Everyone then happened to have a glimpse of all gods including their leader Brahmā. The Lord Maheśa could be visible with his other half, i.e. Pārvatī as well as with his other manifestations. Indra—the ruler of three directions was also visible along with his other halves in the form of Yakṣas, Gandharvas and Kinnaras. The God of wind, i.e. Marūta as well as the guardians of the different quarters of the world could be seen dancing with profound happiness. Siddhas, the Vidyādharas, Vasu, Āditya, i.e. the Sun along with planets, Bhṛgu, Sanaka, i.e. son of Brahmā, etc. could be seen to be dancing equally with heightened happiness. The gods from seven heavens were also making their salutation to Brahmā with all pleasure. Bewildered with happiness in themselves, Brahmā, Īśān, i.e. Śiva and Viṣṇu looked at one another with astonishment and then told Dvārakā.

The gods said:

29-31. It is the same Goddess called Dvārakā where flows the Gomatī. It is the same auspicious place where God Kṛṣṇa abides. It is the best among all regions. It is the best of all centres of pilgrimage. On land, Dvārakā shines in a greater manner than the heaven. It is the same Cakratīrtha for the stones here (i.e. at Dwārakā) bear the impressions of the discus of Śrī Kṛṣṇa. It is a giver of liberation to the sinners in the world. It is also equally worshipped by people from foreign lands.

Prahlāda said:

32-38. Seeing Brahmā, etc. arriving there Nārada, etc. got struck with wonder. Various regions, the main centres of pilgrimage, prominent holy rivers also got surprised. All of them as descended on the earth over and through ages took their turn to offer salutations. O the foremost Brāhmaṇas! seeing the mind captivating procession of Brahmā, etc., as well as of centres of pilgrimage towards Dvārakā, all its (i.e. Dvārakā's) inhabitants got wonderstruck. All gods were too happy to notice that each temple at Dvārakā was resonating with sounds of song accompanied by musical instruments. Noticing Dvārakā in such a state, Brahmā and Maheśa became mentally satisfied and began to utter words in its praise postulating that the city is very dear to Kṛṣṇa. Getting down from their carriers, both the foremost gods then offered their reverences falling flat on the ground. With all happiness both the gods then said in honour of Dvārakā, "O Dvārakā! you are the best/paramount amongst all of us as the immortal Viṣṇu never gave you up. Hence, you please help us to have a look of God Kṛṣṇa and the annihilator of Kaṁsa. Great accomplishment on all our part will materialize by such a sight only."

Prahlāda said:

39-54. After the God's saying so the Goddess-like Dvārakā then took leave of the gods along with all other centres of pilgrimage. Rewarded as it is, both Brahmā and Śiva remained happy witnessing such a great celebration. On her part, Dvārakā was in a state of bewildered happiness with gifts in her hands in the form of songs accompanied by musical instruments, fluttering of flags on its top and holiness. She then told the gods, "O gods! just take note of. The fruits of liberation that are obtained by having a pious look of the Lord of Dvārakā cannot at all be possible even in thousands of universes." After that gods accompanied by all centres of pilgrimage took a look of the idol of Kṛṣṇa— the destroyer of all hardships and which had its face towards the west. All of them, as descended upon the earth through ages, offered their reverences and happiness of the highest order appeared on them. Singing with musical instruments and making proclamations hailing the God, i.e. Kṛṣṇa, all of them kept on dancing. Along with voices of hailing the God, they were equally uttering the word Namaḥ (i.e. obeisance) and repeatatively taking the name of Hari aloud. Brahmā, Śiva, Bhavānī, Indra as well as all other gods had a look of Kṛṣṇa and paid their reverences again and again arousing a sense of devotion within them. Centres of pilgrimage like Prayāga, etc.rivers full of clean water like Gaṅgā, etc. the sages like Śukra and Sanaka, the gods and Gandharvas took a look of the face of great Viṣṇu and offered their reverences repeatedly. Kṛṣṇa! Kṛṣṇa! O hail you Kṛṣṇa! making such utterances, they took bath in the waters of Gomatī especially on the shore where Gomatī flows into the sea. With all happiness, the lotus-seated Brahmā worshipped Śrī Kṛṣṇa. Brahmā bathed the idol of Kṛṣṇa with the milk of his own cow as well as with the holy mixture containing equal proportions of milk, curd, ghee, honey and sugar. Both Śiva and Bhavānī also worshipped with due devotion. Indra as well as other gods, all yogis including Sanaka, etc.prominent rivers like Gaṅgā, etc. worshipped Śrī Kṛṣṇa devotedly with invaluable ornaments, precious jewels, beautiful garlands made of varieties of flowers including those blooming in the garden of Indra known as Nandana and with the favourite basil leaves of Kṛṣṇa. They also worshipped by lighting incense sticks as well as by moving the container bearing lighted camphor of distinct types. They made offerings of varieties of food as a part of worship. They put flowers flavoured with camphor to the deity. They also offered betel leaves after adding peppermint. They also made gifts which Kṛṣṇa is fond of. Reciting highly benedictory prayers they made the auspicious *āratī* (i.e. waving of lamps before an idol) of God and worshipped the great Viṣṇu and Kṛṣṇa— the destroyer of all hardships/calamities. They danced happily. They sang and played musical instruments with great pleasure. Before the God Kṛṣṇa, along with the divine beauties, there were Brahmā with his sons, Indra and the God of wind. Seeing Brahmā, etc. dancing before him, the lotus-eyed (i.e. an epithet of Viṣṇu) interrupted and told them with all pleasure.

The gracious God said:

55. O Brahmā, Maheśa, Maheśvari, holy regions, all centres of pilgrimage, Nārada and Sanaka, etc.! I have been pleased by your devotion. All your desires will materialize.

Prahlāda said:

56. Then all of them wishing for realization of the desires of their minds paid their salutations to Śrī Kṛṣṇa and put forth their wishes to the God with superlative devotion saying:

The Gods said:

57. We have realized our desires spread across all directions by your kindness to grant us the all-pervading boon in this regard. Let our loving devotion for you endure always at your feet.

Prahlāda said:

58-62. Then all of them worshipped Rukmiṇī—the beloved of Kṛṣṇa. Coinciding the same, they all happened to overhear the following words of both Brahmā and Maheśa. Attended with faith of the highest order both happened to address Dvārakā as follows: "You as the Goddess is the best among all centres of pilgrimage and is the best of those considered to be foremost among the holy regions. As the Meru is to the mountains, as the sea holds its place among rivers, as breath is to the body and the senses are to the mind, as heat/glow is integral to fire, as a raised platform is the distinguishing criterion to mark the performance of the religious rite of *yajñas*, as the shining of planets, stars and the moon is a fact but as the sun shines inhering together all their brightness as a collective whole of light, as the great Viṣṇu holds a position of great eminence among all gods, so is the auspicious Dvārakā worshipable among all centres of pilgrimage."

Prahlāda said:

63-84. Saying like this to all other gods, the holy regions as well as to other virtuous sages about the reigning supremacy of Dvārakā, both Brahmā and Śiva then happened to have celebratingly annointed Dvārakā. This is how the reason of ascendance of Dvārakā among the ruling centres of pilgrimage as well as other holy regions has been affirmed by Brahmā and Śiva and other gods, sovereign rulers of people and the blameless sages as well. Then with profound happiness they all performed the great anointing ceremony of Dvārakā. Each of them played a distinct and unique musical instrument in such a large celebration. With the mixture of equal proportions of milk, curd, ghee, honey and sugar collected from all centres of pilgrimage and with the water of the Gaṅgā brought by the leading elephants stated to exist above in the space, they all anointed Dvārakā. They made presents of beautiful clothes for Dvārakā to wear. They also made it to have water in her hands and sip it as a matter of religious ritual. They smeared her face with the paste of sandalwood and decorated her with beautiful ornaments. They then worshipped with flowers circular in shape and with sandalwood. Then the celestial attendants of Hari arrived there. The God's attendants like Viṣvakṣena and Sunanda, etc. were illuminating the ten directions and uttering words like, "hail you God" and "obeisance to you". They were showering flowers. Making proclamations with songs and playing musical instruments, they were dancing in a state of exaltation. They had decorated themselves with a crown on head, with earrings and with necklace made of a special kind of pearls. Having a complexion in between fairness and darkness, each one appeared like the four-armed God and with themselves adorned in yellow dresses and garlands, those attendants of Viṣṇu were shining like the God himself. Brahmā and Maheśvara had happened to see them shining with their own brightness as such. Nārada and Sanaka, etc. saw these sages who were great admirers and devotees of Bhāgavat. They (the sages) were also happy to see them. But equally with their happiness, they remained confused. Seeing the other adorers of Viṣṇu already there, the attendants did welcome them by such gestures like embracing, etc. The sages and other gods also made their salutations to the attendants of Viṣṇu. After their reaching Dvārakā, the attendants of Viṣṇu bowed their head before the Lord of Dvārakā as well as to Dvārakā also. With all faith and devotion they worshipped him with the exquisite flowers that specially grow in forests as well as with varieties of beautiful flowers and the sacred basil leaves which also germinate in forests. With the fruits that grow in forests and by lighting scented incense sticks as well as camphor they worshipped the Lord. By offering rice as food and betel leaves as per laid down procedure, they appeased Kṛṣṇa. Saying that "You are the Lord" "You are the master of the ruling holy regions and the centres of pilgrimage" they made prayers offering salutations to Dvārakā. O Brāhmaṇas! in the meantime, great sounds emanating from the throbbing of big drums of gods could be heard with showering of flowers in an unprecedented manner. The virtuous sages! now listen to the highly wonderful incident that occurred simultaneously with this. Kurukṣetra and Prayāga lifted themselves up respectively on the left and right side of Dvārakā. While stationed in the same position both carried beautiful and white umbrellas with them. They did also fan Dvārakā giving a clean and auspicious touch to the atmosphere. Ayodhyā, Mathurā, Māyāpurī and Vārāṇasī were making calls hailing Dvārakā. All others including all holy regions present there were reciting hymns addressed to Dvārakā. Looking at the lotus-like face of Dvārakā, all places of pilgrimage and rivers were in a state of ecstasy along with gods and the human beings. Then the attendants of Viṣṇu addressed all saying that they were fortunate enough. Before making such a statement they had already seen and taken note of the point that Dvārakā was so holy a place and like a jewel in the entire world. This is how everyone has nurtured a wish in his/her mind to worship Hari by performance of *yajñas*, through meditation and by repeatedly taking the name of God in mind as per Vedic injunctions and earn the happiness onto the self by visiting Dvārakā.

CHAPTER THIRTY-THREE

Dvārakā as an abode to all regions and places of pilgrimage

Śrī Prahlāda said:

1. After hearing all that said about Dvārakā by the attendants of Viṣṇu, Brahmā and Maheśa showed eagerness in the details about the greatness of Dvārakā and then attempted to describe its eminence as follows:

Śrī Brahmā and Īśān (an epithet of Śiva) said:

2-3. O all holy regions, centres of pilgrimage, rivers, seas and places of pilgrimage like Prayāga and Kāśī, etc. which grant liberation! though you all happen to be the ruling centres of pilgrimage, the auspicious Dvārakā is relatively greater amidst you and that way it is like a great king. Hence, you all need to serve it voluntarily while placing yourselves outside its territory.

Śrī Prahlāda said:

4-27. Such words of Maheśa (as well as of Brahmā) unleashed an environment of celebration among the places of pilgrimage and other holy regions. They took rounds of Dvārakā and after offering their salutations they made their abodes there with all happiness. Bhāgīrathī, Prayāga, Yamunā, Sarasvatī, Sarayu, Gaṇḍakī, the holy Gomatī flowing in the east, all other rivers like Sindhu, Śoṇī and centres of pilgimage numbering fifty crore descended down and began to be present at Dvārakā. All of them— greedy as they were— got down to serve Kṛṣṇa and kept looking at Dvārakā again and again. Mandākinī, also the holy Bhāgīrathī, Mahānadī, Narmadā as well as Śiprā, Prācī and Sarasvatī, Cakṣyurbhadrā and Sītā and other rivers equally known as destroyer of sins, along with sixty crore centres of pilgrimage on their banks remained present on the eastern direction. Payoṣṇī. Tāptī, the holy Vidarbhā as well as Payasvinī, the Godāvarī and the very holy Bhīmā and Kṛṣṇā river, Kāverī and the other prominent rivers known as destroyer of sins with all their centres of pilgrimage numbering about ninety-nine crores remained present on the southern direction of Dvārakā with all eagerness and devotion. They began to play merrily either in the waters of Gomatī or on its banks in the vicinity of Kṛṣṇa. The leading rivers known to belong to the seven islands as well as elsewhere and the seven seas remained present in the western side of Dvārakā. All these play merrily in Cakratīrtha as well as in hundreds and crores of other centres of pilgrimage. All of these always keep themselves facing Kṛṣṇa having His face towards the west. The number of centres of pilgrimage in the intermediate zones of all these (already) stated directions is not known. O good Brāhmaṇas! centres of pilgrimage like Puṣkara, Viśālā, Virajā, Gayā as well as those hundreds and crores of centres of pilgrimage at the spot of confluence of Gomatī with the sea vibrate in the intermediate zones—always engaged in the service of Kṛṣṇa creating an environment of celebration. The

Vārāṇasī and Avantī are situated respectively on the north-eastern and eastern side while Kāntī and Mathurā are respectively in the south-eastern and southern direction. Māyāpurī is on the south-west direction and Ayodhyā is on the west. Kurukṣetra is on the north-west, while Harikṣetra is situated further north to it. Śivakṣetra as well as Puruṣottama are on the eastern frontier. Bhṛgukṣetra is also there on the south-eastern direction while Prabhāsa has its abode in the southern side. Śrīraṅga is on the south-western side and Lohadaṇda is on the west. Narasinha is on the north-west and Kokāmukṣya is on the northern side of the former. Kāmāknyā and Reṇukā representing the female personification of divine energy are present everywhere around Dvārakā while other ruling holy regions have found places for themselves as available in the vicinity of Dvārakā. The holy regions called Soura and Gaṇapati are also present completely in the northern side. O Brāhmaṇas! other holy regions have descended in a similar manner and have found their abodes in the vicinity of Rukmiṇī. All of these, viz. Dhenuka, Naimiṣa as well as the Daṇḍaka forests, Saindhava the forest called Daśaraṇya, and the hermitage known as Nārāyana *āśrama* are spread out in all sides of Dvārakā. Mountains like Meru, etc. is also engaged gently and eagerly in the service of Dvārakā. Kailāsa is there on the north-east while Himavat is on the east. Śrī Śaila is on the south-east while Śimhadvādwā is on the south. Tāntrikas and sages like Mahendra have placed themselves on the south-west front. Other holy mountains along with their respective deities are also present there with purpose. Placed around Dvārakā in all its sides, they regularly worship it. Gods like Brahmā, and sages like Sanaka along with other holy regions, centres of pilgrimage and all other virtuous souls usually come to have a look of Dvārakā attended with faith and devotion of higher order during the period of Guru, i.e. Jupiter's transit through the zodiac sign of Virgo and they do so very much with happiness.

CHAPTER THIRTY-FOUR

Dilīp's visit to Dvārakā and sins committed at Kāśī as a prelude

Śrī Prahlāda said:

1-8. O leading sages! this is the wonder of greatness of Dvārakā. It is a remover of great sins on the part of all regions and places of pilgrimage. Specially, it is a great abductor of sins of people irrespective of their varṇas and their committing sins while passing through any *āśrama,* i.e. the four stages of life. It is said to be an enhancer of great virtue. In all appropriateness, it is therefore remembered as a cemetery for all those seated on extreme sin. O Brāhmaṇas! this just results from a visit to Dvārakā. So what to speak about dwelling at Dvārakā? O the leading Brāhmaṇas! Brahmā, etc. along with centres of pilgrimage remain specially visible here at the time of transit of Guru (an epithet for Jupiter) through the zodiac sign of Kanyā, i.e. Virgo. Sinners obtain a divine passage by simply touching the dust particles of the feet of those men who visit Dvārakā every year. Purify your bodies with the water of Gomatī and thereafter take a look of Kṛṣṇa. Sins of those earned through one hundred births go away by their having a look of Kṛṣṇa in this manner. O the foremost sages! listen to the saying made in history in this regard. The message from the dialogues between king Dilīp and the sage Vasiṣṭha which underlies this, adds one with wonder of the highest order. Kāśī is the only place where sins having a firm foundation like that of a cemented floor get destroyed all-together. Hearing that this can only happen by having a look of it Dilīp had made such a statement.

Dilīp said:

9-10. Horrible sins having a cemented foundation get destroyed at Kāśī. In that case do all the great virtues earned on one's part remain intact or not? O the best Brāhmaṇa (i.e. Vasiṣṭha)! please speak about any such place where sins can not sprout or for that matter speak about such holy place where sin virtually ceases to exist or has disappeared.

Vasiṣṭha said:

11-36. There used to be a master advocate of liberation at Kāśī known by the name Tridaṇḍī. With all sincerity he used to recite the Gāyatrī mantra repeatedly there placing himself at the backside of Daśāśvamedha. At some point of time a young girl walking in a slow and stately manner like that of an elephant came there. Taking off her clothes and leaving them on the banks of the river she entered into Gaṅgā to relieve her off tiredness. Bare-bodied, she entered into the water and engaged herself in water sports. Seeing her naked and playing, the ascetic (i.e. Tridaṇḍī) got completely struck. Fully enthralled, his mind by chance, got into an unstable state and he got instantly deviated from his path. With her mind equally overcome with libido, she also began to desire the company of the young sannyāsī. In this way both of their union materialized with derogatory action as its basis. Infatuated with her, the sannyāsī followed her and kept himself engaged in earning wealth by unjust means. One cannot get rid of sins committed through making of wealth by unfair/black means, by donating the same at night even without taking a bath. At some juncture of time, he headed towards a forest in search of meat. But the sinner sannyāsī always indulged himself there in stealing money at night even without taking a bath. At some juncture of time, he headed towards a forest in search of meat. But there (again) he got into a state of madness to see a woman and especially her intoxicating eyes. Encountering her youthfulness at the very first sight, arrogance dawned on his sinful mind. Prompted by intoxication, he had sexual union with her in some desolate corner of the forest. Infatuated with her he committed sins along with her in food and drinks. Like one driven to the edge under liquor, he, driven by licentious pleasure, also ate cooked beef. Then he—the voracious eater of everything died in his house. But due to the influence of Vārāṇasī, he did not get to hell then. However, the sins committed by him there were severe enough to acquire a strong foundation like that of a cemented floor. His relation with a woman in Śūdra, i.e. an untouchable caste was a ground enough for him to be born (again) in a womb that heralds harmful effects due to his misdeeds. He got rebirth in the form of a wolf, a tiger, a snake, a fox successively as his actions had made for so well in this direction and met with death in due course in each stage. He was severely afflicted and peace or pleasure to the slightest degree was not visible in him. In this way, all his sinful deeds spanning a thousand of his (re)births and the sins that resulted from his mad association with the outcaste woman did not drift away for ten thousand yugas. He got reborn as a rabbit in his seventh rebirth. Then he got birth again as a demon and in this birth as a sinful soul he indulged himself in all sorts of food. In his continuing spree of devouring living beings, he reached the Vindhya mountain. After this he got born as a strange chameleon. The sins having roots in his relationship with a Śudra (i.e. untouchable) woman made for his birth in the womb of insects. Companion of an untouchable woman has always been decried and disapproved. In a similar manner, its fruits have been spoken of. He underwent severe suffering for one thousand years and even in multiples of one thousand years. Then there occurred a highly surprising incident of unprecdented nature. Dilīp! listen to it. Incidentally, he happened to see someone who returned from Dvārāvat after having a look of the graceful face of Kṛṣṇa. The entire Vindhya region got so much brightened up with his presence that every one there got struck with wonder. After purifying himself with a bath in the waters of Gomatī, the traveller had reached Vindhya. With all happiness he was carrying a part of the gift on his shoulders, granted by the grace of Kṛṣṇa. While on his way towards own home, the demon happened to see him. Seeing him, the demon having a cruel nature hurried up to devour him. By a mere look of him, i.e. the traveller all the terrible sins having a strong cemented foundation on the part of the demon turned into ashes in a moment only, like at Vārāṇasī where all sins get thrown away. Crores and hundreds of birth could not succeed in taking away his sins. But he got himself free from his mountain-like heap of sins by a sight of a traveller who had a look of Kṛṣṇa. All his temperament towards cruelty got burnt up and he became free like the moon showing up with its brightness after the passing out of the curtain of cloud. All his ethical and moral bankruptcy went away by the benedictory light of having a sight of the traveller who had taken a look of Kṛṣṇa. Then with all pleasure, he came before the traveller who had already visited Dvārakā. Lying down on the ground he offered his salutation to him with due reverence and celebrated in a big manner for having a sight of him. With his head kept down he then told him with an element of surprise, "Oh! my ferocious temperament has gone away by taking a look of yours. I have approximated a good state of accomplishment. O good soul! where have you come from? Moreover, how could you have such an impact as had been visible on me? My sins committed at Kāśī and having a firm foundation like that of a cemented floor has got burnt up by my having your look."

Vasiṣṭha said:

37. After hearing the demon speaking like this, the traveller so-called as of Kṛṣṇa (for his already having a look of Kṛṣṇa) was taken aback completely and then with all pleasure of mind said:

The Traveller said:

38-39. O demon! I have come here after having a look of Dvārāvatī. All this power of mine to take away sins having a firm foundation like that of a cemented floor has been due to my having a look of Kṛṣṇa. The good action of taking a bath in Gomatī and thereafter having a look at the lotus-face of Kṛṣṇa rescues one from all sins having the potentials to burn up the three worlds.

Vasiṣṭha said:

39-43. After his saying so, the demon got very pleased. His self was already purified. Attended with devotion, he bowed down to the traveller and after taking circumambulation of him (i.e. the traveller) he then left for Dvārakā. (In course of time) he left the body and obtained the position of a Vaiṣṇava. Gods like Brahmā, Śiva and the Gandharvas began to sing hymns in his honour and also showered flowers on him. This is how the great impact of Dvārakā has been extolled. Sins do not (even) grow by having a sight of its travellers. So what more to speak about the power of Dvārakā in arresting the growth of sins? O blameless king! this is all, I have to tell you about the best of the holy regions having the power to destroy sins having a firm foundation like that of a cemented floor.

Śrī Prahlāda said:

44-45. Dilīp became pleased mentally after hearing the lofty words of Vasiṣṭha. He became surprised to learn that Dvārakā is a king among the holy regions. He went to Dvārāvatī to have a look of God of gods, i.e. Śrī Kṛṣṇa with all regards. Then after having a look of Kṛṣṇa in the God's temple there, he obtained that ultimate state of purity and holiness.

CHAPTER THIRTY-FIVE

Dvārakā: Eminence of name

Prahlāda said:

1-11. The eminence of this place extends everywhere constituting ten yojanam. Those placed in the heaven take notice of all those taking a look of the Four-armed God, i.e. Viṣṇu. The greatness of this area lies in the fact that after watching each resident of Dvārakā taking a look of the four-armed God all those residing in heaven pay their salutations to him/her. The greatness of this area has been celebrated in all the Śāstras. The blameless sages! now listen to the eminence of this place. All those staying here and always attached to the service of Kṛṣṇa with eagerness never aspire for liberation. According to them, even the stones here are enough to grant liberation to one. Even the insects, grasshoppers, animals, snakes and sinners—all of these attain liberation by the grace of Dvārakā. So what to speak again about the humans who reside here regularly. The passage that remains very much within the reach of all animals as well as of human inhabitants in Dvārakā, is certainly difficult for ascetics placed higher to them. Fruits attained by residing for a crore of years in all places of pilgrimage, can be obtained by presence at Dvārakā for just a fraction of moment every day. All men and women putting up at Dvārakā can be seen similar to the four-armed God, i.e. Viṣṇu. A look of an inhabitant of Dvārakā kills all sins. O best Brāhmaṇas! this is the undesirable truth that those who take look of the inhabitants of Dvārakā become very dear to Kṛṣṇa. Men censuring the inhabitants of Dvārakā are considered to be stupids. Devoid of love and affection for Kṛṣṇa they fall into the ocean of sorrows. Such censurers are terribly threatened by Jayanta (considered as the guardian of Dvārakā). They are dragged to sit on the sharp edge of an iron bar. They are made to get tormented in this manner and are helped to rise themselves only on the brink of their getting unconscious. Helpless out of fear they keep yelling out "rescue us, Jayanta!" And tortured in this way by Jayanta they get reminded of their past sins.

Jayanta said:

12-16. O unfortunate beings! what could I do? You people have committed such sins which are quite terrible. Fruits of all meritorious deeds can only be earned by a stay at Dvārakā which is good (and that way desirable). It is for sure that there is no sin greater than censure of inhabitants of Dvārakā. One cannot retrieve oneself from such sins as Dvārakā is known as the supreme Goddess. Hence, it is as per the instructions of Kṛṣṇa that I punish such sinners. Due to condemnation of the Vaiṣṇavites, any censurer has to face ferocious consequences. Only after that, a birth heralding well being can occur (for one) at Dvārakā and the resultant attainment of purity and holiness of the highest order by appeasement of Kṛṣṇa which in any case is very difficult to obtain. Hence, one has to suffer the fruits that arise from deprecation of Vaiṣṇavas. The wishes of Yama do not prevail here, but that of Viṣṇu who is the most powerful God.

Śrī Prahlāda said:

17-26. Hence, the leading God, i.e. Viṣṇu needs to be worshipped by visiting Dvārāvat. O Brāhmaṇas! (now) listen to the fruits that come out of donating some wealth religiously after sheltering oneself on the bank of Gomatī. (As you all know) one can reap fruits by making donation of one thousand *karat* gold on Sunday in the name of the Sun. Similarly one does get fruits by donating elephants, horses and chariots at Kurukṣetra. I can tell you about thousand times the fruits of the same and this is an undeniable truth. Donating just half the amount of gold (stated above) fits in well enough to yield the same fruit (i.e. thousand times as stated earlier). O Brāhmaṇas! by worshipping Lord Kṛṣṇa with offering of flowers and food in container of any size, limitless fruits amounting to the innumerable number of grains of boiled/cooked rice in the food so offered result. Brahmā, Śeṣa (an epithet of Viṣṇu) and Maheśvara themselves, have not been able to tell the fruits that result from donating cooked rice at Dvārakā. Any human being—be a Brāhmaṇa, a Kṣatriya, a Vaiśya, a Śūdra or even outside the caste system and a woman—if they reside at Dvārakā with faith, they liberate a crore of their clan members and themselves. They go to the great abode of Viṣṇu. O best Brāhmaṇas! I may repeatedly tell you all that this is the truth. (As you all know) I never tell a lie. By looking at the inhabitants of Dvārakā and especially by touching them, they all (i.e. as specified above) get free from the severest of sins and get entitled for residence in Heaven. Even the dust particles of Dvārakā which flow in the air, throw away the sins. So what to speak about the land of Dvārakā?

Śrī Prahlāda said:

27-50. O the best of Brāhmaṇas! listen to the destructible power of Dvārakā with regard to severe attachments and infatuation. Such greatness of Dvārakā is due to its vicinity to Gomatī and Kṛṣṇa. After taking a revolution of Kuśābatī (i.e. the city known as capital of the kingdom of Rāma's son that is Kuśa) and surpassing the farthest limit of the sea, the divine priest (an epithet for the planet Jupiter) in its transit through the zodiacal sign of Leo passes over this centre of pilgrimage, i.e. Dvārakā. A bath at Gomatī during this juncture yields fruits equivalent to taking bath at Godāvarī for two hundred times. Efforts to dive into Gautamī during this coincidence of Jupiter's transit through Leo are blessed with good fruits by Gautamī. The Brāhmaṇas! the meritorious fruits that result from putting up for a number of years on the banks of Godāvarī, can equally be reaped by service of Gomatī. Taking a bath at Gomatī with faith on the day of transit of Guru, i.e. Jupiter in the zodiac sign of Leo multiplies the bath at Dvārāvat by thousand times. Hence, O the greatly fortunate souls! go to Dvārakā. It has been said that all sins go away by just having a look of it. "Dvārakā is everything". By muttering this while on way towards Dvārakā, it is for sure that one becomes a claimant in his/her share for liberation by the grace of God Kṛṣṇa. Those who remember Dvārakā, the holy Gomatī, Rukmiṇī and Kṛṣṇa everyday with devotion get to enjoy the fruits of Dvārakā. Despite their staying at a distance of thousand *yojanas,* (i.e. eight thousand miles away from Dvārakā) if people keep Dvārakā in their minds (i.e. they give Dvārakā an uppermost place in mind) they get an opportunity to visit Dvārakā and have a look of its lord at some point of time in their life. People get free from all sins. That human society is fortunate where the sanctifying river Gomatī flows. What to speak about those human beings who undertake visits to Dvārakā and have a look of the master/lord/ruler of Dvārakā, i.e. Kṛṣṇa? Sins committed by killing of friends and cows, even Brahmicide, sins yielded by kidnapping others' wives, sins like matricide, patricide and taking away or depriving one of Brahmahood—all such sinners as well as others attended with any other sin of ferocious nature—get rid of all their sins by virtue of having a look of God Kṛṣṇa. Moreover, what use giving discourses of Veda without faith or for that matter of making charity of gold measuring one thousands *karats* at Kurukṣetra on the day of solar eclipse? Similarly of what use making gifts of elephants, horses and chariots, or setting up temples, or for that matter of performance of religious acts/ ceremonies subsequent to realization of desires on one's part? What can be derived by conducting the *Rājasuya yajna* (i.e. the sacrificial fire on the occasion of coronation of a king), the *Aśvamedha yajña* (i.e. the sacrificial fire making offering of horses to fire) and all kinds of *yajñas*? Similarly what fruits can be yielded by serving centres of pilgrimage and by undergoing varieties of penance? What is the need of perseverance for liberation or undergoing the arduous task of meditation or for that matter remaining wholly immersed/engrossed in Yoga if one has got (the opportunity) to take a look of the God of Dvārakā, i.e. Kṛṣṇa. One may listen to the greatness of Dvārakā. In particular, one must remember Lord Kṛṣṇa sitting awake throughout the night in the month of Vaiśākha, i.e. April. Also remembering the God specially in the months of Māgha, i.e. January-Febuary, Phālguna, i.e. February, Caitra, i.e. March and Jyeṣṭha, i.e May is also quite profitable even today from the point of view of reaping goodness/well-being. From evincing generosity to arranging facilities like provision of drinking water in public places, one can make mansion, raised platforms and set up temporary tent houses on the banks of river Gomatī which serve as retiring places or as places of rest for the ascetics. One can restore wells including those having a provision of steps into them and ponds in a dilapidated condition. After placing the idol, one can invoke Lord Viṣṇu into the same by offering luxurious items/ articles. The Brāhmaṇas, listen to the excellent fruits that can be derived from such acts as I am telling. With realization of all wishes in the mind (by such acts) one gets entitled to the favour/blessings of Kṛṣṇa. Enjoying all attachments/ luxuries in successive series in the shining world (such) men get to the abode of Viṣṇu after making their salutations to other gods. Those who place the idol of Viṣṇu made of either wood or stone at Dvārakā, they tend to earn intimacy of Viṣṇu in the three worlds. Sin no more grows in them. Goodness on the other hand enhances in a well-founded manner with them. O Lord! where from such distinguished quality of Dvārakā arise! All of them keep on speaking about such surprisingly unique quality of Dvārakā among holy regions and all centres of pilgrimage.

CHAPTER THIRTY-SIX

Validity of rule governing visit to Dvārakā and a bath in Gomatī

Sūta said:

1. After hearing such words of Prahlāda, Bali who was present in the assembly asked with all curiosity in mind as to how could there be a relatively greater fame of that region, i.e. Dvārakā?

2. After listening to such words of him (i.e. of Bali) Prahlāda himself got full of admiration. Then after conveying his greetings to him, he began to speak with all love.

Prahlāda said:

3-37. On each step of the living being towards the city of Dvārakā, awaits thousands of virtuous fruits. Those who nurture a wish as an attitude to visit Dvārakā, ten thousands of sins committed on their part in previous lives get destroyed. Formidable crimes continue with the beings till they visit Dvārāvat in the Kaliyuga. Even one visiting Cakratīrtha at Dvārakā out of some greed or with lot of impediments on the way or out of conceit and deceit, does not get entry again into material life/existence. Despite his committing excessively formidable crimes in the Kaliyuga if a man, whether a sinner or belonging to the lower varṇa dies at the city of Kṛṣṇa, he never indulges in any sin by just having a look of the (gracious) face of Kṛṣṇa. Kāśī, Avantī and Mathurā rule in the minds of living beings till they happen to see the city known to be reared/protected by Kṛṣṇa. O leader of demons (i.e. Bali)! in cases of those whose life-force exits from their bodies here, re-entry into material life never happens to them till the subsistence of creation for hundreds or crores of years. Opportunity to reside at Dvārakā, having a look of Kṛṣṇa, to take a bath in Gomatī and to have a look of Rukmiṇī is quite difficult to have in the Kaliyuga. While at home, those who always remember the beautiful city of Kṛṣṇa, sins can hardly ever remain with them so long as their life-force remains in body as a resort/ support. O king! cooked rice from those homes is not only unfit for consumption but also rated as non-edible where worship of Keśava is not done. Like the absence of heat with the moon or of coldness with fire, so is the absence of sin with Vaiṣṇavas observing the fasting meant for the eleventh day (of a month). O highly fortunate being (i.e. the king)! there is no *yuga* similar to the Kaliyuga. By remembering Viṣṇu and making *kirtans* addressed to him one can obtain that imperishable position. The husband of Satyabhāmā (i.e. Kṛṣṇa) is present here (i.e. at Dvārakā). The holy Gomatī too flows here. Men can obtain liberation in the Kaliyuga by taking a bath there (in Gomatī). If the twelfth day of a month meant for observance of religious vow called *Trispruśo* coincides with the brighter day of the moon specifically addressed to religious act for Mādhava, there is no more such fortunate occasion for religious observance at Dvārakā than this. By going to the Kṛṣṇa city as the twelfth day meant for observance of *Trispruśo* sets in and by rising to fulfill the duties required in connection with devotion for Hari, a man attains the fruits of *Aśvamedha yajña.* If in a lunar month, days known as Nandā (i.e. the first day in the brighter fortnight of the moon) and Jayā, coincide with Bhadrā (i.e. the day having characteristic of both the seventh and the twelfth day) worship of Kṛṣṇa near Him by fasting and singing, is indeed a difficult/rare fortune for one to have. If the eleventh day sets in as the Moon rises, but the thirteenth day advents as the same day gets over and in between the twelfth day just squeezes in for a short while, then such a twelfth day is usually considered as a full day. *Trispruśo* is the name of such a day which is quite dear to Hari. Fasting for just a single day on this day yields results equal to ten thousand fastings. Sitting awake throughout a night in the worship of Kṛṣṇa yields hundred times of one thousand results. Dancing in admiration of Kṛṣṇa gives crore times of fruits in the Kaliyuga. These fruits are available to the mortals who put up regularly at Dvārakā for having their homes there. So what more to speak about those who remain present in the temple at Dvārakā and that way in the vicinity of Kṛṣṇa? People having their minds vitiated with sins and on whose part sins cannot be thrown out easily either from their words, temperament and over all being together, get free from all these at Dvārāvatī by taking a look of the auspicious face of Kṛṣṇa. O king of demons! men who visit Dvārāvat deserve admiration. Among the centres of pilgrimage this (i.e. Dvārakā) is quite difficult to get. Difficult are also the best mountains. Attainment of the abode of Viṣṇu as well as dwelling at Dvārakā are quite difficult to get in the Kaliyuga. Fruits accruable to donation of crores and thousands of cows as well as to gifting of crores and hundreds of gems can be obtained in the same manner by nearness to Kṛṣṇa. Sins like Brahmicide, etc. get destroyed by entering into its (Dvārakā's) boundary and by a look of it. So who will not like to serve this city of Him (i.e. Kṛṣṇa)? There are stones with imprints/marks of Kṛṣṇa's *cakra,* i.e. the discus here at the confluence spot of Gomatī with the sea. Worship of such stone blesses one with liberation. So who will not like to serve this city of Him, i.e. Kṛṣṇa? The fruits that the Brāhmaṇas get entitled to by a bath in/at Godāvarī during the time when Guru, i.e. Jupiter transits through the Zodiac sign of Siṃha, i.e. Leo, can be had just by a bath in Gomatī in the vicinity of Kṛṣṇa. Remaining present at Dvārakā, if a man drinks the water (of Gomatī) for six months, his body begins to bear marks of *cakra,* i.e. the discus without any doubt. Fruits that result from residing at Kāśī for a time measuring thousand times the sustenance of creation as per Manu can be had equally by a residence for (just) five days at Dvārakā. O the foremost demon! that unfortunate woman's children continue to die till she takes a look of the favourite city of Kṛṣṇa with all devotion during the Kaliyuga. In addition to this they (i.e. such women) do also need to worship Rukmiṇī,

Satyabhāmā, Goddess Jāmbavatī, Mitrabindā, Kālindī, Bhadrā and Nāgrajitī. Thereafter they have to worship Lakṣmaṇā and Vaiṣṇavī—the favourite of Kṛṣṇa. After a sincere worship of all of them as per prescribed procedure, they get the best son. A man remains troubled up with the fear of worldly life as well as with idiocy of break-up of home until he takes a look of Kṛṣṇa's city with devotion in the Kaliyuga. Every place having confluence of rivers with sea does not yield liberation by a bath. Liberation is only possible at the confluence of Jāhnavī with the sea and of Gomatī with the sea. (Liberation is possible) through contact of the body with Gomatī's water at the vicinity of Kṛṣṇa. Master of rivers, i.e. the sea has said, "By taking a look of me after having a bath in Gomatī, m n never get rebirth." An individual meeting death on his way to Dvārakā does not have to enter material life again till the thriving of creation for hundreds and crores of years.

CHAPTER THIRTY-SEVEN

The Ultimate and Eternal Sudarśana Cakra on Stone at Dvārakā

Śrī Prahlāda said:

1-8. "Kṛṣṇa and Kṛṣṇa"—muttering like this, if an outcaste keeps worshipping Kṛṣṇa unfailingly sitting awake throughout the night in the Kaliyuga, he gets the form and appearance of Kṛṣṇa. "Kṛṣṇa and Kṛṣṇa"— one who says, day and night like this persistently in the Kaliyuga, he/she reaps the fruits accruable to performance of thousands of *yajñas* as well as those arising from crore of centres of pilgrimage. If the eleventh day of the Lunar Month has already been completed, but the same somehow lingers into the twelfth day, then such a time is well-known as *unmīlinī* and is considered propitious for pilgrimage. By sitting awake throughout the night in the worship of Kṛṣṇa on the day called *vaṇjulī*, meritorious fruits attended upon performance of thousands of *yajñas* can be had in just half of a moment. If the twelfth day of the lunar month is completed, but somehow extends over to the next thirteenth day, then such a day, the best of sages, is known as *vaṇjulī* which (in any case) is quite difficult to avail in the Kaliyuga. As the religious time known as *unmīlinī* approaches and people observe the same by sitting awake throughout the night (in the worship of Kṛṣṇa) meritorious fruits attended upon gifting of a crore of cows can be availed by them in just half a moment. In a lunar month if after the completion of the eleventh day, the duration of the onward following days keeps increasing either till the new moon day or the full moon day, then such a time is known as the enhanced period in the lunar month. After the coming into being of the enhanced period in the lunar month, those who comply by worshipping Kṛṣṇa by sitting awake throughout the night, they reap the fruits attended upon gifting one crore cows even in half of a half moment.

Śrī Prahlāda said:

9-24. By a bath at Cakratīrtha, a man gets exonerated of all sins. He reaches that supreme place which is free from getting burnt up and destruction. Kṛṣṇa himself had washed his discus there (to clean it after killing the demons). This is how the well-being giving Cakratīrtha sings the glory of supreme Hari. The stones bearing marks of the discus of Viṣṇu there are the givers of liberation. If a stone bearing marks of twelve discuses together is found there it is known as the twelfth Supreme Soul. As a giver of liberation, its glory has been sung vividly. There are also stones at Dvārāvat adored with just a single discus. Called Sudarśana, bestowing one with salvation is its single (i.e. only) fruit. The Stone bearing marks of two discuses is called Lakṣmī-Nārāyaṇa and its fruits are both granting of luxuries and liberation. The stone with marks of three discuses is called Achyuta and it grants one with the position of Indra of heaven. The stone with marks of four discuses is known as Janārdana. It takes away all difficulties and grants one with property. The Stone with marks of five discuses is called Vāsudeva and it throws away fear of life and death. The stone with marks of six discuses is known as Pradyumna and it blesses one with both Lakṣmī, i.e. wealth and a beautiful body. The stone with seven marks of discuses is called Baladeva and it enhances the fame of one's clan. The stone with eight marks of discuses is known as Puruṣottama and it grants fulfillment of all wishes/desires. The stone with nine marks of discus is a giver of everything and even that which is difficult for the best of gods. It is called Navavyuha. The stone with marks of ten discuses grants one with kingdom and is known to represent the tenth incarnation of God Kṛṣṇa. The stone bearing eleven marks of discuses is known as Aniruddha and it grants one with supemacy of power. The stone bearing twelve marks of discus is known to represent the twelfth Supreme Soul and grants one with salvation. The stone bearing marks of higher number of discuses in comparison to all these is usually referred as 'limitless' and it grants one with both happiness and liberation. Stones to be found anywhere here, but bearing marks of discuses like coins on them, make one free from all sins by just touching them. All sins like Brahmicide, etc. as well as those earned intentionally (by actions) and by words get obsolete by a sincere worship of the stones bearing marks of discuses like pictures engraved on them. Wherever in the region/country inhabited by the outcastes, the stone bearing imprint of the God's auspicious discus is found, that region becomes the God's lovely region upto twelve *yojanas*, (i.e. upto about ninety-six miles in its stretch/expanse/ territory). One who bears this (i.e. the discus-marked stone) on chest as the time of death approaches, the stone bearing imprints of discus crushes one's sins and he gets himself on the way towards ultimate passage. By taking a bath in the spot of confluence of Gomatī with the sea as well as at Bhṛgu

Tīrtha one does not come again in a mother's womb despite being a sinner. Despite having a vicious nature or a passionate nature, with the very act of worship of Viṣṇu, virtue essentially penetrates the interior being of an individual like the lower portion of an afloat object remains submerged in water.

CHAPTER THIRTY-EIGHT

Eminence of sitting awake throughout the night at Cakratīrtha on the banks of Gomatī

Śrī Prahlāda said:

1-46. O grandson! listen to the greatness of Dvārakā as I bring it to light. It is certain that liberation materializes for one by the grace of Kṛṣṇa by listening to it or by speaking about it. A man feels honoured by having a son. Grandchild causes limitless happiness for him. Hence, with son and grandson he gets opportunity to ascend onto heaven. A son adept in good qualities, well into observance of religious righteousness since an early age in life and performing duties in consonance with devotion for Viṣṇu is always considered to remain in the forehead as a son. He continuously makes gift of the Kapilā cow with its horns decked up with gold, its hooves adorned with silver, its milk collected in a bronze bucket and the same cow having a calf. Fruits that are reaped by gifting of cow in this manner to the learned Brāhmaṇas, can equally be yielded by having a bath in the pure water of Gomatī. One can feed barley to the Brāhmaṇas staying at Dvārakā. O the best of Brāhmaṇas! fruits multiply by one lakh times by such good alms. It has also been stated that fruits grow by one lakh times by feeding Brāhmaṇas in the time of drought in the vicinity of Kṛṣṇa. Thus, one needs to offer alms to those seeking for it in conformity with religious *dharma,* i.e. duty. Will there be a virtuous man born in your clan who can feed the ascetics for the purpose of contentment of forefathers in the Kaliyuga ? Can there be anyone—who for the sake of good deeds especially at Dvārakā in the vicinity of Kṛṣṇa—to give cooked rice to the ascetics and gift them with clothes to cover up their bodies including private parts of the body? Neither on part of yourself have you at all done any pilgrimage nor is there any one in your family who can be regarded as good enough to fulfill the necessity of pilgrimage. Either here or there, pleasing the ascetics (therefore) is always your duty. Even the outcastes have become fortunate by going to the city of Dvārakā. After availing for themselves a sight of Bhāgavat, they have also, as part of their duties as sons, performed the religious act in honour of their forefathers. They worship with all devotion as well as by making gifts of clothes and other donations in plenty. (The Forefathers have happened to say) "we do not get the same satisfaction by offering balls of cooked rice in *śrāddha* at Gayā as the genuine motivation behind worship of Viṣṇu gives rise to." People observe the religious activities required for the twelfth day in the month of Vaiśākha, i.e. April in the proximity of Kṛṣṇa by sitting awake throughout the night in the worship of Kṛṣṇa. As far as possible it is desirable to read the great accounts of Dvārakā which is quite auspicious. Also one needs to read the childhood accounts of Kṛṣṇa and take a look of Kṛṣṇa in the form of a child. One must also listen to the playful pastimes of Kṛṣṇa both at Gokula* as well as with the mistresses of cowherds. Acts of Kṛṣṇa in His several incarnations are also worthy of listening once and again. Give a cow already having calf to the Brāhmaṇa required as an offering to the sacrificial fire. The cow must be decked up with gold in its horns while its hooves and tail need to be adorned respectively with silver and pearls. Fruit of the religious act of sitting awake throughout the night in the worship of Kṛṣṇa can be derived by just touching a part of the idol of Kṛṣṇa for a fraction of moment. Sins committed and accumulated to whatever extent by a

* Name of the village where Kṛṣṇa was reared.

human being spanning crores of birth, get burnt up beyond any doubt by sitting up awake throughout the night in worship of Kṛṣṇa. Those who read the Bhāgavat Purāṇa— a favourite of Kṛṣṇa at night they will reside at heaven till the sun shines and the moon beautifies the night and till the seas, the earth and mountains of high standing continue to exist. There will be nothing otherwise to this as I say. Hearing and seeing their own son to be engaged in worship of Kṛṣṇa as far as possible, forefathers appear to bloom forth before one and grandfathers of one become very delighted. Sanctity forsakes that place/region like that of the region inhabited by outcastes, where the accounts of greatness of Dvārakā are not read out and where sitting awake throughout the night in the worship of Kṛṣṇa is never done. Give up that house, even that highly well-being - causing place of pilgrimage and that auspicious temple where there is no stone known as Śāligrāma (i.e. the stone from which the evenly-levelled statue of Viṣṇu is made) or no devotee for Bhāgavat. So also give up that particular home as well as the forest where activity required in connection with the religious observance of the twelfth day of the month specifically addressed to Kṛṣṇa is not undertaken. That country having a good name for itself becomes a matter of depreciation for its inhabitants not observing religious vow(s) addressed to Viṣṇu. On the other hand, a country having a bad name gets holier for promoting Bhāgavat (i.e. devotion towards Viṣṇu) in the Kaliyuga. One born in a caste with limitations gets purified by becoming a devotee of Madhusūdana, while one hailing from a higher caste is like an outcaste if he does not have devotion in Janārdana. After putting (the idol of) Madhu Mādhava on a chariot, those who pull it, they obtain liberation along with crore of members of their clan. Those who make themselves the prisoners of the chariot meant for the son of Devakī, i.e. Kṛṣṇa, they happen to reside in the abode of Viṣṇu along with their forefathers till the exhaustion of the measured time of creation. Listening to the greatness of Dvārakā in the Kaliyuga evokes the motivation for attendant i.e. complementary action in men by which they reap hundreds of fruits. The sinners usually head towards some other place without worshipping the God, i.e. Viṣṇu. In such cases, virtues earned on their part through a crore of earlier births, are usually taken away by the husband of Rukmiṇī. The king of demons! listen to the fruits I am describing, that arise from people always putting/bearing a mark made out of the earth of place of the pilgrimage known as *śaṅkhodhāra* on their bodies. Any human being who gives/ distributes the earth of the same centre of pilgrimage to ascetics and the Vaiṣṇavas to put on as an auspicious mark on their forehead, he gets fruits equal to one hundred karats of gold. A human being in whose house the earth of Śaṅkhodhāra Tīrtha is always present, i.e. found, virtues integral/inherent to his daily deeds get multiplied by a crore times. He, whose forehead always bears the mark made of the particular type of sandalwood called *Gopīcandana*, Lakṣmī—the favourite of Kṛṣṇa never deserts his home. Neither there will be any hurdle (on the path of such an individual whose forehead is always beautified with the mark made of *Gopīcandana*) from planets, by diseases and demons. He will not also have to bother about ghosts, spirits, the demon called Jambha and about boils/eruptions on his skin. Neither he will have fear of fire and thieves. He will also remain free from the fear of enslavement of beautiful women. He will also not have the fear of unforseen circumstances that may arise in the wake of lightning and falling of shooting stars. He will also not have the fear of misfortune, of anything that may be injurious/harmful and of anything that can have causeless/unreasonable foundation to affect him for his good act underlying devotion for Viṣṇu and worship of the Śāligrāma stone. O intelligent man! by drinking the water offered at the feet (of Viṣṇu), by eating the food offered in worship of Him and by leaving the water offered to Viṣṇu at the time of His worship near the basil plant, all bad acts of an individual get obsolete. Listen to what the God Himself has stated earlier about the individual worthy of His grace as a favourite of Him. He has said, "I am a servant of him for whom Bhāgavat is lovingly dear. Mathurā, Kāśī, Avantī, Māyāpurī, Kāñcī and Ayodhyā enable one to get rid of all sins and with the arrival of Kaliyuga, I have begun to put up at Dvārakā with all my attendants/followers. Through pilgrimage at Dvārakā, by observance of *vrata* (i.e. religious vow), through knowledge, charities, by pleasing Rūdra and utterances of words of Veda as per the rendering of the best sages, through faith, sacrifice and devotion, everyone there (i.e. at Dvārakā) strives/wishes to earn my pleasure/appeasement. It is desirable on the part of everyone to have a look of mine in the Kaliyuga by undergoing the necessary visits to the beautiful Dvārāvatī. By purifying fully all the existing centres of pilgrimage in the three worlds, I have established the holy Cakratīrtha near Gomatī. Just a single day's bath here in the Cakratīrtha on the banks of Gomatī entitles one to have the well-being that results from taking bath successively in all centres of pilgrimage in the three worlds. A man doing so (i.e. taking a bath at Cakratīrtha) gets free from crore of sins on his part and lives like me in my abode. (Not only he) crore of members in his clan get entitled to the same beyond any doubt. He does not commit crimes nor does he involve himself in sin of terrible nature. Lakṣmī happens to stay in his house spanning hundreds and thousands of his rebirth."

CHAPTER THIRTY-NINE

The eminence of religious vow (vrata) of the twelfth Day

Śrī Prahlāda said:

1-14. Anniversaries like Jayā and Vijayā and observance of religious rituals meant for *vratas* like *banjulī* and *unmīlinī* called *Trispruśo* falling on the eleventh day of the brighter fortnight of the moon are destroyers of sins. Those people earn the merits as laid down in all the Purāṇas if they eat the rice cooked with ghee everyday. One needs to offer food cooked with *ghee* and wave the lighted earthen lamps full of *ghee* before the God to worship Padmanābha (an epithet of Viṣṇu) by sitting awake throughout the night. To perform the worship of Viṣṇu by staying up awake throughout the night one needs to do so before the Śāligrāma stone. Hence, it is desirable that one does so before the idol of Viṣṇu made of Śāligrāma stone. People can dance, play musical instruments, put colours on one another and cover the Śāligrāma stone with flowers. In particular, Brāhmaṇas can offer the idol of Viṣṇu bearing the mark of discus with sandalwood paste, camphor and the perfume made out of the wood called *agar.* Then after preparing a paste by mixing the sandalwood known as *Gopīcandana* with the scented substance called *kastūrī* (which generally emits from the navel of the deer so-called) and by applying it on the idol, the religious observance of the twelfth day of the month addressed to Kṛṣṇa can bc complied with. Let me tell you in brief about its fruits. Its fruits are the same as that of the temple at Ujjainī which assembles together the virtues obtainable at crores of centres of pilgrimage. The fruits obtainable at Vārāṇasī, Kurukṣetra, Mathurā, Tripuṣkara, Ayodhyā, Prayāga and at all those places of pilgrimage located on the confluences of rivers with sea, all the well-being reaped by performance of *yajñas,* observance of thousands of *vratas* and by plenty of charities at all the holy centres of pilgrimage as well as at temples, virtues acquired by reading of the Veda as well as a deeper understanding of Purāṇas, by undergoing penance, by following the four-stage *āśrama* system—fruits, O son! stated to be integral to all these by the sages and Vedavyāsa—can similarly be had by sitting awake throughout the night in the worship of Kṛṣṇa in the brighter period of the lunar month. In olden time, the God known to be related to the snow-covered Kailāsa mountain and the bearer of the trident in hand (i.e. Śiva) had happened to tell Nārada near Brahmā "that in olden time when asked, Arūṇa (i.e. Sun) had told the bearer of thunderbolt (i.e. Indra) that Brāhmaṇas can derive fruits by sitting awake throughout the night in the worship of Kṛṣṇa on the twelfth day (of the brighter period of Moon). I had made the same such statement. Hence, all the Brāhmaṇas must sit awake throughout the night to perform *yajña* on the day specially meant for Viṣṇu."

Sūta said:

15-48. After saying like this to the Brāhmaṇas, Prahlāda then told his grandson Bali that he should also perform the very act of sitting awake throughout the night with all reverence in the worship of Hari. By bearing Dvārakā in mind and through Kīrtans there, sins brought upon one through one hundred births and all sins having risen their heads over one hundred births, get burnt up without any doubt. Sins that have raised their heads over a thousand of births just go away by taking a single step towards Dvārakā. With the taking away of sins by Dvārakā, one certainly attains liberation by virtue of taking a look of Kṛṣṇa. If a man cannot go to Dvārakā, he better reads the account of its greatness as far as possible at home. As making of gifts to the Vaiṣṇavas is desirable, so is the listening of the greatness of Dvārakā with due devotion. Specially it is necessary to read the same while sitting up awake throughout the night meant for the twelfth day in worship of Viṣṇu. By this a man obtains the good fruits as obtained at Dvārakā out of the grace of Vāsudeva. This is the truth. O grandson! Mathurā, Dvārakā, Avantī, Māyāpurī, Prayāga, Kurukṣetra, Tripuṣkara, Naimiṣa, Gaṅgādvāra (i.e. Haridvāra), Śaṅkara, Candreśa, Kedāra, the Rūdra great temple, Vastrāpatha, Mahādeva, Mahākāla, Bhūteśvara, Bhasmagātra, Somanātha—the husband of Umā, Koṭiliṅga, Trinetra, Bhṛguvanecaram, Dīpeśvara, Mahānāda, the God Acaleśvara, and Gods like Brahmā, etc. remain ever present in his house who observes the eighth day of the waning period of the moon in the month of Bhādra, i.e. September which is generally referred to as the birthday of Kṛṣṇa. Besides all of these, one's forefathers, the community of Nāgas, Gandharvas, sages, practitioners in the pursuit of siddha, i.e. accomplishment, all centres of pilgrimage here and there and yajñas like Aśvamedha, etc. remain present in his house who particularly observes the Kṛṣṇa Janmāṣṭamī (i.e. the eighth day of the waning period of the moon in the month of Bhādra i.e. September). Like the Bhāgavat Śāstra is the devotee in Bhāgavat. There is no difference between the two like that of Hari and Hara. Like by going to a savage, i.e. an untamed area one has to eat radish, so one involved in barbaric activities cannot have respite from hell irrespective of the fact of creation lasting for hundred or a crore of years. If a Brāhmaṇa, infatuated with greed does degraded acts he cannot reap the fruits for whatever good deeds, he might have done. No one will be there to buy his arguments however loudly he may put them across. The universal Self does not get pleased by offending the Vaiṣṇavas. If one cuts down one peepal tree each as per the series of religious festivals, he remains in the terrible hell known as *rourava* even after the completion of time-period of creation as per estimation of Manu. O king of demons! even if one performs the act of worship with a broken/impaired piece of wood at any point of time, Bhāskara (i.e. Sun) does not accept his worship and the offerings made during worship. O demon! if one cuts down the *arka* tree he remains poor and diseased for one hundred (re)births. That best man who plants a sunplant and nourishes it further, he remains in the proximity of Bhāskara for a period spanning seven creations. The fruits that are associated with planting of a lakh and crore of heavenly plants can be had by just planting of one peepal tree. Similar fruits also accrue by planting a gooseberry tree. Comparatively surprising to this is the planting of basil which gives more results. Those who do so attain immortality. Hence, there is no need for considering any other action. After getting up in the morning, one who makes prayers addressing the glory of Dvārakā in the Kaliyuga, he gets free from all sins and goes to heaven beyond any doubt. He who has not observed the twelfth day of the month of Śrāvaṇa having togetherness with the star Rohiṇī, he remains enjoined with great sins and gets heaven only after the completion of the time-period of creation. Without the sun, days cannot be possible and without the moon, the nights. Is it ever possible to have a village without trees? So, how can observance of any religious vow be possible without the twelfth day of the month addressed to worship of Kṛṣṇa? His house is similar to hell and is like a second abode penalised with the punishment of Yama where the *śāstra* containing one thousand names of Viṣṇu is never read out. That hell-like house of him is the second place being ruled over by Yama where Bhāgvat Purāṇa is not sung in the Kaliyuga. Getting burnt up in fire, such houses get dumped in dark well. Those who nurture disinterest in or disregard for Bhāgavat and those houses where the accounts of Hari are not read out everyday, are always taken away by the attendants/messengers of Yama and these people keep repeatedly coming back to the earth (i.e. they get rebirths once and again). Those who do not listen to the accounts of Hari's character, they get terribly tortured as if being cut into pieces by saw under the impact of Yama's rule. Those evil-minded who always deprecate the great-minded Vaiṣṇavas, they remain dumped in Hell till the final deluge, i.e. the final dissolution of creation. Relatively greater results are obtainable by having a look of the earth, i.e. sandalwood here called *Gopīcandana* than that of baths at crores of Gotīrtha. Fruits associated with a bath at Gaṅgā result beyond doubt for them by this sight. Those who offer paste of sandalwood known as *Gopīcandana* to Vaiṣṇavas or as far as possible bear a mark made of the paste of *Gopīcandana* on their foreheads, or those who sit up awake throughout the night on the twelfth day in the worship of Viṣṇu with a mark made of paste of *Gopicandana* on their foreheads and read the *śāstra* containing one thousand names of Viṣṇu—all such people attain liberation. After getting up in the morning, those who regularly do prayers singing the glory of Vaiṣṇavas as well as remember the Gomatī, they obtain the position that can be comparable to Kṛṣṇa Himself. There can be no doubt about this. After getting up in the morning, those who regularly mutter the word Dvārakā within they derive the well-being that results from undergoing a crore of pilgrimage per day.

CHAPTER FORTY

Virtue of bath, charity and *śrāddha* at Cakratiīrtha during the month of Kārtika

Śrī Prahlāda said:

1-28. By worshipping Śrīpati, i.e. the Lord of prosperity i.e. Śrī Kṛṣṇa with leaves bearing markings of names of God, one gets seven worlds and becomes a sovereign of seven islands. By worshipping Hari regularly with *bel* leaves (i.e. leaves of wood apple) one earns the fruits of well-being equal to that of ten thousand Aśvamedha *yajñas* in the Kaliyuga. By worshipping Lakṣmī, Sarasvatī and equally the Goddesses Sāvitrī and Caṇḍikā with *bel* leaves as far as possible one goes to heaven. The impact of *bel* leaves has been stated to be more than that of basil leaves. Hence, Acyuta (an epithet of Viṣṇu) needs to be worshipped with *bel* leaves with all sincere efforts. If on the twelfth day falling on a Sunday people worship the *bel* tree, they get free from the sin of Brahmicide, etc. which they might have committed or have indulged themselves in. As other feet get assimilated in the feet of a very big elephant, so all well-being earned get merged in the day, i.e. the twelfth day of the month addressed to Hari.

When decay lurks every moment in the transitory body then why should living beings not observe the twelfth day sitting awake throughout the night in the worship of Śrī Kṛṣṇa? The previous seven generations in a man's family as well as his fourteen future generations successfully tide over the hell by his singing the prayer addressed to Kṛṣṇa. They never come back to life again here and there wherever the human species are (stated to be) present/found. Those people who put up at Dvārakā (and visit the Kṛṣṇa temple regularly there) they are usually admired in the three worlds. Those who make shelters for ascetics at Dvārakā and give them food, they reap fruits equalling that yielded by performance of one hundred *yajñas*, on every mouthful of food so offered. O king of demons! listen to the fruits of well-being that result by making presents of clothes which include that of both the inner and outer garments to the ascetics and by feeding them as per one's capability, which I am narrating in brief. The fruits that people having love and affection for their fathers, reap by feeding crore of learned Brāhmaṇas in Veda at Gayā, can be obtained by feeding just one ascetic at Dvārakā. The grandson, just feeding one monk here induces this kind of result even if one has to sell oneself to give cooked rice to him. O the king of demons! fortunate are all those ascetics who having taken resort of Kṛṣṇa have been putting up on a regular basis at Dvārakā in the Kaliyuga. If the mortal beings go near Kṛṣṇa at Dvārakā, despite their being sinners, they obtain that ultimate position after piercing through the solar system. All those best of men who happen to dwell at Cakratīrtha at Dvārakā can be presumed to have found the preventive remedy of keeping the attendants of Yama at bay. To say anything about them who after a bath at Gomatī, take a look of Kṛṣṇa—the snatcher of all dirt of the Kaliyuga—is beyond our imagination. Even insects, grasshoppers and trees which have made their shelters there (at Dvārakā) go to the abode of Kṛṣṇa and hardly ever return again to the worldly life/existence. So, what is the need of describing about the Brāhmaṇa and the Kṣatriya varṇas in particular? Even the Śūdras stipulated to be engaged in the service of the other three varṇas higher to it in the *varṇa* system get freedom from their handicaps there (by having a look of Kṛṣṇa at Dvārakā). With food for only one time at night and with full awareness of their purpose, the Brāhmaṇas who read the Gitā before Kṛṣṇa for the entire month of Kārtika (i.e. October-November) and observe the quite difficult *cāndrāyaṇa* vrata for three nights or taking barley as food, do arduous perseverance for half of the period of lunar month or observing the month-long vrata for Kārtika month (i.e. October-November) take bath in the water of Gomatī as well as that of the Rukmiṇī lake—all such followers bearing conch, chakra (i.e. the discus) and mace in hands assume form and appearance like that of Kṛṣṇa for they observe the fasting meant for the eleventh day which, as it is, is quite clear of any remnant influences/affectations characteristics of the tenth day. Those who perform the *śrāddha* on the twelfth day at the sacred Cakratīrtha and offer honey, *pāyas* (i.e. a pooding of rice boiled in milk with addition of sugar) and melted *ghee* as food to Brāhmaṇas and please them as per followed practice with due reverence and with religious fee as per ability which may include gifting of cows, land, deer, clothes, betel leaves with areca nuts, fruits, footwear, umbrella white in colour like flowers, earthen pots full of water, cooked food along with fresh fruits, etc., they are sure to earn for themselves the pleasure of forefathers like Mārkaṇḍeya as they fulfill the duty of observance of religious vow meant for the month of Kārtika addressed to the worship of Kṛṣṇa with all sincerity. Earning the imperishable satisfaction of Kṛṣṇa as well as of all gods in the three directions can be possible by such acts. Attended with observance of vrata (i.e. the religious vow) and making charities, those virtuous men who stay here at this Rathāṅga Tīrtha (i.e. an epithet for Cakratīrtha) for the entire month of Kārtika and after purification of their bodies by a bath here and by singing *ślokas* perform their *vrata*, they obtain that position of virtue free from any sign of decay.

CHAPTER FORTY-ONE

Virtuous fruits of bath in Gomatī, worship of Kṛṣṇa, śrāddha and offering of food and charities to ascetics

Śrī Prahlāda said:

1-14. Fortunate are the people in the human world who get the opportunity to take a bath in the Gomatī and thereafter follow it up with worship of Kṛṣṇa with *ketakī* flowers and basil leaves. People who do so, do not enter the terrible worldly life again. They do not die again for they seem to have already attained the path of immortality. Fruits which are obtainable by doing good to a crore of ascetics in other places can be had by just offering food to only one monk at Dvārakā. All sins of the past, the present as well as for the future simply get burnt up by remembering Dvārakā with all intent of mind. Aware of the fact fully that pain/difficulty would be the order of the day during the fierce Kaliyuga solely due to people's ignorance/lack of understanding, the best of men do not give up Dvārakā with the full conviction that they would be rewarded for such good action on their part. Even the animals dying here continue to always remain present here in this island known after the God—bearer of conch, as the *śveta* island. The sacrificial fire after getting blown out by the wind from outside as well as those feeding on melted ghee, the drinkers of Soma, i.e. the drink of gods and one's forefathers spanning twenty-one generations—put up at Dvārakā. Places of pilgrimage like Puṣkara, etc. rivers like Gaṅgā, holy regions like Kurukṣetra, such regions like Kāśī where no sin can germinate (i.e. it operates as a saline ground for sins to sprout), centres of pilgrimage identified as fit places for performance of *śrāddha* in memory of one's forefathers such as Gayā and other holy centres like Prabhāsa and many other holy villages also remain present here, i.e. at Dvārakā.

Holy cities like Kāśī which could not get obsolete in the Kaliyuga, remains always present here in the temple of Kṛṣṇa always granting liberation to the sinners. O foremost among the demons! sitting awake in the night on the twelfth day of the brighter fortnight of the moon in the month of Vaiśākha, i.e. April in the worship of Kṛṣṇa surpasses all fruits that can be imagined for the time the Creation lasts encompassing different *yugas*. O leader of demons! such fruits are also obtainable without any doubt by worship of Kṛṣṇa at Dvārakā during the period of solar and lunar eclipses as well as on that specific auspicious day as per estimation of Manu and his (fourteen) descendents. Especially one may adopt himself to worship the Lord on the day of *saṅkrānti* (i.e. the specific day of the month when the Sun transits from one zodiac sign to another) which is stated to be marked with difficulty/disfavour. Making devoted offering of sesame and of libations of water to one's forefathers here preceded with a bath at Gomatī have been stated to yield undecaying happiness/appeasement for them. Those who do *śrāddha* for their forefathers by offering balls of cooked rice in front of the pool of water here, they (certainly) help generating undecaying satisfaction for them.

CHAPTER FORTY-TWO

To donate bull and listen to the greatness of Dvārakā

Prahlāda said:

1-33. Those who donate bulls here either in the months of Vaiśākha (i.e. April) and Kārtika (i.e. October-November) their grandfathers, if at all gone to the state of ghosthood, get free from the same out of influence of Dvārakā. Brahmicide, drinking of liquor, theft, outraging the modesty of teacher's daughters—all such sins as provided in the rule of law and even sins greater than these, and committed for hundred and crore of times in the span of creation, get obsolete, O king of demons! by just a bath in Gomatī and having a look of Kṛṣṇa. If men in the Kaliyuga take a devoted look of Rukmiṇī and thereafter taking repeated rounds of the city mutter the thousand names of Viṣṇu, such taking rounds by them of the city can undoubtedly be taken for as their having taken round of the entire cosmos. Fruits of great charities as have been sung for being made in places other than Dvārakā can simply be made for by having a look of Rukmiṇī and as a result of the impact of Dvārakā. There is a greater side to the reading of *śāstra* dealing with Viṣṇu near Him as the twelfth day approaches. Listen, I am describing the fruits of the same. With his actions getting to rule over everyone in the world, he gets carried by a lotus-coloured chariot decked up with chains of ringing bells. The chariot gets pulled by robust horses white in colour. He gets to have his happiness as per own desire. He happens to remain engaged in merriments with the divine beauties till the unprecedented final deluge, i.e. destruction of creation. They (such people) remain fortunate in creation lasting for crore of years. Like fire becoming visible through friction of two pieces of wood so also radiance shines on the man observing the twelfth day meant for worship of Kṛṣṇa. Now Bali, let me tell you the precious wish of forefathers in this regard. It has always been their wish if they could be blessed with a son in their family who after taking a bath in Gomatī with faith would perform *śrāddha* for them with due offering of balls of cooked rice. Similarly it is also their constant wish if a son could be born in their family who would always observe the practice of taking a bath at the spot of confluence of Gomatī with the sea and thereafter take a look of Kṛṣṇa for their emancipation. It is also their wish if there is (or will be) anyone in their family who would have the earnest urge to listen to the greatness of Dvārakā from the mouths of Brāhmaṇas and accordingly worship Dvārakā with devotion. They also wish if there is the possibility of any son in their family who would go to the city of Dvārakā and would sit awake throughout the night in the worship of Kṛṣṇa as the holy twelfth day comes. In a similar vein they do wish for either a son or a daughter in the family to mutter and read the book containing one thousand names of Viṣṇu before Kṛṣṇa. They wish if it will be possible in their family to have one member who, as a follower of religious vow, will please the Vaiṣṇavas by gifting sandalwood known as *Gopīcandana*. They think if there is someone in the family who can have victory over his senses and will read out the greatness of Dvārakā near the Vaiṣṇavas. Similarly for them it is a desirable wish if there will be someone in the family who will write down the greatness of Dvārakā as it unfolds in course of time and make the flow of the same trickle down to his own house for appeasement of Kṛṣṇa. It is because one has enabled trickling down of the greatness of Dvārakā to the four corners of his house in the Kaliyuga he/she has equally availed the benefits of making donations of gold, cows and land. A living being can be understood to have undergone very difficult and arduous penance as well as to have observed fasting for a month by his listening to the accounts of greatness of Dvārakā in the Kaliyuga. He can be presumed to have undergone repentance as a means of destruction of sins by canvassing about the greatness of Dvārakā here and there, in the Kaliyuga. Sins of Brahmicide, etc. persist with man till he happens to write down the greatness of Dvārakā. What utility, making charities as well as taking bath at all centres of pilgrimage can have for one who has happened to inscribe the greatness of Dvārakā on the walls of his house? Adding onto the faith in Hari (on part of one) everyday acts as an alleviator of all sorrows and giver of accomplishment/achievement to everyone in the four-fold-*varṇa* system. He will not have any sort of mental and physical worry. He will certainly have nothing to fear about Yama, for reading about the greatness of Dvārakā in Dvārakā itself induces such results. The very centre of pilgrimage of Dvārakā happens to remain always present in that house with its walls bearing inscriptions of its greatness. Listening to the greatness of Dvārakā is itself a powerful means to give effect to such a distinctive mark to one's house. Lord Keśava also acknowledges his worship done without observance of any specific attendant rule, mantra and ritual if the greatness of Dvārakā is always written on the walls of his house. Despite his coming into worldly life (i.e. rebirths) for thousand times, such a man never indulges himself in any unbecoming acts/deeds. By his reading or listening to the greatness that germinates from Dvārakā, one does not get upset with any untoward thought about defects or imperfections about his past nor does his mind get agitated over the point that Dharma, i.e. righteousness has lost its hold. One who, after getting up in the morning, reads the accounts related to greatness that arises from Dvārakā, reaps all those fruits which have been stated to dawn on everyone out of the observance of the twelfth day stipulated for worship of Lord Kṛṣṇa. Gods from the three (i.e. all) directions as well as those persistently engaged in the pathways towards perfection/accomplishment salute those who read the greatness that evolves out of Dvārakā. The eternal Viṣṇu dwells there wherever Dvārakā may be. All centres of pilgrimage including all gods besides Indra remain present there. All *yajñas*, the Vedas, the sages, even the three worlds encompassing both the mobile and immobile, abide there. O Son! if a man is not able to visit Dvārakā, he can derive the virtue integral to taking a look of Kṛṣṇa by reading the greatness of Dvārakā. All his qualities, viz. truthfulness, purity, knowledge of *śāstras*, wealth, good conduct and forbearance become futile if one has not listened to the accounts of greatness of Dvārakā. A son gets born in six months in his family and Lakṣmī, i.e. the Goddess of wealth gets magnified in his house who listens to the accounts of greatness of Dvārakā with all faith and devotion.

CHAPTER FORTY-THREE

Giving ear to Dvārakā's greatness and eminence of basil wood— the message of Prahlāda

Prahlāda said:

1-21. One having a genuine wish towards attainment/ fulfillment of his desires needs to worship Sāvitrī, Bhavānī, Durgā and Sarasvatī, with basil leaves. It is desirable to worship Viṣṇu with basil leaves in hands. All gods, demons and human beings get worshipped equally by such act of worship. Maheśa is to be worshipped on the fourteenth day of the brighter half of lunar month while the grandfather God, i.e. Brahmā and Gaṇapati are to be worshipped respectively on the full-moon day and on the seventh day of the brighter half of moon. Water offered in a conch during worship is considered more exalted than that of the water of the leading centre of pilgrimage. So is the water offered at the feet of God which is considered to be relatively higher than the best of the centres of pilgrimage. The food left-over from that offered to God in the act of worship is considered similar to performance of a crore of *yajñas.* The left-over flowers from those offered to God in worship (i.e. Nirmālya) which are but naturally waned out in freshness are considered comparable to charities made as part of the observance of *vrata,* i.e. religious vow. If one takes the left-over boiled rice offered to Mukunda (an epithet of Viṣṇu) in the very act of worship everyday, he/she derives merits more than that made for through observance of one hundred *candrāyaṇa vrata.* If a man takes the left-over food offered to Murāri (an epithet of Kṛṣṇa) after adding basil leaves and the water, in particular, offered at the feet of Viṣṇu, he obtains meritorious fruits equal to that made for by performance of a crore of *yajñas.* He who, during the time of performing *śrāddha* offers, the remaining portion of balls of cooked rice made to Hari, to his divine forefathers with due faith after adding sesame to it, his forefathers remain contented for the period of creation lasting crore of years. At the time of performing the act of bathing the idol of God and its worship, he who rings bells before the God, obtains the fruits similar to that made for by gifting crores of cows to Vāsudeva. All instruments of music bringing out sounds of tingling bells are always dear to Keśava. By making bells to ring, a man earns fruits of a crore of *yajñas.* It is the desirable duty on the part of all men to ring bells, if there is a paucity of music at the time of worship of God, for the tingling sounds of a bell accommodate/inhere all music. One who offers basilwood to Hari after applying a paste of sandalwood on it, he burns up hundreds of sins committed in previous births. Even offering of basil wood applied with paste of sandalwood along with balls of cooked rice in performing *śrāddha* makes one's forefathers satisfied in the same way like the one conducted at Gayā. Basilwood with paste of sandalwood is a favourite of all gods. Particularly in the Kaliyuga, it is dearest to Hari and the forefathers. While claiming themselves to be devotees of Hari and believers in Bhāgavat, those who do not always offer basilwood with paste of sandalwood to Viṣṇu, cannot be taken for as such during the Kaliyuga. A body put on fire of pyre made of basilwood with application of sandalwood paste (after death) if taken by Yama, also goes to the abode of Viṣṇu. If there is just one piece of basilwood with applied paste of sandalwood on it amidst the pile of wood in the funeral pyre, the same dead soul gets free from crores, hundreds and thousands of sins while the dead body is in the very process of burning. If one happens to witness the human body burning on the funeral pyre having basilwood applied with paste of sandalwood,he/she can be assumed to have pleased Janārdana (an epithet of Viṣṇu) for hundred and crores of times of his/her cycle of birth. Witnessing human beings burning on the funeral pyre made of basilwood with applied paste of sandalwood, the gods seated on aerial vehicle and carrying flowers in their palms joined together in shape of cups, appear to shower those on them. O king of demons! divine beauties dance and sing with a melodious voice where the holy basil wood is put on fire. And Viṣṇu along with Śambhu remain pleased to have a look of them. Śourie (an epithet of Viṣṇu) holds that man by hand and proceeds ahead. And under the watchful eyes of Gods, he (i.e. Viṣṇu) cleanses all his sins. The gods celebrate greatly by sounding "hail you and victory to you".

Sūta said:

22-26. Hearing about the greatness of Dvārakā brought to light before them by Prahlāda—all the sages as well as Bali, the master of demons, became very happy. Then they all greeted Prahlāda—the leader of the demons. With all intention to have a look of the lotus-face of Kṛṣṇa, they began their journey towards Dvārakā. Then with king Bali all the sages who were minute observers of religious vows, i.e. *vratas*, after reaching Dvārakā performed the ritual of bathing at Gomatī as per due procedure. They followed up their visit to Dvārakā as per rules by having a look of Kṛṣṇa and His worship. They also made plenty of charities there and felt themselves to have been gratified by that. Then they got back to their own homes. Bali returned to his own world underneath the surface of earth. On their part, they felt themselves to be gratified by saluting Prahlāda.

CHAPTER FORTY-FOUR

The Skanda Mahāpurāṇa—virtues of its listening to, reading, gifting and worship of Vyāsa.

Sūta said:

1-21. This is how Skanda had deciphered this Purāṇa in olden time. Bhṛgu—the son of Brahmā learnt it from him, who in turn had passed it on to Angirā. The sage Cyavana learnt it from Angirā and through him other sages got acquainted with it. In this way, the code of the Purāṇa percolated down and got delivered amongst all in the general public of the world. Kumāra, i.e. Kārtikeya had laid bare the complete summary of Skanda Purāṇa. Listening to it in a religious assembly relieves a man of his sins. (Further) age gets added to one's life by listening to it. This Purāṇa accords happiness to everyone in the four-fold *varṇa* system for its contents have been discernably laid down by the good and great soul Ṣaṇmukha, i.e. Skanda. This glorified account as has been brought home by Skanda induces welfare of everyone. The virtuous fruits that result on the part of one by reading or listening to the seven parts that the Skanda Purāṇa is decorated with cannot be counted by a man. One who makes a gift of this Purāṇa elucidating great accounts of righteousness and good conduct to a Brāhmaṇa, he/she gets entitled for residence in the heaven amounting to that many years of the letters that the Purāṇa contains. Like the raindrops not countable, innumerable dazzling stars in the sky beyond count and the unlimited particles of sand underneath the water-bed of Gaṅgā cannot be counted, so are the fruits of merit which accrue from listening to the Skanda Purāṇa. By listening to it with due devotion for sometime for days together as well as by reading it, a man becomes accomplished in all sides and entirely. Those desirous of having a son obtain a son. People desirous of wealth get the same. Desire for a husband gets materialized. So is also the desire of a man to have a beautiful girl as wife. By reading it people get their friends outside their land to make a come-back. By listening to Skanda Purāṇa, a man obtains all his desired objects. Listening to and reading this Purāṇa grant all desires of human beings. People get long life by listening to this auspicious Purāṇa while a king gets victory over the world with full domination of his enemies. The Brāhmaṇas get learned in the Vedas while the Kṣatriyas get kingdom by reading it. The Vaiśyas get the fortune of wealth and remain gratified while its reading blesses the Śūdras with all happiness. By listening to one chapter or just a *śloka* (i.e. verse) or half of a *śloka* one goes to the abode of Viṣṇu. Listening to the various accounts integral to the Purāṇa and following it up with a worship of its narrator is equivalent to worship of Brahmā, Viṣṇu and Rūdra (an epithet of Śiva). If a Guru (i.e. a preceptor or teacher) imparts learning of a single letter of the Purāṇa to his disciple, there is hardly any such object available on the earth by gifting which can he be brought under the burden of debt. Hence, Vyāsa who has been reckoned as the adviser/ recommender of learning of the Skanda Purāṇa is worthy of worship by gifting of gold, cows, clothes and all other desirable goods and through offer of food to him. Listening to the Skanda Purāṇa attended with faith, following its injunctions in the best possible manner and worship of its adviser entitles one to obtain the position of Śaiva. Listening to the Purāṇa absolves man of sins accumulated over series of births on his part and entitles him to obtain the fruits associated with all centres of pilgrimage. Despite having nectar in their stomachs, all gods do not abide that long, while despite himself being full to the throat with poison, the God Nīlakaṇṭha always keeps an eye upon us.

Vyāsa said:

22. After Sūta's saying like this all the great sages like Śounaka, etc. worshipped him according to rules and greeted him with all praises.

The Sages said:

23-27. You have told us everything count by count as had happened. You have described us the intergenerational accounts as per sequence in the Purāṇa. You gave us the proof with regard to the culmination of the time period of creation as per estimation of Manu. You also described us all about the cosmic expanse. You have also told us about the basic characteristic of astrology as has been spoken about and described. We feel ourselves to be fortunate. We have been gratified and consider ourselves to be successful after hearing the Skanda Mahāpurāṇa from your lotus-mouth. We are very happy and exalted. We—the Brāhmaṇas and great sages, give you our blessings. Let you— the disciple of Vyāsa attain the height of wisdom, get a long life and be always happy. Blessing him in this manner and gifting him with clothes as well as ornaments, the sages then permitted Sūta—the son of Lomaśa to take leave and got themselves engaged in their usual practice of performance of *yajñas.*

INDEX

S

T

U

V

W

Y